"Don't worry about me, Mr. Cobb." She chiseled out the words as if striking them in stone. "My problems are not your concern."

"You're wrong there, Doc. You are my problem. And I've got to decide on how to deal with you."

She drew herself up with a fiery indignity. "You don't get to decide anything. You're just the hired help here, along for the paycheck. You've got no stake whatsoever in this."

"That's right. I've got nothing invested except my life and, excuse me, but I do tend to place some value on that. And I do get to decide where I'm going to risk it. If I'm going to go out there and put it on the line for, as you so succinctly put it, the paycheck, I need to know if you can keep it together. If you have any doubts, you stay behind."

"I'll be fine, Cobb."

"Will you? Are you? Then tell me what you saw earlier tonight in your room. Can you do that?"

"A mask on the wall."

"Bull."

"I didn't see anything." His steady stare wouldn't let her leave it at that. "I didn't see anything real, okay. Is that what you wanted to hear? That I'm nuts, bonkers and all the rest? That I see things that aren't there? That I have a hole in my memories large enough to drive a Mack truck through? That I can't trust myself to know what's real?"

"Trust me."

His sudden intensity dragged her back from the edge of hysteria.

"Why, Cobb? Why should I trust you?"

"Because I can protect you if you let me. Because I know you're not crazy."

"Nancy Gideon's latest supernatural romance will embellish her deserved reputation for entertaining novels. This story never slows down on either the paranormal or the romantic fronts. Another triumph!" – BookBrowser

Other "Midnight" Books by Nancy Gideon

Available from ImaJinn Books

Midnight Enchantment
Midnight Gamble
Midnight Redeemer
Midnight Masquerade (coming in October 2001)

From Pinnacle (Out of Print)

Midnight Kiss
Midnight Temptation
Midnight Surrender

Also available from ImaJinn Books

In the Woods
(Novelization of the horror movie In the Woods)

Midnight Shadows

***

Nancy Gideon

MIDNIGHT SHADOWS
Published by ImaJinn Books, a division of ImaJinn

ISBN: 1-893896-47-1

10 9 8 7 6 5 4 3 2 1

PUBLISHER'S NOTE:
This book is a work of fiction. Names, characters, places and incidents are products of the author's imagination or are used fictitiously. Any resemblance to actual events or locales or persons, living or dead, is entirely coincidental.

Books are available at quantity discounts when used to promote products or services. For information please write to: Marketing Division, ImaJinn Books, P.O. Box 162, Hickory Corners, MI 49060-0162, or call toll free 1-877-625-3592.

Cover design by Patricia Lazarus

ImaJinn Books, a division of ImaJinn
P.O. Box 162, Hickory Corners, MI 49060-0162
Toll Free: 1-877-625-3592
http://www.imajinnbooks.com

PROLOGUE

Hide.

Instinct had kept him alive and unchanged for a century. Quinton Alexander knew he had to escape Seattle before enemies, new and old, found him. A creature of little courage and much craft, he recognized the wisdom of burrowing in like a tick until danger passed and memory faded. Time was his best friend, and distance would be a close second.

But another instinct, deep and pulsing, drew him out perhaps foolishly on the foggy night.

Hunger.

The desire to feed pushed safety from the forefront. Need writhed within him. Emptiness withered his veins and roared in his belly, demanding appeasement in a loud, agonizing voice. First he would feed, then he would flee.

And once safely in his hiding place, he would scheme. Even if it took decades, he would have his revenge upon those who had out smarted him and forced him from this comfortable existence into exile once more.

He hunted in shadow, slipping along the silent pre-dawn streets from doorway to alleyway, searching, sniffing like a hound trained for a particular scent. He paused, inhaling deeply.

There.

Rich, warm, life-sustaining.

Human blood.

Perched like a dark bird of prey upon a recessed stoop, he watched her hurry toward a parked car, fishing in her purse for keys and cursing softly under her breath. She'd come from the hospital. The acrid bite of that clinical atmosphere clung to her, a bitter condiment to spice his meal. It reminded him of his most recent prison. He almost let her pass. Almost. He had no time to be picky. So he continued to watch and wait for opportunity, knowing it would come soon. She rushed out of weariness not worry. After all, the city slept securely, believing the serial killer stalking their streets to be a threat no longer. And they'd be right . . . after he finished here.

Impatient in his thirst, he swooped down upon his victim. There was no time for the luxury of the cat-and-mouse play he usually enjoyed. Just eat and run.

She never knew what hit her. Her keys dangled from her vehicle's door. Her purse lay open, its contents strewn upon the ground while he feasted deeply, carelessly draining the life away from this mortal who meant less than nothing to him. Good to the last drop.

Bloated and slightly intoxicated by his over-indulgence, he sat on the curb, reveling in his sated satisfaction. And for that fleeting moment, he was vulnerable and unaware that he was not alone.

The sound of a footstep startled him from his lethargy. Suddenly, a brilliant flood of light bathed him and the empty shell lying in the gutter at his feet. His first thought was the police.

His second was Frank Cobb.

With bloodied fangs horribly exposed, he faced the intruder from the coil of a crouch, ready to spring, yet unable to identify the threat beyond that blinding light.

"I've been looking for you."

It wasn't Cobb. A relief.

"You've found me, unlucky for you," he responded with a promising hiss.

The soft chuckle perplexed him.

"Oh, I would say very lucky for the both of us. You see I have a proposition for you, one that will prove beneficial to both you and me."

"Why should I make bargains?" He grew bolder now that the immediate surprise and danger had faded. Coming out of his crouch, he struggled to see beyond the glare to the owner of the unfamiliar voice.

But just because he didn't recognize the speaker, didn't mean the speaker didn't recognize him.

"Because it's in your best interest to listen. I know what you are, and I have no fear of you."

A shape appeared, haloed by the light behind it. Alexander howled in dismay, turning away as the holy cross burned his eyes. Slowly, he glanced back, relieved to find the offensive tool was gone. If his unidentified assailant meant to capture or kill him, the crucifix would still be wielded to hold him at helpless bay. So if not to trap or destroy him, what did this human have in mind? Clever thoughts working now in search of an advantage, he relaxed his cornered stance.

"Who are you?" he demanded. "What do you want? You must want something or you wouldn't have come looking for me."

"I'm a friend. A friend who is going to take you away from all your troubles here and then make us both very, very wealthy."

Slowly, the vampire smiled.

"Tell me more."

ONE

Some Indian tribes in the Amazon had a hundred words for green.

To the three men chopping their way through the tangle of squirming vines, only one term applied.

Green hell.

Hot. Steaming. Hell.

Though nothing moved, the heavy, wet air held the sense of stealthy activity, scurrying just out of the line of sight, in the impenetrable canopies overhead, beneath the dense, umbrella-like palms concealing the decayed forest floor. A memory of life, a shadow of what had passed by before or perhaps now lay in wait within that verdant, unrelieved green. Something watching, something dangerous, something stirring a cold shiver of sweat under damp shirts and hat bands as the trio continued to toil. But greed overcame harbingers of dread. They worked faster, harder, focusing on their goal until foliage ripped away to reveal their reward.

"It's here," one of them breathed in a hush of avaricious amazement.

Spurred on by the discovery, they continued to chop and tear and pull and bare the ancient walls the jungle sought to bury. Stepping back at last, they regarded the fruits of their labor, panting with an excitement tempered by inbred superstition.

"Who goes in?" the eldest asked of no one in particular.

"You go, Mano. You are the smallest."

"And the bravest, no?" Teeth as rotted as the spongy matter beneath their feet flashed in the swarthy face. "Just make sure you warn me if anyone comes before you take to the lowlands like a pair of capybaras."

Not caring for the too-accurate likening to those sheep-sized rodents, the eldest struck his spade against the ancient mortar with offended zeal.

Powder sifted through the vines.

They went to work again, gouging between stones that had stood as protective sentinels since pre-Columbian time. But old and worn away by the seeping dampness, the rocks could not hold against this latest assault. First one, then another rolled away, and a narrow path into darkness beckoned, promising secrets to the bold.

Mano shrugged out of his pack. There'd be no room for anything except his flashlight and his small hand pick in the pitch-black tunnel ahead. A rope was quickly tied to his jute belt and knotted. If he was victorious, he would use the rope to haul in bags to steal away his illegal harvest. If he encountered something more sinister than a dead ruler laid out in his tomb, the rope would be his lifeline, dragging him back to safety. He made sure the knot was tight, then with a nod to the expectant pair, he wriggled through the tiny opening into the unknown.

He'd inched his way for a cramped ten feet when he met with another stone barrier. Not discouraged, he went to work on it, chipping in the confined quarters with his hand tool until he had a groove notched between the stones. He cleaned the loose debris away then caught his breath as his fingertips brushed against something foreign embedded within the sealing mud. He shone the dim light on the golf-ball sized pellet nestled in his palm. A bead left between the stones. A pearl of pure gold for the owner of the tomb to take with him to the afterlife.

Now they would be Mano's reward for going first.

Quickly, he scooped out several more beads, tucking them into the pockets of his chinos, then he went back to work, driven by the need to know what riches lay beyond. If the size of the beads was any indication, wealth beyond imagination.

And he could imagine quite a lot.

He squirmed his way through the next opening, dropping

several feet down onto an earthen floor that had last hosted foot traffic in 600 BC. Dusting himself off, Mano straightened then directed his light down either corridor. The passageway gave no clues as to destination. Picking his left, he started down the narrow tunnel while the sun began to set on his nervous friends waiting outside. He gave no thought to their trepidation or the time as he abruptly came upon an arched opening that left him gaping in awe.

The chamber was huge, soaring upward like a cathedral before narrowing into a sort of chimney through which the fading daylight filtered in a weak downward stream. Standing in that fragile pool of natural light was a creature carved in native stone, a creature so fearsome and fantastical that Mano was distracted from the large emeralds inset for its eyes, from the hammered collar beaten from solid gold. He sucked a fearful breath, tasting the sour, almost acrid odor of the burial temple laced with his own tangy sweat.

The creature sat on powerful animal-like haunches, clawed hands gripping upthrust knees. A ridge of spines was cut down its back, and its face was lifted as if baying at the circle of sky so far out of reach overhead. The human features were pulled back from a great gaping maw, exposing hideous fangs in that wide-open mouth. And from the corners of that mouth, seeded like glittering droplets of blood, were rubies by the dozens, trickling downward.

Even as a shudder rippled through him, Mano's gaze fixed on a pattern upon the floor. More rubies just there for the picking? Lust for treasure pushed away his caution just as night overwhelmed the last of the day, plunging the chamber into complete blackness. Using his flashlight to direct him, Mano crossed to the foot of the monolithic being, sweeping the beam in search of gemstones. But what he found wasn't rubies, it was the faded brilliance of dried blood.

Someone else had been here. Recently.

Did that mean they were too late to claim the treasure?

As disappointment and dread warred within him, Mano felt a faint breath of movement behind him. Thinking one of his friends had decided not to wait after all, he turned, eager to share what he had found.

But whatever words he sought to say strangled upon a fateful scream.

By the time the sound reached the two waiting restlessly in the jungle, it was barely louder than a whimper but still enough to make the hair quiver on their napes. The rope snapped taut in their hands, and they began to draw upon it, slowly at first, then more frantically as they puzzled over what weighed down the other end. Gold? Carved stone antiquities that would fetch a small fortune from their supplier? The rattling in the tunnel grew louder, and their anticipation increased apace. But what emerged from the dark cavern was a pair of worn boots bound by their rope at the ankles.

"Mano!"

They dragged him from of the hole but, from the way he flopped to the ground limp and motionless, they knew it was already too late. Kneeling down, they shone their lanterns onto features frozen in nameless horror and eyes round with the recognition of impending death. If his expression wasn't enough to send them fleeing into the forest, it was the cause of his demise that came nipping at their heels: a hound from that Green Hell.

Mano Mendes's shirt was black with blood from where his throat had been torn wide open.

***

Mid-1970s in the Rio Grande Valley of South Texas, sightings of what may have been a condor are linked to a rash of mutilated cattle. Blood was removed to the last drop.

Early 1970s in Brownsville, Texas, a rancher finds a bull dead with no blood around it and no tracks.

March 11, 1995, Ornocovis: eight sheep are found dead with three unexplained marks or punctures in the chest, through which they are completely drained of blood.

August 1995 in Canvanas, Puerto Rico a name is given to a legend. The Chupacabra is blamed for the deaths of approximately 150 animals.

December 7, 1995, near Guanica, Puerto Rico chickens and cows suffer unusually bloodless deaths.

December 18, 1995, Puerto Rico, animals found dead from a single puncture mark and drained of blood. The local tabloid suggests giant vampire bats infiltrated the island in a cargo shipment from South America.

January 4, 1996 in Isabella County, Michigan eight calves are discovered frozen and dead, skinned from head to hooves.

March 1996 in rural Miami 40 animals are killed. A woman reported a dog-like figure rising up onto hind legs with two short hands in the air.

May 2, 1996, Rio Grande Valley, South Texas, pet goat dead with three puncture wounds in its neck: the telltale marks of the Chupacabra. On the same day in Juarez, Mexico, small mammals killed by tall "animal-like" being with three-toed feet and hands, on haunches with forearms at chest level like a kangaroo. A row of spikes or feathers project from the back of its head and down its back that glow with their own light.

May 3, 1996, a rash of similar sightings in eight states in Mexico: bat-like creatures sucking goats dry. Numerous animals drained of blood, dead cows and sheep.

May 9, 1996 at 2:00 a.m., a Latino family has its front door opened, and a creature with scaly skin, clawed hands, red eyes and a row of spines from its skull down its back "mumbled and gestured."

May 10, in Florida reports of a Chupacabra among Hispanics.

May 12, Chiapas, Mexico, 28 rams found dead with puncture marks.

Chupacabra. New Jersey Devil, Spring Heeled Jack. Large, slanted, glowing red eyes, Simian-like face, spikes on its head and back, three-toed foot, seen to hop or fly, leaves puncture wounds resembling the classic vampire bite. Speculation that the Chupacabras might be from outer space.

Fiction. Folly.

Relieved, Sheba Reynard set down her pencil and stared at the time line and the huge stack of notes she'd meticulously gathered since her arrival in Puerto Rico almost seven months earlier.

She'd done thorough investigative research, approaching

the topic more like a scandal journalist than the scientist she was. Taking advantage of her fluent Spanish, she'd gone beyond the basic records checking, taking her questions to the people who crossed themselves at dusk and prayed their livestock would survive the night. It was easy to laugh at their nonsensical stories...until looking into the somber faces, into the haunted eyes of those who believed, who'd seen, firsthand, what the island's favorite legend had done. These weren't the people who created colorful web sites or hawked cute tee shirts selling the Chupacabra as Puerto Rico's answer to the cuddly ET. They'd gone into their fields, their corrals, their barns to discover unimaginable horrors. They had no interest in feeding the media frenzy or joining fan clubs that glorified the startling and inexplicable deaths of their animals, which came without warning, without clues. They lived in terror, victims of the unknown, prisoners of their own ignorance.

Chupacabara. An invention of superstition. The product of an unlearned mind. The perpetuation of a media hungry for sensation and a marketing tool for those eager to capitalize from misfortune that hadn't touched them personally. Those were the things this creature was. What it was was myth not monster.

There were no monsters.

Behind the hysteria and rampant fear, there was a manipulation of the truth born of rumor and legend. That's why the Puerto Rican government had supplied her with a grant. Find the truth. She'd dug; she'd snooped; she'd listened; she'd sympathized. But what she'd never done was believed.

And on the bottom of her notes, she jotted a short, blunt sentence: The work of angry neighbors, a jilted lover and mostly likely, a stray dog. A logical conclusion to years of fright and panic. Just reality once the trappings of religion and legend were stripped away. Sheba had more respect for the latter than the former, but both she considered dangerous follies.

Case closed.

Finally.

Wearily, she rubbed at her eyes and wondered what time

it was. Hours, days, weeks and now months had escaped her notice while on this latest quest for truth. A hoax. A coincidence. Nothing mysterious or inexplicable. Satisfied with her answer, she could return to...what? What did she have when not out chasing myths and disproving beliefs? What did she have besides a battered suitcase and the reputation of being a ruthless faith-basher?

She'd been out of touch with civilization too long, or such ruminations wouldn't bother her. She had a good life, a full and meaningful profession earning respect from her peers and the gratitude of those she liberated from their own misconceptions.

She provided a useful and necessary service.

And once she'd had a long shower, she'd remember that.

Gathering her notes and the dozens of audiotapes she'd made over the past months, she deposited them into a large portfolio, closing the flap the way she'd meant to close her mind to the remembered awe and terror in those voices, those eyes.

There are no monsters.

Hadn't she proved it, again?

When would it be enough for her to begin to believe, for her to have a dreamless night's sleep?

Perhaps tonight while the sense of victory was sweet and strong.

Now that her almost zealous focus was gone, Sheba glanced about and noticed in some surprise that she barely recognized her surroundings. She'd lived out of this small, nearly airless room for more than half a year, yet the only thing she'd brought to it was the big suitcase that had toured the globe with her. She'd never looked at the childlike rendering of a still-life hanging over the hard double bed. She hadn't recoiled at the garish colors of the bedspread that repeated in horrifying boldness in the splashy pattern on the drapes. Nor did she know what she would see if she opened those curtains to look beyond. What was outside the window, anyway? A view of the sprawling city? Could she see the jeweled waters of the Carribean? She'd never taken the time to look...or to care. This place was like any other, a base to which she would return each night to surround herself with the stuff of legends. Her safe retreat from out of which she would battle ignorance using knowledge and logic as her crusader's sword, slicing through superstition, rending apart traditions to get at the bare bones of fact. When possessed by her passion for truth, the world around her ceased to exist. And most of the time, that didn't bother her.

Tonight it did.

When had she stopped looking out the windows to appreciate the view? When did it cease to matter where she was, only what she was doing?

When had she become such a drudge?

She rolled her shoulders and massaged at the tension bunching at the back of her neck. Tonight, she'd shower and go out for a decent dinner accompanied by too much wine. In the morning, she'd type up her findings, call for flight reservations back to the States and arrange a meeting with the nervous officials that had sought her out in desperation. Her manner would calm them, her words would relieve them, her report would vindicate them. But would it be enough to keep the grass-roots panic at bay? Would her logical conclusions control the hysteria of a people fiercely protective of their cultural icons? That wasn't her problem, was it? She was the Myth-buster sent down from the prestigious Eastern university to abolish their beliefs. And that's what she had done.

No monsters. Only man-made, media-perpetuated fears.

She'd steeped herself for too long in the whispers of superstition. Time to get back to the realities of finding a new grant with which to support herself and pay the rent on the apartment she never stayed in long enough to call home. She'd touch base with her mentors, arrange to have her papers published, maybe even book a few speaking engagements. But who was she kidding? She wasn't looking forward to any of those things.

She was already anticipating the next hunt.

The sluice of tepid water rinsed away the panic and poverty of the people she'd lived among for more than half a year.

Now, it was time to wash away the memory of their faces and their fears, to put them neatly away as research and move on. She'd done all she could to conquer those fears, and in doing so had managed to forestall her own, for a little while anyway.

At least until she stepped out of the tiny shower stall to hear the phone ringing.

Wrapped in a thin, ineffectual towel, Sheba dropped down onto the edge of the bed to answer the shrill demand. Probably the desk clerk asking if she wanted some food brought up in exchange for an exorbitant tip. The last thing she expected was for the past to reach out through those inconsistent lines of communications to cruelly snatch her smug sense of accomplishment from her.

"Sheba? It's Paulo. Can you hear me? I've been trying to reach you all day."

"Paulo? Oh, my gosh! How are you? It's been ages. Where are you?"

"Home."

Home. Tightness clutched within her chest, spreading upward to paralyze her throat, preventing an immediate response. A response she didn't fully understand or want.

"Sheba? Are you still there?"

She swallowed hard. "I'm here. What are you doing in Peru? I thought you were taking the scientific world by storm in, where was it this time?"

"Ha, ha. Very funny coming from a world-weary traveler like yourself. Actually, I'm doing some research right in our backyard."

"Oh." The thought of that big, untamed backyard rose up in a tidal wave of unfounded alarm.

"That was always the plan, wasn't it? For you and me to do good at home? Well, here I am. When can I expect you?"

Sheba closed her eyes, opening them quickly when her mind's deep, scary recesses brought threatening shadows from the forgotten realm of danger and dread accompanying thoughts of home. She didn't know where those feelings came from—the claustrophobic sweats, the clawing terror, the glassy shards of panic and pain. But she knew she could never go back to the source of those miseries. Never. A defensive wall of distance slammed into place.

"Paulo, I'm right in the middle of some important work myself. I can't just walk away from it."

"Can't or won't?

Never, never, never.

"Don't be silly, Paulo. I'd love to see you. I really would. Now's just not a good time. I've got notes to put together and–"

"Yadda, yadda, yadda." The warm, forgiving laugh reached across the continent to soothe her. "Don't worry about it. Who am I to throw the first stone? It's not like I don't thrive on being a workaholic, too. It's just that I miss you so much sometimes."

A wad of emotion got the best of her for a moment, skewing her vision and burning in her throat as she thought of the only link to the past that she could return to.

"I miss you, too, *mi hermano, mi amigo*," she managed to whisper.

"But all gooey sentiments aside, there was another reason I called."

Sheba smiled at the runaway enthusiasm in his voice. "I'm crushed. But not surprised."

"A couple of *huagueros* have everything in an uproar down here."

What did the misadventures of some Peruvian tomb robbers have to do with her? She was suddenly terrified to find out.

"Oh? Some new find my colleagues might be interested in?" Did she sound normal, her curiosity genuine? Or did her reluctance and fear shiver through the lines to touch her oldest friend in the world? Apparently not, for Paulo continued excitedly.

"They found a tomb, Sheba. Buried out in the jungle. Maybe *the* tomb. I thought you'd want to know."

Dizziness swam up to engulf her senses. Sickness sloshed in her belly and roared upward to sear her throat and nose with the acrid bite of remembered fear. The world went momentarily black then green.

Then red.

"Sheba? Are you still there?"

She bent over, tucking her head between her knees as nausea thundered in her ears and left her trembling.

"Sheba?"

"I'm sorry, Paulo, but I've got to go." How weak and wobbly her voice sounded.

"Sheba, I thought you'd want to know." Apology and the first strains of regret colored his words.

"Thanks, Paulo. I've really got to go now. I'll talk to you soon."

She tried to hang up the phone, missing the cradle once, twice, then just letting the receiver fall to the worn rug. The world reeled as she dropped to her knees, swaying in the thrall of a shuddering sickness she couldn't name.

No, that wasn't quite true. She knew the name. It was Peru. Paulo called it home. But to Sheba, it would only mean one thing.

Death.

The smell drew him out of the darkness. Not the rich aroma wafting from the stew pot, nor the bite of cheap alcohol filtering outward on each softly snored breath, but a more subtle bouquet, one rich and bold and vital. One stirred up, not by a wooden cook spoon or the pull of a cork, but issued forth with a steady, timeless beat.

The scent of life. The fragrance of renewal and eternity. It beckoned, an irresistible pheromone from the figure slouched and slumbering drunkenly on the front steps.

The lone predator crept in closer, nostrils quivering, mouth moistening in anticipation of the feast to come. So easy, so unaware of the danger. The man on the porch muttered. The empty bottle fell from his slack hand, hitting the ground with a hollow thud. Just as the unsuspecting victim soon would after the swift attack left him an equally emptied vessel.

Closer. Easing through the brush without sound, more a shadow than a man. A deadly shadow.

The door to the shack burst open, flooding the dirty yard with light. A large woman's silhouette filled the opening, hands on hips in the picture of indignant fury. The killer sank back into anonymity. Patiently, he waited in the shadows, waited and watched for his chance to come again.

The angry woman advanced upon her hapless husband, waking him rudely with the smack of her spoon against one ear.

"Paco, you useless piece of dung! I work all day at the lodge to put food on the table and here you sit, too drunk to taste it."

Rubbing his ear against abuse both physical and verbal, Paco Ruis struggled up from the pleasant embrace of liquor to confront the shrew he'd married. She's been pretty then, with tiny feet, good teeth and a waist he could span with his meaty hands. Now, her teeth were almost gone, and he could barely get his arms around her. The teasing laugh of that young girl had aged to the harping chatter of a squirrel monkey, always barking about how she provided for them by toiling at the lodge while he drank up her precious earnings. It wasn't his fault there was no work. He'd made a good living as a street vendor until the government ended his right to hawk his wares on the sidewalks of the city. He and others like him were pushed from their shanty town, forced to follow the north-south highway bulldozed into the jungle where they were promised resettlement and work.

Only there was no work, no way for a proud man to provide for his family. His wife, his once beautiful Maria, didn't understand a man's shame in letting his woman bring home the means for their survival. She couldn't comprehend the misery that coaxed him to the bottle. She could only nag and belittle, carving away at his machismo pride until little was left of the man he'd once been.

"You were supposed to have brought in wood for the stove, but instead you've spent the day wallowing in the comfort of cheap liquor."

"It's the only comfort I get here, woman," he roared, satisfied when she took a few cautious steps back as he wobbled to his feet. He'd been an imposing man with a hot temper. Now he was a pitiful one, and the temper was quicker. Only when it had its way did she give him the respect he was due. Perhaps it was time to show her who was boss. His eyes narrowed at the thought, and a thin smile gave her warning.

For all her bulk, she was still fast on those tiny feet. She dodged back into the house and barred the door as he crashed into it, bellowing her name in impotent rage.

"Maria, open this door. I am the man of this house. Let me in."

"Man?" she shouted back through the surprisingly strong door. Neither would yield to his bullying. "Then act like one. Do a man's work instead of whimpering into your bottle like a child. Go out into the jungle and find wood. Once you've cut and stacked it, perhaps the honest sweat will clear the fumes from your brain, and I can open the door to you once more."

"*Puta*!" He battered the barring portal one last time, but it was only for effect. His shoulder was sore, and the hinges showed as little sign of relenting as the she-dog on the other side. "Bah! Find your own wood, woman. You are the man of the house now. I will find myself another bed to lie in."

He waited to see if the oft-tendered threat would sway her. A stony silence was his answer. He sighed. With his bottle empty, he had only two choices, cut the wood and grovel his way back into his still-pleasurable bed...or go find another bottle.

He reeled off the porch, stumbling down the steps and into the dirt patch yard. Finding a bottle would be much easier and more rewarding on this steamy night than chopping wood. That decided, he started down the narrow path that would take him to the village. There he would find more drink and perhaps a more malleable female to share it with.

He'd gone twenty yards, surely no more than that, when he began to have second thoughts. He could still see the flickering lights from the windows of his home, and they looked more inviting than a long walk in the dark. Besides, his pockets were empty. Wondering how much wood it would take to calm her mood and earn him a way back under her covers, Paco left the path in search of fallen timber. He'd drag a few branches back, make a grand show of chopping them into kindling, then romance his wife from her evil temper. And perhaps tomorrow he would go with her to the lodge to see if they offered any work a man could do.

He'd bent to wrestle a limb from a tangle of vines when he heard a faint sound behind him. Could Maria have followed him, worried that he might not come home? He refused to turn and greet her. Let her make the first apologizing overture.

But when that overture came, there was nothing apologetic about it.

Powerful hands clasped either side of his skull. He was jerked upright, then off his feet with a strength that defied even the biggest men he knew. Then, with a quick, savage wrench of those hands, Paco Ruis knew nothing at all.

And later, when a woman's screams echoed through the trees, startling birds into flight, a soft chuckle teased about that cacophony of sound.

"That's right, my dear. You run. You tell them all what you've found. Tell them what terror walks among them in the night. Tell them to be afraid, very afraid. And tell them to get ready to pay."

TWO

Frank Cobb appeared at ease as he regarded the man on the other side of the big mahogany desk, but his thoughts were far from relaxed. Anything that had to do with Greg Forrester or Harper Research pushed him right to the razor edge of self-preserving caution.

He had every reason for his suspicions. He'd sat in this same spot before, only then, the office had been bigger, just as the other man's reputation had been bigger. But Cobb had learned that when things got smaller, they weren't necessarily less powerful, only more driven and, therefore, more dangerous. Forrester had that stink of danger about him even in the cool of the climate-controlled facility. And Cobb had to wonder what was making the man sweat and how that would affect him in the long run.

"There's a flight leaving for Lima in two hours." Forrester pushed an airline packet across the gleaming desk top.

"Lima, Ohio?"

"Lima, Peru."

Cobb looked at the packet but didn't pick it up. "What's in Peru that interests you and Harper?" *And me?*

"One of the Center's pursuits is in biological prospecting. The Amazon is rich in plant life with properties no one's ever cataloged. There are alleged blood-cleansing seeds in Peru, cancer-killing vines in Iquitos, the *burseraceae* bush and samples of *una de gato* known to alleviate cancer and AIDs. The possibilities are limitless."

Cobb was unimpressed by his humanitarian fervor. "Along with the profits."

Forrester ignored Cobb's dry summation as if it were beneath him to comment. "The only problem is researchers run into a lot of governmental red-tape. They aren't allowed into some parts of the country."

"And you want me to smuggle a group of Seattle scientists across the borders into Peru. That's certainly a new twist."

This time, Forrester expressed his annoyance with a brief, brow-lowering scowl. "No. Harper is funding a young economic botanist named Paulo Lemos. He's a Peruvian. So far he's been very successful in penetrating jungle areas that have been off-limits to us before."

"Sounds like you've found an economical answer to the problem. So what's the problem?" And there had to be one if Forrester had asked for him by name. He was on retainer to Harper as a problem solver.

A dirty job, but . . . but the pay more than made up for it. Usually.

Forrester's irritation grew more difficult to hide. It didn't take a huge leap for Cobb to make the connection between the administrator's struggle to regain face with the Center and the Peruvian botanist. Lemos was Forrester's project, and Forrester's star would rise or fall with the young man's success. Cobb had learned that the smooth-spoken, grandfatherly Forrester's ambition was like the cancer his center studied—voracious, unpredictable and totally merciless about what it devoured. He'd almost been swallowed whole once before and didn't like the sensation of being chewed and spit out according to Forrester's taste of the moment.

Apparently, the man was now teething on Lemos, and Frank didn't envy the boy's position.

"There's been some . . . trouble," Forrester conceded at last.

Wasn't there always? Here it comes. Cobb could imagine Forrester's maw opening wide, getting ready to take a bite out of his butt.

"Could you be a bit more specific?"

"There have been some grumblings from the indigenous population, nothing too overt or threatening up until now."

"Gee, I wonder why they wouldn't fling their arms wide open to welcome a new plague of resource-stripping locusts among them."

Forrester's hard stare cut Cobb's sarcasm off at the knees. "There have been killings."

Suddenly, Cobb was all attention though he never actually moved. "Who and why?"

"Just natives at first, random choices. The local authorities thought it some kind of new cult-thing rising up in one of the isolated tribes. No reason to get involved or to worry us."

"Until?"

"Until one of the guests was murdered at an exclusive ecotourism lodge. The wife of a very influential political supporter."

Cobb got the picture. The deaths of a few natives were no big deal. Write it off to jungle law or some such nonsense. But touch one of the elite . . .

"And so?" Cobb prompted.

"And so the government is thinking of closing down the entire area. Surely you can see what that means?"

Sure. The area would revert back to its rightful owners, and the killings would stop. Secretly, Cobb applauded the official reasoning. But those weren't the officials paying his salary. "No more research. No more potential cures. No more potential profits."

"Exactly."

"So what do you want me to do about it?" For Cobb, it all boiled down to that.

"Go to Peru. Stick close to Lemos. The government is still on the fence, so I want him to get as much work done as possible in case they pull his ticket."

"You want me to babysit."

Great.

Manicured fingers fanned wide and pressed down on the shiny desktop as the executive leaned forward for emphasis. "I want you to do what you do best. Observe, investigate and eradicate the problem."

"The problem being?" If Forrester thought he'd be game

for a little high profile assassination, he was wrong. Cobb wasn't in that business anymore.

"I want you to stop whoever's behind the killings. Or whatever is."

"Isn't that what Peru has a police force for? Won't I be stepping on some pretty big official toes?"

One elegant hand flicked the problem away with a flourish. Why not? It wasn't going to be his problem for much longer. If Frank decided to take the job.

"The situation down there is murky at best. There are no clear-cut lines of authority. I'm not even sure what the chain of command for investigation is, whether it's military or local considering the importance of the last victim. I only know that you have a certain expertise that they may not."

"I'm sure Peru has its share of snipers."

"You misunderstand me, Cobb. I'm not talking about your history as a killer. I'm speaking of your experience as a hunter."

Now, it was Cobb's turn to frown. Hunter? Of what?

Forrester didn't keep him guessing for long. "Some hysterical grave robbers spread all sorts of wild stories about unleashing some ancient evil that killed their partner. Panic is growing, and I'm afraid our time in Peru is getting uncomfortably short."

Cobb's frown deepened, all his alarm bells and whistles going off at once. "How were these people killed?"

Forrester's grim smile told him he'd hit the proverbial nail dead center.

"The local reports called it in ritual fashion. Their throats were torn open, and their blood was gone."

And Cobb's blood temperature took an icy plunge. "And you suspect?"

"I suspect nothing. I want to know for sure. And I want you to find out for me. Lemos is important to the Center. He's doing valuable work that could have wide-spread consequence. But you and I, better than anyone else, know how much greater the potential could be if these killings are following the pattern we saw here in Seattle. This is more than profits, Cobb. It's personal, and I don't have to explain that to you, of all people, do I?"

"No, sir." His own voice reflected the same glass-cutting edge. No, Forrester didn't have to explain anything to him. The executive's reputation wasn't the only one to take a tarnishing hit from the last unfortunate turn of affairs. His jaw tensed, the movement pulling at the barely healed slash across his cheek. It would take more than a few dozen stitches to close that ragged wound and repair the damage done.

It would take retribution.

He picked up the plane tickets.

"Where do I meet this Lemos?"

"You'll have to make your own arrangements once you get to Lima."

No problem. He was a resourceful guy.

"There is one more thing."

Forrester's approach was delicate, almost cagy in its caution. Cobb tensed, waiting for that shoe to drop right where his nerve endings were the most sensitive.

"Lemos would accept our help on one condition."

"Condition? He calls in the cavalry and makes his own conditions?"

"Lemos didn't call us in. His uncle did. Peyton Samuels. He owns the ecotourism lodge where the last murder occurred. Lemos is a reluctant participant, but he agreed to let you come down as long as you brought someone with you."

"Who?" He wasn't liking this at all.

"A Dr. Reynard, Lemos's childhood friend. An archaeologist from what I gather, someone who knows the language and the people. An asset to you."

A pain in the asset, was more like it.

"And where do I meet this Dr. Reynard?"

"In Lima. Can you be ready in an hour?"

"I've had all my shots."

And in just over two hours time, Frank Cobb was jetting toward South America.

***

With its jagged and mysterious landscapes, Peru ranked amongst the world's best known centers of ancient civilization.

Before its traditional world was crushed by the invading Spanish, a long line of highly developed cultures, including the sun-worshiping Incas, had left their mark thousands of years before the first European set foot within its diverse borders. A land of stunning variety, it contained 83 of the 103 possible ecological zones, from the icy peaks of the Andes down into the steamy jungles and to the world's driest desert running the length of its coastline. Half of its 23 million people were of pure Indian origin, many still speaking Quechua or the Aymaran tongue of their ancestors. Some tribes of the deep Amazon had never been disturbed by the new invasion of the modern world which came to find not only the gold that had drawn the bloody Spanish, but rubber and mahogany amongst the country's other precious resources.

When Frank Cobb exited the airport, he left that greedy modern world behind to enter the decaying colonial splendor that was Lima. Draped by a blanket of low clouds, the City of Kings sprawled before him like an oriental bazaar beneath the softening patina of desert dust. Conspicuous in the suit coat that had felt comfortable in the damp clime of Seattle, he set down his single duffle and began to scan the bustling thoroughfare for the faceless Dr. Reynard. He'd pictured some elderly scholar looking like the distinguished and slightly addled character Sean Connery played in the last of the Indiana Jones trilogy, so he was more than a little surprised by a breathy and very female overture.

"If you want a change of clothes tomorrow, you'd better hang on to that bag. You must be Cobb."

Features schooled to betray none of his astonishment, he regarded the speaker as if he'd expected to find an ethnologist with the face of an angel. "That obvious?"

"Umm." She bent to pick up his bag, giving him a quick assessment from black wingtips to muted tie and dark glasses. "You have the easy mark of tourist stamped right on you. I'm Dr. Reynard." A wry smile quivered on her lips. "Not that obvious, right? You weren't expecting a woman, I see."

Surprise. That was a pertinent piece of need-to-know data he really needed to know from the start. The cunning Greg

Forrester must have guessed at his reluctance and decided silence was a virtue on this particular subject. He'd let Cobb assume what was now obviously not true. There was nothing scholarly, aged or the least bit masculine about this doctor.

She was tall—looking him almost directly in the eye—slender, almost boyish in the baggy khaki pants and an unbuttoned denim shirt over a faded Grateful Dead tee. She wasn't wearing a bra, probably because she didn't see the need to. There wasn't much to see. It was the short bob of her not-quite-naturally blonde hair that defined her femininity with a riot of wash and go curls. And her face . . . no mistake there. Pure woman. Round, soft, and sun-kissed. Old-fashioned was the first description that came to mind. None of the artfully made-up, cosmopolitan sleekness of the urban socialite, but a casual, unpretentious beauty that was found down on the farm. Or in the Peruvian jungles. When she spoke, the faintest trace of a Southern dialect softened her syllables.

He might have been taken in by that overall innocent appeal if not for her gaze. Oh, her eyes were big and brown and doe-soft, but there was an unswerving directness to her and an edge of caution that warned there was more to this one than bronzed skin and Clara Bow lips. And that made him nervous.

Not liking to be caught off guard, he kept his response short and crisp.

"Dr. Reynard. Where to?"

She took his curt reply in and adjusted her own stance into one a bit more tense and adversarial. When he didn't move to take back his luggage the way a true gentleman would have, he could see her redrawing the picture she'd created of him, as well, into a less flattering portrait. He didn't think she needed to know he preferred to keep his hands free just in case he had to reach for the revolver it had taken all sorts of string-pulling for him to bring into the country. Despite his buttoned up apparel, he wasn't in Peru to play tourist.

"We leave first thing in the morning," she told him at last. "I've booked us rooms here in the city for tonight. Nothing fancy, so I hope you aren't too attached to your creature comforts."

"Just as long as the bed doesn't come with creatures of its own."

She smiled again, somewhat reluctantly, and he found himself looking at her lips. A cupid's bow. He'd heard that expression before but had never witnessed it in full, pouty detail. A small, ripely contoured mouth perpetually pursed as if for a kiss. He turned away, jaw tensing, to speak through clenched teeth.

A real asset. He could see it now.

"Lead on, Dr. Reynard."

He knew his attitude confused her, but that was all right. They both needed to be on their guard, with one another and with the hostile world around them. They weren't in this as best pals nor adversaries. More like as necessary evils.

"I'll get us a cab," she replied in an equally frigid tone.

Lima's idea of a taxi was an ancient VW Beetle, with the absence of paint on its exterior leaving an even finish of rust. As they wedged themselves into the microscopic back seat, the little bug took off with a sputter and explosion of oily exhaust, bouncing them against one another to create a flash of discomfort before they settled in with Cobb's duffle in the middle to provide a neutral buffer.

Frank didn't know where to look to find the least unsettling distraction, at the quixotic doctor beside him or out the side window to chronicle the driver's headlong rush down pot-holed back streets strewn with garbage, dead dogs and roaming livestock. The windshield had been shattered so many times, the poor man had to risk life and a possible decapitation leaning out the door to see where he was going. But that inconvenience didn't slow him down as he raced toward intersections, blowing his horn in sharp bursts to claim right of way before tearing through the impoverished urban sprawl without hesitation.

Frank fought the inclination to cling for dear life because his companion seemed so at ease with the reckless roller-coaster ride. Soft shell, tough interior, he surmised. A good thing, considering where they were headed. He'd been in the jungle before, not in Peru but in places a lot less welcoming, and not as a tourist then, either. It wasn't for the faint of heart or delicate natured. And apparently, she was thinking the same thing.

"I hope you have some footwear that's a little more sensible in that bag." Her scrutiny fell upon his leather street shoes.

"I've been dressing myself for quite a few years now, Doctor. I do all right on my own."

"So I've heard."

At the provoking lift of his brow, she elaborated.

"Your reputation precedes you. I've done some checking."

That shocked him. As far as he knew, his background was available only to those with the highest clearance. So who did she know, and what strings had she pulled?

"Well, don't believe everything you read, Doc. Life's full of little surprises."

And that effectively ended further conversation until their wild ride ended outside a stately old building. His optimism took a cautious step up. Maybe it wasn't going to be so bad after all.

He climbed out of the claustrophobic cab and put out a hand to his companion. She took it with some reluctance, as if wondering what price would come attached to the courtesy. Then she stood by, raising an impressed brow that he'd already exchanged his American currency for the sol and spent it like he knew its worth.

When he hoisted his bag and took a step toward the grand front doors, the good doctor caught his sleeve.

"Not here. Over there across the street."

He pondered the subtle humor in her voice until he turned and got a look at their accommodations. Where the other building had stately elegance, their hotel was simply old. The squatting two story looked as though it had housed the original Spanish invaders. Its facade was as weather beaten and tired as the corner crone with her begging cup, dependant upon the pity of strangers for her existence. Noting his expression, his companion managed a half-hearted apology.

"It looked a lot better the last time I stayed here."

"And when was that?"

"Twenty years ago."

Before he could comment, she darted across the cobbles, dodging a pickup truck and a pair of bicyclists and leaving him no alternative but to follow at a more prudent pace.

So much for comforts of any kind.

If anything, the interior was worse than the weary face it presented to the world. Footprints marked a floor where the dust hadn't been disturbed for ages. The lobby was little more than a narrow hall with the attendant backed into a closet. Frank knew enough Spanish to catch the irony of them getting the key to the presidential suite. As if any kind of president would deign to stay here.

Upstairs the view only grew bleaker. Low ceiling, non-existent lighting and the smell – he didn't want to guess what that was about. He had to admire the doctor's cool. She was unruffled by the squalor and picked her way around the questionable items littering the hall without a downward glance. The sign of a seasoned traveler. Or an exhausted one. He'd forgotten to ask where she'd arrived from. Perhaps over dinner there'd be the chance for more civilizing small talk. If the surroundings could yield up a decent place to eat. He hoped this wasn't a 'Catch Your Own' type hotel.

Their suite was a surprise, and he was ready for one of that nature. Not that it was large or new, but it was clean, done in cheerful colors splashed across the floors and single couch woven in local patterns. The main room had a sofa, a chair and a café table upon which the only light was found. Doors led off to two separate bedrooms and a tiny bath. In his earlier visits south of the equator, Frank learned that 'with bath' meant shower and toilet, not a tub and sometimes not even hot water. If they were lucky, they'd have soap, towels and toilet paper. If not, they'd have to make do.

Then their host was gone, closing the door upon two strangers alone.

It was after six. Cobb was thinking food, but his companion had another objective in mind.

Without once looking in his direction, the good doctor

headed for one of the rooms.

"I've been up for thirty-six hours. I'm going to grab a little sleep."

"I'll just check out the hot water situation–"

She closed the door on the last of his comment.

So much for small talk.

After dropping his bag on the twin-sized bed in the other room, he was pleased to find all three necessities in the bathroom and a tepid drizzle from the shower head as icing on the cake. A quick shower proved revitalizing but not relaxing considering the circumstances. He was reminded of them the minute he swiped the fog off the mirror with his forearm.

The scar ran several inches in a lateral slash across his cheekbone then made a diving 'L' to his jaw. He followed the harsh line with his fingertip, not needing the reflection to go by. He'd mapped it enough to know the distances by heart. He wasn't a vain man. The fact that his looks were destroyed hadn't been anywhere near the blow of having his competence questioned. He hadn't been able to protect the last woman in his care. What made him think he could provide safety for this one if they were to confront the same evil?

He caught sight of the cross he wore out of habit, not religion, and considered the irony of that small sliver of silver offering more protection than any of his brutal training regimes. He fingered the delicate shape. It had been an unexpected gift. Though not a bold piece of man's jewelry, he enjoyed the fragile dimensions because they brought to mind the giver and the reason for the gift.

He etched that same design in the air out of vaguely remember childhood catechisms and mouthed the words, "Protect us."

And as if in answer, the steamy air in the bath was rent with a scream of terror.

THREE

Sheba sat up with a gasp, covered in the sweat of dread from a familiar, if unremembered, dream. Her heart pounded with the fierceness of a tribal drum, aching within her breast as she struggled against the panic.

Leave me alone! What do you want from me?

She could scream out the words but who would hear? Who or what haunted her mind and fragmented memories every time she closed her eyes?

She'd just oriented herself within the shabby room when the door flew open, its frame filled with the startling silhouette of a half-dressed man with gun in hand.

"Are you all right?"

The terse voice centered her. Cobb. She forced a stabilizing breath to expand the crushing pressure about her heart. She never thought she'd be grateful for his presence. But then, how must she look to him? Quivering like a child afraid of the closet monster, crouched in the day's heavy shadows, her cheeks slicked with a residue of tears?

Not a great first impression.

"Of course, I'm all right," she growled with the rusty timbre of fading fear and mounting humiliation. Her hands scrubbed away the dampness on her cheeks in angry, stinging swipes. "Or I will be once I have my privacy returned. If you don't mind."

For a moment, he didn't move from that alert and dangerous pose, and she began to wonder if she'd have to further embarrass herself with an even more rude and unforgivable dismissal. Then he relented, the gun lowering, his posture easing from its readied tension.

"Well, excuse me all to hell. Next time, I'll wait for an invitation before trying to play hero."

He took a step back and let the slam of the door echo his indignation.

She let him go. How could she reach out with an apology or explanation? What reasoning could she give that didn't sound crazy to her own ears? Besides, Cobb was acting out of bruised male ego, not from any real affront to his feelings. They were strangers. He had no emotional investment in her, so how could he take her rebuff personally? She hadn't asked him to become involved.

She didn't even want to be here.

You shouldn't be here, whispered her prophetic inner voice.

Angrily, she took control of her shaken nerves and watery limbs, driving herself up off the sheltering bed where she huddled like a coward. Get up, get out, get busy, her answer for the near-paralyzing attacks of fright. She'd made the decision to return, so there was no point in wallowing in regrets. Only Paulo had the power to bring her back. Her love for him was the only force on Earth powerful enough to conquer her reluctant terror.

He needed her. How could she say no?

And how could she keep running from the answers she knew lay in wait out there in the jungle? Answers to twenty years of night-sweats and not knowing why. Answers she wasn't sure she'd ever be strong enough to face.

But she had to be, didn't she? She had to be if she was ever going to make something normal out of her life.

Damn Paulo for his second phone call and his plea for her assistance.

For forcing her to put her head in the lion's mouth.

***

Cobb stood at the single window, staring out through filmy panes at nothing in particular. He didn't turn when he heard her behind him and he didn't make the mistake of asking after her well-being again. Once the fool, shame on you, twice the fool, shame on me, was his motto.

"I'm going out to get something to eat." Her statement

was followed by a long pause he did nothing to ease. Then with a snap of irritation, she added, "Would you care to join me, Mr. Cobb?"

"Delighted."

If she could make an effort, so could he. And he had to eat, after all, even though the dinner conversation promised to be agonizing at best. He turned, the last of his irritation dissolving away at the sight of her. She looked so haggard, it would have been like kicking a puppy to treat her with other than graciousness.

He'd changed from his professional intimidation wear into practical clothes. She noted the slouchy cargo pants and plain black tee shirt with obvious approval, even managing a faint smile at the sight of his battered hiking boots. Adapt to the environment. Another credo he'd found useful in the past. He slipped on his suede-fronted varsity jacket and discreetly tucked his pistol in the band of his trousers at the small of his back. Pays to be ready should she happen to issue that invitation for his help.

Or even if she didn't.

He planned to stick close and be alert. Maybe her dream was just that, a bad dream because she was tired, and he was being over-sensitive because of his last assignment and what he knew to be at stake here in Peru.

Better safe...

He wasn't sure exactly who knew they were coming. But he was sure someone wasn't going to like it.

***

The Restaurant Cordano was another pleasant surprise. Situated across from the Desamparados Station which boasted the world's highest track until rail service was discontinued, they were seated in an old-fashioned dining room and presented with a list of traditional Peruvian foods.

"What do you recommend?"

At his question, Sheba took a moment to regard her companion. True, he'd gone out of his way not to mention her breakdown earlier, but he hadn't exactly proven to be a nurturing soul of support. Frank Cobb was as tightly buttoned up as that white shirt she'd first seen him wearing. His manner, his aloof air of anticipation, all suggested Federal government – one of the more elite and not talked about agencies. One of the scary ones. He had that look about him, the calm cool, the casual demeanor stretched like lamb's skin over the wolf inside. When he'd burst into her room, the taut sense of competence and unhesitating violence he exuded had made her feel safe for the first time in decades. But she couldn't afford to forget that he was not here to protect her. He was there to see to Harper Research's investment in Paulo. She was just along for the ride – a ride she feared would be one way. Cobb wasn't here to deal with her demons.

But he'd looked damned fine half-dressed in her doorway.

Not a tall or overly imposing man, he was solid power compressed tightly into the guise of an average build. That bulk of upper body was neatly hidden beneath the suit coat but not so successfully by the tee shirt. Thin black knit hugged to carefully honed contours of sculpted chest, broad shoulders and arms defined by muscle strength. Not a sleek Doberman but a stocky pit bull. He was a man who could do some serious damage even without the deadly sidearm he carried.

Another deception came with his pleasantly average, All-American features. Hard jaw, nice facial angles. Brown hair cut close and conservatively. Brows that arched in a cocky, Jack Nicholson way over hazel eyes to express more than he would in that wry, slightly smoky voice that held the faint bite of a Jersey Shore accent. A tempting mouth when it relaxed its intense line into a slightly cynical smile. Pleasant. Average. Except for a gaze that penetrated like x-rays and a wicked scar lending a lethal imperfection.

Too bad he wasn't on her side. How wonderful it would have been to rely upon him. But that wasn't the case. She had no one but herself. And Paulo was the only one she had in her corner. That's why she'd returned.

Cobb was staring at her with a patient expectation. Waiting.

Startled from her thoughts, she remembered his question and looked at the menu. Food was a nice, neutral topic, so she let herself relax.

"The cuisine in Peru focuses on three main ingredients—potatoes, corn and hot peppers. There are over two hundred different varieties of potatoes, or *papas,* grown here. Corn is, of course, a sacred pre-Hispanic crop that was used both as food and for barter. They use a purple variety to make a palatable drink called *chicha morada*, rather like beer, actually." She paused because he'd begun to smile. Heat rose in her cheeks. "I'm sorry. I'm rattling on rather like a history professor. An unfortunate habit, I'm afraid, to force knowledge upon the unwilling."

"There are worse habits." His smile grew slightly wolfish. "And I'm not all that unwilling."

Sheba reared back.

Was he flirting with her?

Having little experience there and next to no practice with intimate banter, Sheba quickly dropped her gaze back to the menu before she lost herself in the sudden warmth of his intense stare. She hurried on with the safe discussion of their meal.

"Picante from the highlands is an art form in itself in terms of degrees of spiciness. How hot do you like it, Mr. Cobb?"

When he didn't answer right away, she glanced up in question and found herself devoured by his sultry, green-gold gaze.

"The hotter the better, Dr. Reynard."

For a moment, she couldn't breathe. Confusion fluttered through her like a band of Morpho butterflies on frantic wings, heightening her alarm and scaring up a rather dizzying loss of control. For another long moment, she considered experimenting with the odd sense of sexual attraction teased up between them. What would his kisses feel like? Hard and dominating or wooingly sweet?

The image of him in her doorway returned to tantalize. Could the stroke of his strong hands upon her body brush away the film of anxiousness left by her unsettling dream?

Would the nights be so dreaded if not spent alone?

But then shyness and caution tempered her reactions. She was not here to play pat-a-cake with a quixotic stranger, and she'd better do something fast lest things get out of hand.

"Let me order for you then," she offered with a disarmingly innocent smile. Without looking away from Cobb's smug demeanor, she gestured for their server. She requested *papa rellena* for herself and for her daring companion, *lomo saltado* with rocoto peppers. Before the waiter could contest her choice, she merely said, "Don't worry. He's a tough guy. He likes it hot."

When their glasses of cold whitish beer arrived, Cobb took an appreciative sip and leaned back in his chair.

"You're right. I was expecting a man. It threw me for a minute."

Lulled by his honesty, she was prepared to give a little. "Perhaps it would have helped to have my full name, Dr. Sheba Reynard."

One brow arched. "Sheba? As in Queen of the Jungle? Someone had a sense of humor."

"That's Sheena. It's Sheba, as in Come Back Little."

"And have you?"

"What?"

"Come back?"

Her mouth tightened, and her words bit like rock salt. "Only under pressure, Mr. Cobb, not by choice."

Taking his cue from her hard tone, he became all business. "How much have you been told about what's going on?"

The temperature in the elegant restaurant seemed to plunge as chills of gooseflesh broke out on Sheba's arms. "About as much as you, I suspect," was her evasive answer. "More than I care to know."

She wasn't ready for this, for what lay ahead in the jungle, nor did she want to spend this oddly enjoyable dinner rushing the inevitable.

That would come soon enough.

Cobb was studying her carefully. What did he see? What dare she show him of her real reluctance and fear? Nothing, rumbled her inner pride. Show him nothing. She took a deep drought of beer and forced her mood to calm.

"But here I am."

"I was told you were some kind of expert in the area of native culture. A real asset." His sudden smile was lightning quick in response to some joke that went over her head. Was he laughing at her? Annoyance braced her.

"I'm an ethnologist. I study the effects of legend and myth upon indigenous societies."

He made a sound that might have meant he was impressed. But probably not. "In other words, you're a one woman National Geographic Society."

"And what are you, Mr. Cobb?" she countered with a pointed verbal thrust.

Unflappable, he remained smiling. "A babysitter, Dr. Reynard."

She was about to protest the need for his protection when their meals arrived, hers a fried oblong of mashed potatoes stuffed with meat, onions, olives, boiled eggs and raisins; his, French fries combined with strips of steak, onions and tomatoes...and screamingly torrid rocoto peppers.

"Smells good," he pronounced before diving in with obvious relish.

She took a few small bites of her own meal while watching him make quick work of his. Waiting, perversely, for the dappling of sweat to pop along his brow, for his eyes to well up in misery. When neither happened, she felt both cheated and ashamed.

"I'm here to make sure Dr. Lemos finishes his work," Cobb went on to explain with cut-and-dry clarity. "What that might entail, I'm not really sure at this point."

Sheba could have told him, but Frank Cobb, with his city clothes and cosmopolitan belief system, wouldn't have understood. He was here to do battle against superstition, against an enemy that was imagined, not flesh and blood. An enemy far more dangerous than one that was real.

"And how about you, Doctor?"

Alerted by the sudden skewering of his gaze, Sheba held on to her control. "What about me?"

"Aren't you the least bit worried?"

Her heart started pounding faster. What did he know?

"Worried about what, Mr. Cobb?"

"About stepping into the middle of a potentially dangerous situation?"

Now the sweat was on her brow. "I grew up in these jungles, Mr. Cobb. You're the outsider here. You're the one who has no idea what you're getting into."

A certain flintiness gave his gaze a cold, metallic gleam. "That's not quite true, Doctor. I understand more than you know." With that, he reached for his wallet to pay for the meal, ending the conversation and the awkward companionability of their evening.

And inexplicably, Sheba was sad to see it end.

She'd started to push back in her chair when an odd look crossed Cobb's face. He began to blink rapidly, his gaze losing focus.

"Oh, my God," he wheezed, tears rolling down his cheeks.

Then she understood, quickly intercepting his reach for the bottled water she'd requested.

"No, don't drink. That'll spread the heat and make it worse." She pushed the bread toward him. "This will help absorb it."

He chewed and sucked for air as the hot peppers seared him from the inside out. He looked so wretched, she felt childish and a bit nervous as to how he'd react to her treachery.

"I'm sorry. I should have warned you." Then a mischievous grin got the better of her. "But you did say–"

He glanced up at her, his eyes still swimming. "I'm an idiot. Don't listen to what I say when I'm being an idiot."

Her mood abruptly softened toward him. In a quiet voice, she said, "And I'd ask that you do the same."

He paused in his desperate stuffing to demand a further explanation with his look.

"Earlier tonight, I spoke harshly." The words came uncomfortably, as hard to swallow as Cobb's peppers. "I didn't mean to offend you. I appreciated your concern."

He continued to stare at her, suddenly less at ease with her honesty than with her trickery. "It's my job," he stated bluntly. Then, when her features began to freeze up, he added,

"And my pleasure."

Upon leaving the restaurant, Cobb, who was breathing easier by then, glanced at a battered taxi loitering by the door, noting the way its front wheels seemed to be sitting at odd angles.

"I've had enough E-ticket fun for one night. Do you mind if we walk?"

"Fine," Sheba was quick to agree, not eager to return to their room where her nightmare awaited. "It'll give me a chance to do some shopping."

They wandered the crowded walks of the market which, even after an attempt at government control, was still run with the vitality and larceny of an ancient bazaar. Sheba was an expert haggler, enjoying the challenge. With a practiced air alternating between contempt and indifference, she picked through the merchandise, her comments knowledgeable and often complimentary, making the vendors beg for her purchase with a banter of price until it was often below their cost. She bought shawls woven from crude wool still embedded with flecks of thistle from a nearly blind woman and a jacket featuring a serpent design brilliantly depicted in fine yarns dyed from seeds, herbs and vegetables. The excellent quality would have fetched a small fortune in an urban boutique in the States. She sorted through stacks of alpaca sweaters, llama rugs, blankets and cotton cloth, speaking rapidly to the women in layered skirts who had drop spindles dangling from their fingers. Cobb didn't recognize the language as Spanish. That made him give her another, closer look.

True, her skin was a soft shade of gold, not Brazil nut brown. Her hair was rinsed with streaks of blonde but was it, in reality, a glossy black? Though her features were somewhat delicate, her face was broad through the cheek bones and round. Did she share some of the same heritage as these Peruvian people?

As she led him from booth to booth, she explained with a tour guide's rhetoric that it was illegal to buy or take pre-Columbian or colonial antiques out of the country or to purchase anything made from vicuna fibers, feathers, skins or shells of rainforest creatures. She sounded defensive. Because she was protecting her own?

"Is this real gold?" he asked, fingering the delicately spun filigree shaped to resemble doves on a pair of earrings.

"The stuff of Conquistador dreams."

He wasn't much of a browser. After the gold earrings, his selection was quick and generic. Six silver crosses on fine chains. Funny, he didn't strike her as a particularly ardent Catholic sort.

As he paid for the jewelry without questioning the price, Sheba found herself wondering who they were for. A gift for his mother or sister, perhaps? Or a wife or girlfriend? No wedding band, but that wasn't proof positive that he was a free agent. Though it was none of her business, she couldn't help considering what kind of female influence he allowed into his life. Certainly, there must be someone. Most people didn't live alone by choice, the way she did.

Feeling a bit melancholy at the thought of some woman waiting a half world away to receive Cobb's gifts, Sheba paused to listen to a trio of traditional street musicians weaving a pentatonic harmony into a mournful tapestry that suited her mood. One teen played the zamponas panpipes, another the Andean harp, both to the percussion accompaniment of a deep-voiced frame drum upon which the player thumped out the rhythm soulfully by hand. As she bent to drop a scattering of coins into their donation basket, her necklace slipped free of her tee shirt, swinging once, twice before being snatched up by a dexterous hand. A rough jerk broke the cord about her neck, surprising her into a sharp cry of alarmed dismay. Her hand instinctively reached for where her treasured necklace no longer hung.

No!

But as the bold and clever market thief spun to make good his escape into the teaming crowds, he found the barrel of a pistol wedged beneath his chin, effectively stopping his flight the way it could easily stop his life.

"I believe you have something there that doesn't belong to you."

Cobb's voice was a soft ripple that didn't quite cover the deadly jagged rocks below. The thief wisely released the medallion into Cobb's outstretched hand. The instant the pressure of the muzzle lessened, the thief dodged and darted away.

Cobb examined the ancient oval of tarnished precious metal. A strange image was beaten into an age-softened relief. A face of some god, most likely. Half man, half beast. Old. Old enough to be one of those illegal antiquities she'd spoken of.

"This is yours," he announced, passing the piece into her anxious possession. "If you want to wear it tomorrow, I suggest you hang onto it more carefully."

She didn't even smile at the return of her own cautioning from the airport. Her fingers closed about the medallion with knuckle-whitening strength as she brought her fist up to rest over her heart. Her features were pale, her manner shaken by the near loss of something that must have had special meaning to her. For a moment, her eyes glimmered in the uneven light.

"Thank you," was all she said before turning to continue along the market street.

Leaving Cobb to trail behind, wondering over the intriguing facets to the thorny ethnologist who pretended to be all business yet gave rare insights to a raw and vulnerable soul.

Damn. Just what he needed. Another wounded bird in his palm.

***

Lying back on her bed, Sheba studied the medallion she'd carried with her for twenty years. Its value went beyond the rarity of the piece, which itself was worth a fortune to certain pre-Columbian collectors. In all her years of travel and exploring, she'd never come across this same design, yet somehow it was as familiar to her as her driver's license photo. Its origin was just as much a mystery as how it had come into her possession.

And Cobb had saved it for her.

Dropping the warmed circle back atop her skin, she let

her thoughts drift to Frank Cobb. He was a mystery to her, too. Sometimes teasing—right up to the edge of intimate innuendo—then retreating behind a cold, professional veneer. But even though logic couldn't support it, even though experience denied it, she felt she could count on him.

Frank Cobb would keep her safe.

She closed her eyes, and for the first time in a long while, she slept without dreams.

But in the room across from hers, Cobb didn't rest so easily. He lay in a pose of relaxation, but his senses were active and alert for any sound from the other bedroom. He hadn't expected his job to start so soon, but he'd learned never to disregard his innate alarm systems. Dr. Reynard was a troubled woman. But was she also a woman in trouble?

And was that going to be his problem?

He couldn't afford to let it be, not when he had a job to do.

Once he was sure she slept soundly, he slipped out of the room and asked directions for the address he had scribbled onto a piece of paper. Following the clerk's verbal map, he found himself burrowed into the seedier side of Lima, a side tourists would shy away from for its lack of charm or appeal. Visitors didn't want to see reality or snap quaint pictures of poverty.

Cobb paused outside a rundown bar, rechecking his address against the sagging plank hung over the open doors. From inside, the stench of drink and sweat mingled with the loud assault of up-tempoed traditional music and laughter that overpowered his senses the moment he crossed the threshold. He went to the bar and yelled over the aggressive drum beat.

"I'm looking for Andres and Felipe Mendes. I was told I could find them here."

"Why should they want to see you, *señor*?"

Cobb littered the stained bar top with coins. "Because I have more of that."

The silver was quickly swept up, and the bartender nodded toward a smoky corner. After making a purchase, Cobb murmured his thanks.

The Mendes brothers weren't exactly the cream of Lima society. They were dirty, unshaven and smelled like llamas. And they were drunk, getting drunker. Cobb set the bottle he carried upon the cluttered table top. Two pairs of narrowed eyes regarded him as a possible threat.

"*Buenas noches. Habla usted ingles?*"

"*Si.* What do you want?"

"I want you to tell me a story. Pretend I'm your priest."

"And you will forgive us our sins?"

"Depends upon the sins, *mi amigo.*"

They laughed and gestured to an empty chair before diving into the fresh bottle of liquor. When they made no offer to fill Cobb's glass, he took care of it himself.

"Now that we're old friends, tell me about the night your other brother died."

Both grimy faces closed up tighter than a whore's generosity. The older one crossed himself while the other growled, "It is not a story to tell to strangers."

Cobb placed an impressive pile of money on the table. "There. Does that get us better acquainted?"

The two exchanged uncomfortable looks, but the younger raked up the cash, saying, "There is not much to tell, *señor.*"

"I'm not the law. I don't give a rat's hindend what you were doing. I want to know what you found...or what found you."

The younger, more talkative one leaned forward. "We found death, *señor*. We went looking for treasure and we found death."

"Where?"

"We do not remember the way."

Or were being well paid to forget, Cobb suspected. But by whom?

"Could you take me there?"

"No. The SIN has made the area off-limits to those without special passes."

What interest would the Peruvian intelligence community have in the murder of a tomb robber?

"Because of what you found?"

The elder spat on the table top just shy of Cobb's hand. He didn't move it.

"We tell them nothing but they hear anyway."

"Hear what?"

"That my brother, Mano, rest his soul, woke something that should have been left undisturbed."

"Something? Explain that to me."

"Our legends are not for your amusement, *civilazado*."

"Tell him, Andres. What does it matter now that Mano is dead?"

The elder Mendes brother considered this then shrugged. "We intruded upon the sleep of the Ancient One. Now he hunts the jungle at night until someone puts him back to rest."

"How is that done?"

"First, we apologize by making offerings, and then there will be a sacrifice of–"

Andres halted his younger brother's words with a cautioning shake of his head. But Cobb was all over the significance of what he didn't say.

"Sacrifice? What kind of sacrifice? Human?"

Andres laughed. "You watch too many bad movies, *señor*. That is not how it's done any more."

"How is it done?"

"We have said too much already. You go away now. And leave the bottle."

"Just one more thing. How was your brother killed?"

Andres's gaze took on a flat, black glaze. "He was drained of blood, *señor*. Does that answer your question?"

Oh, yes. It most certainly did.

FOUR

Their small plane took off just before dawn. The privately chartered six-seat Cessna would take them to the junction of the Madre de Dios and Manu rivers for an exorbitant price but would cut days off from overland travel. Though there was a government-run air service out of Lima that shuttled passengers to the mission towns of Sepahua and Pucallpa at the gateway to the Amazon's southern jungle, it was extremely unreliable, and Peyton Samuels was anxious enough to get them there to foot the extra bill.

Sheba stared out the window, watching as the big buildings and boulevards became square-cut fields chopped from the encroaching jungle, and the pindots of light and life went from an electric glow to the fires of shanty towns. Then a thick blanket of clouds swallowed them whole, and she was forced to turn her attention inside the small plane's cabin.

Her own nervousness abated when she cast a look at her companion. He sat stiff and straight in his seat, his hands curved into white-knuckled talons over the ends of the arm rest, his features granite-set and his eyes closed. She didn't think he was breathing.

Funny, she wouldn't have thought anything scared Frank Cobb. At least anything so ordinary.

"We're off the ground. You can exhale now."

He answered her comment with a shaky gust of breath as his eyes flickered open to regard their surroundings uneasily.

"Don't like to fly?"

"I don't mind the flying. I'm just not too fond of unscheduled landings."

She smiled at his terse reply. "After all the puddle-jumpers I've been on, some of them pre-dating World War II, this is a Cadillac."

His return smile with thin and unconvincing.

"I've learned to place my faith in a higher power, Mr. Cobb, and to just relax."

"God?"

"The pilot."

He made a soft sound of disbelief but much of the tension left the harsh angle of his jaw. A sudden curiosity came to her. *Frank Cobb, what do you do for fun*?

Would her question startle him? Or would it confirm what she'd already guessed, that she and her traveling partner were sad cases when it came to the extra-curriculars of life?

Why was he really here? She'd had a quick, unauthorized glimpse at his record while visiting a colleague in D.C. She was certain that what it said was a lot shorter than what it didn't say. What it didn't say was that a man like this wouldn't be sent to babysit anybody. Something fishy was going on to bring a man of Frank Cobb's dangerous caliber into the picture. And that made her wonder what kind of trouble Paulo was really in.

His message had been short and sweet. He'd run into some problems—some political, some practical. Their mutual uncle Peyton Samuels wanted to call in the marines, but Paulo would settle for the 'security expert' Harper recommended...only if she would come along. He needed her to run interference with the locals and with Samuels, who'd always held a soft spot for her.

Now she was wondering if she was soft in the head for agreeing.

But she couldn't keep Paulo from getting the protection he needed, nor could she turn away from his almost desperate sounding request. Not after all he'd done to keep her sane.

Would she even recognize him? It had been, after all, twenty years. Twenty years of letters and phone calls and grainy photos staring out at her from professional periodicals.

But no amount of passing years could place a wedge

between the loyalty and love she felt, not even her fear.

She could only hope that Frank Cobb was darned good at his job.

She should have used the flight time to discover what Cobb knew about the situation ahead. In particular, what he knew about her connection. But a self-avowed coward in this particular arena, she put off such inevitabilities for as long as possible. She didn't want to think about their destination. Besides, Cobb might have some uncomfortable questions of his own. Better she not provoke them lest she be forced to come up with a palatable answer.

Taking a deep, forestalling breath, she slumped back in her seat and tried to unwind. Maybe it wouldn't be so bad. What could be worse than the relentless night sweats, than the not knowing? Wasn't it time she faced the truth, if indeed, there was one to find? Maybe after all these years, the jungle had devoured those truths. Maybe if left alone, they would have remained safely covered by time and a tangle of forest green. Until some greedy tomb raiders ripped through that pretense of serenity and distance to expose the horrors of the past. She fingered the shape of the medallion beneath her cotton shirt. Maybe nothing awaited her in the jungle. Maybe it was just a tomb, just a coincidence.

And maybe pigs could fly.

She closed her eyes, trying not to appear as small and terrified as she felt inside.

She must have drifted off into a fitful sleep because a sudden bout of turbulence had her head bouncing against the unyielding curve of Frank's shoulder. She straightened in her seat, slightly embarrassed at the liberty she'd taken, but Cobb seemed unaware of it. His attention was focused ahead, his breath hissing through clenched teeth.

They were about to land.

Their plane dipped down through the cloud cover until the impenetrable solid blew into wispy threads of white, finally revealing the jungle below. From the air, the Amazon looked like an unbroken sea of green sponges. The sight of that endless canopy filled Sheba with a confusing mix of welcome and dread. *Coming home*, Paulo called it.

Home to face her destiny.

The plane banked abruptly, angling to slip through what, at their altitude, seemed like a tiny crack in the surface of this jungle planet. The movement tossed Sheba against Frank and had her grabbing at his knee and forearm for balance. As tense as he was, it was like seeking purchase on a rock face. She immediately started to push back, but his hand clapped down over the one she'd placed on his thigh, holding it there at first with a flattening pressure and then within the crushing curl of his fingers. It was all she could do not to yelp in discomfort.

The hair-like fracture in the green below widened, becoming the twists and turns of a good-sized river and the runway their pilot sought. As they grew close enough to scare up a ripple on that lazy water surface, Sheba could see their destination: a single dock stretching out into the river, its pilings decorated with the gargoyle-like black vultures waiting patiently for the opportunity to scavenge for whatever carrion might be dumped into the still waters. Though ugly while at roost, when provoked by the plane's arrival, the village's sanitary engineers took to the air on long, dark wings, their flight strangely graceful and evoking a sense of tranquility. Odd harbingers of welcome.

Their plane skimmed along the water's surface with scarcely a bump, bringing them up to cozy against the warped dock. The second the engine was cut, Cobb was out of his seat, grabbing for his bag, unwilling to even wait for the propeller to slow in its rhythmic slicing of air.

"Ladies and gentleman, thank you for surviving your trip on Fly By Night Air," he muttered in cynical relief, pausing only long enough to put down a hand to Sheba. She held up the one he hadn't mashed in his fretful and apparently unconscious grip, and let him haul her from the narrow seat to balance on slightly shivery legs. Whether her weak stance was due to the cramped quarters or her anxiety, she was now grateful, nonetheless, for her companion's supportive hand beneath her elbow.

They ducked through the small door to step into the steamy

air of the Amazon.

Sheba held a hand up to shadow her eyes from the glare of the sun off water so she could scan the shoreline for a familiar face. Behind her, Cobb passed a wad of currency into the pilot's hand with the pronouncement, "Thanks for getting us here alive."

The pilot grinned and nodded, not understanding the words but recognizing the universal symbol of money.

Then a joyous cry was heard.

"Sheba!"

At the sound of his voice, all Sheba's anxieties melted away in a bittersweet rush. She dropped her suitcase and ran carelessly down the dock's uneven boards. Right into the open arms of her best friend from childhood. After a long, whirling hug, Paulo Lemos held her back for a warm, reacquainting look.

How tall he'd grown! How handsome! How wonderfully familiar.

The Paulo she'd left behind in the jungles had been a shy, chubby boy of ten hiding behind a somber demeanor and Coke bottle-thick glasses. At approaching thirty, he was cosmopolitanly gorgeous, with Peruvian-bronze complexion, whipcord physique and eyes like melting chocolate behind contact lenses. But there was the same hint of grateful camaraderie in the blinding flash of his smile.

"*Una regla*, how beautiful you are!" he declared, bringing a blush of denying pleasure to her cheeks. "Last time I saw you, you were all ears, elbows and knees, a stick figure girl with pigtails I used to tie in knots."

"And I've never worn my hair long since then, you awful beast of a boy. Though I am still as flat as a ruler." She cupped his face between her palms, adoring him with her gaze. "It's been too long."

His expression grew suddenly serious as he bent to kiss her brow. "Welcome home, little Sheba."

It was then he glanced over her head to see Cobb regarding the two of them together through inscrutable eyes. Keeping Sheba tucked within the curl of his arm, he confronted the other man with a cool formality.

"You must be the American mercenary the Center sent down to protect me. I am Paulo Lemos." He put out his free hand.

For a long beat, Cobb ignored the outstretched hand as he searched the other's features, reading signs of character and checking for shortcomings. He didn't misread the territorial bristle of one man warning off another, though he hadn't thought of the two scientists' relationship that way. Sheba had given him to believe that Lemos was an old friend. That's not the impression the Peruvian was telegraphing with his rigid posture and enfolding arm. The attitude was typical possessive male – a threatened male.

Finally, Cobb clasped his hand for a firm shake. "Frank Cobb. I'll be your shadow from now on."

"Does that mean you disappear from sight when the limelights go on?"

Cobb snapped his fingers then opened his hand wide. "Invisible. Unless you need me."

They exchanged steady, gaging stares, then Paulo broke the contact to gaze fondly upon Sheba once more. "How can I object to you being here? Look what you've brought me."

Sheba beamed up at him, and Cobb realized that she didn't have the slightest idea that Paulo Lemos was out to change the basis of their relationship from roughhouse to romance.

Well, it wasn't his job to enlighten her. It was his job to stay out of the way. Invisible. A shadow with no opinions, no input and no reason to get involved. The only way he could perform his duties was to stay objective, and that didn't entail feeling just a wee bit envious of the young scientist for the way Sheba was gazing up at him like he was her moon and stars.

Dismissing Cobb as if he were transparent already, Paulo exclaimed, "Come, Sheba. I have a surprise for you."

"Seeing you again is gift enough, Paulo," she assured him happily but still allowed him to steer her away. Neither of them looked back.

"I'll just get the bags," Cobb grumbled to himself. "No,

don't thank me. Happy to do it."

He shouldered his duffle then lifted Sheba's suitcase.

"Good God, woman, what are you traveling with? The kitchen sink?"

Amazed that the slender Sheba Reynard that been toting the massively weighty bag about without a word of complaint, he hoisted it manfully and followed the couple to dry land. When she stepped ashore, Sheba looked back over her shoulder to give him a grateful smile. It wasn't much in the way of a tip, but it would do.

The village they entered could have been a backdrop for a Tarzan movie or a new Disney theme park. Rustic buildings leaned haphazardly in a drunken line along the main road, which was little more than a dirt two track that would become impassable with the first good rain. To Sheba, the *caserios* was typical of the countless settlements she'd passed through as a child. Some, like this one, where the residents made their living gathering Brazil nuts, served as a frequent collecting point where ancient trucks would carry the harvest to a processing center and would offer a lift to a traveler for $20 U.S. It was almost frightening the way she slipped so easily back into the pattern of their language and way of life, for it had been hers for only the first third of her accumulated years. No wonder, really, since the time spent in similar circumstances far outweighed her experiences in civilization.

There was an honesty here that couldn't be found in the American city. True, it was mostly a hand-to- mouth existence, but there was a sense of pride and community to these people she'd never experienced during her visits to the States. She could relax her defenses and be herself with the one person she trusted above all others.

She smiled as Paulo lingered in the village's small marketplace to inventory the medicinal plants supplied by the local *curandero* to cure the ills of the Indians. After he had soothed the old vendor's suspicions with his fluent use of their region's dialect, he spent several minutes discussing the properties of each sample, going so far as to peel skin off several of the fruits to suck at their pulp for taste. He ended up bagging two of the specimens then jotting down notes in the battered spiral notebook he carried, including a quick sketch of the sample and a location as to where it could be found.

Catching Sheba in her indulgent study, he grinned rather sheepishly but didn't apologize for being what he was, first and foremost—a scientist. How well that profession suited the boy she'd once known, whose curiosity had gotten them into trouble on more than one occasion.

How she'd missed him.

"Where's my surprise?" she asked as they continued down the rutted road.

"It comes in this evening with our boat."

"We're not leaving until morning then?"

"I've got some supplies coming in that I must wait for. And it will give us a chance to reminisce. There's a little café that serves the best *ceviche*. The hotel isn't much, but it has mosquito netting and cold showers."

"What more could I ask for?"

Behind her, she heard Cobb mutter, "Cable, A/C and a wet bar," but she pretended not to notice.

"You might wish to rest in your room for an hour or two. The boat ride tomorrow is six hours and not very hospitable."

"I'm not a tenderfoot, Paulo," she scolded mildly.

The scientist's dark eyes cut over to Cobb. "I wasn't thinking of you."

Cobb supplied a narrow smile and a chilly, "Don't concern yourself over me. This isn't my first jungle tour, and I'm sure it will be a lot more friendly than what I'm used to."

Paulo shrugged and turned away with an indifference that surprised Sheba. She was about to apologize for her friend's rudeness when an innate loyalty held her silent. Cobb wouldn't take such things personally, and she wouldn't hurt Paulo for the world even with such a small correction. She let the matter go, making her own excuses for Paulo's attitude. He didn't know Cobb and was leery of outsiders, even though many would consider him one as well. He would relax once he realized Cobb wasn't a threat.

Their rooms were the best the jungle usually offered.

Sagging beds surrounded by a swaddling of net with no luxuries of air-conditioning, television or hot water. Frank was shown to his room first, and as he stood surveying the dingy interior with a stoic acceptance, Sheba leaned close to whisper, "If I were you, I'd plug up those holes in the walls in case they're part of a roach run."

"Terrific," he muttered, stepping inside and closing the door between them.

Feeling strangely adrift without her abruptly taciturn protector, Sheba sought out the quiet of her own room. Even after her brief nap on the plane, exhaustion weighed heavily upon her. She hadn't enjoyed a decent rest since Paulo's call. She hadn't known an unbroken night's sleep in twenty years. She grabbed for sleep when and where she could find it. And now was a good time, while it was still daylight. Paulo left her with a hug at the door. Then the silence settled in, with only the broken rhythm of the overhead ceiling fan to create a stir of life.

After thoroughly checking the corners and under the bed for potential creature infestations, she stretched out on the lumpy mattress and let the shivers of anxiousness overtake her. She couldn't shake the sense of unease. It was the jungle with its invasive scent of decay and moisture, and another remembered odor that seemed interlaced with the rest even though it wasn't actually present, one that held a metallic bite and a coppery after-taste.

The scent of blood.

***

Not one for taking siestas, Frank stowed his gear, and after checking to see that Sheba was also safely stowed for the moment, decided to do a quick sweep of the perimeter. It was then he noticed Paulo Lemos seated in an open air café across the street. He hesitated a moment, not exactly eager for the man's company. One of the benefits of his job was not having to mingle or socialize with the client. He was there, in fact, to be invisible. But he had an unfortunate weakness that drew him across the road, one that he wouldn't admit to even as it got the better of him.

He wanted to find out more about Dr. Sheba Reynard.

Lemos regarded him with a steady, somewhat hostile stare, but when it became clear to him that Cobb wasn't going to graciously go away, he gestured toward a second chair.

"Join me, Mr. Cobb?" He waved the waiter over as Cobb sat down. "A pisco sour for my...friend."

Cobb held up his hand to halt the waiter. *"No, gracias."*

"Ah. You speak the language.."

"Not much and not well, but I can find the restrooms and cigarettes in just about any country."

Lemos nodded to the waiter and murmured a quick pattering of Spanish, overruling Cobb's objection to Peru's national drink of brandy, lemon juice, bitters, egg whites and sugar. Then he took one of the filter-tips Cobb offered and exhaled a thin stream of smoke in the other man's direction. His narrowed gaze told Cobb that things were about to get sticky.

"So, Mr. Cobb, what do you think of her?"

"Of whom?"

Lemos scowled impatiently at the bland response. "Sheba, of course."

"Dr. Reynard? We only met the other day. I can't say that we've gotten personal enough for me to have formed an opinion of any kind."

"Good," the scientist muttered under his breath with just enough attitude for Frank to perversely want to taunt him.

"But I've found her to be smart and capable and amazingly strong considering that suitcase she lugs around."

"And attractive?" The question jabbed like a knifepoint, ready to eviscerate him.

"I suppose, if you like skinny women. I prefer more than a handful, myself."

Lemos smiled thinly, encouraged by that crudely offered opinion. "What she lacks in inches, she more than makes up for in IQ."

"If you like brainy women." Which he did, but he didn't feel obligated to share that with his forced companion. No sense in antagonizing the man beyond prudence if they were going to be spending time in the jungle with Sheba Reynard between them. Sheba shouldn't have figured into the equation at all, but she was the reason Cobb had joined the rather snotty Lemos in the first place.

"You've known her for a long time?"

Lemos nodded and stated with a territorial intimation, "All my life. And there's no one I'd rather spend the rest of it with."

Now, that was putting it on the line so there could be no misinterpretation. Lemos was either in love with her or had to have her. Either way, the gloves were off, and it wasn't in Frank's best interest to interfere. But he found he couldn't leave it gracefully alone.

"Does she know that you've got her future all neatly planned out?"

That added query brought a degree of tension back between them. "She will soon enough. She still sees me as a childhood playmate. Soon, she will see me as more."

"Congratulations."

Lemos accepted the flat comment with a nod. "Yes, I am a very lucky man. Few women are as versatile and accomplished as Sheba. Or as fragile."

That surprised Cobb. Delicate wasn't how he would have described Sheba Reynard. Troubled, definitely. Neurotic, perhaps. But fragile? "I'm afraid I don't see her as some fainting hothouse orchid."

"That's because you share no history with her. How could you understand without knowing what she's been through."

Now, he was all attention. "What's that?"

"You could ask her to tell you about it, but you see, she remembers none of it. She was found wandering alone in the jungle, in shock and covered in blood."

"What happened?" Cobb asked, dreading the answer.

"She'd witnessed her parents' murder."

***

Sheba dozed fitfully as the heat of the day turned sultry while the hours stretched into early evening. She stumbled through her veiled dreams, her breath quickening, her hands and feet twitching like a pup chasing rabbits. Only what followed her through the leafy green corridors of her familiar nightmare was nothing so harmless.

She was running for her life.

Moaning softly, she thrashed beneath her sheet, unaware that she was no longer alone in her room. The mosquito netting rippled as an indistinguishable shadow brushed by on the other side. As Sheba ran from imagined dangers in her dream, a real threat drew back the gauzy curtain to peer at her in her restless sleep.

"How much do you remember, Sheba?" the figure whispered in a soft, sibilant hiss. "You will live for only as long as your memory stays blank."

Sheba sat up with a gasp. Her bed curtain fluttered. Through sleep-glazed eyes, she thought she saw something or someone moving in her room.

"Who's there?" Her voice trembled slightly then firmed. "Paulo? Cobb?"

Had someone been there, or was it a lingering fragment of her dream?

She sat clutching her bed covers as a new horror shivered through her. What if she could no longer tell the difference?

What if her relentless monsters had stepped from the realm of nightmares into the realities of her waking moments?

Wasn't that what she'd been afraid of all along?

That returning to Peru would give substance to her fears and a name to her night terrors.

And then she noticed it. A soft fragrance on the slowly moving current of air. And all the hairs prickled up on her arms and nape.

She hadn't been dreaming.

FIVE

"And what are you boys talking about?"

Two pairs of eyes lifted, and Sheba got the uncomfortable impression that they were looking at the topic of their discussion. Paulo had the decency to seem embarrassed, but Cobb's stare was keen and unblinking as he rose to hold out a chair for her. As she settled into it, did she imagine the light brush of his fingertips along the outsides of her arms? A sensual or a sympathetic touch?

What had Paulo been telling him?

Feeling as though her towel had just been yanked off as she stepped out of the shower, she did her best to act unaffected as her question hung in the air.

"Your friend was saying that the two of you grew up together."

"Yes, we did."

Sheba waited, but Cobb didn't follow her succinct answer with another intrusive question. Perversely, she found herself offering more.

"My parents were missionaries. Paulo's family hosted them. His father and my mother were distant cousins. My earliest memories are of this place and these people."

"Your people?" Cobb slipped that loaded question in with a silky skill, a question too complex to answer with a simple yes or no.

As Cobb was probably well aware, or he wouldn't have asked.

"Technically, at least on my mother's side. Her family had moved to the States before she was born, so my grandfather could get an engineering degree. My mama and daddy met during their first semester at a small Bible college in Alabama."

She noted his small smile of discovery. He'd been wondering about the accent. It had hung on tenaciously regardless of the fact that two decades had passed since she'd heard her father's drawling voice reading Scripture aloud each night. She'd tried to breed it out while attending the snobby Eastern schools where she was teased and called a hick. But now she didn't mind so much. It reminded her of the familiar.

"My parents belonged to an offshoot of the Summer Institute of Linguistics program working with indigenous tribes to give their language a written form. The idea was to translate the Bible for them, a noble goal that only earned criticism for their destruction of cultural identity."

"And is that what you think they were doing?"

She didn't try to avoid his penetrating stare but rather matched it boldly. "Their beliefs aren't mine."

"And what do you believe, Dr. Reynard?"

"I believe I'll order the *cuy*. I've heard it's quite delicious spit-roasted."

Their gazes held for another long minute, then Cobb's eyes crinkled at the corners in appreciation of her deft evasion.

"And what exactly is *cuy*? Does it involve hot peppers?'

Sheba relaxed into a smile. "No. Did you ever have a pet Guinea pig as a child? If you did, it may seem a little cannibalistic."

Though there was no discernable change in his expression, Frank Cobb was suddenly locked down as tight as the National vault. "The closest thing I had to a pet were rats. And we didn't eat them, spit roasted or otherwise."

He said it so blandly. Was he telling the truth or just playing another game with her gullibility? Something in the flat sheen of his stare told her it was the former, but Sheba had no time to respond to the shocking nature of his claim.

Feeling excluded from the conversation, Paulo announced, "I'll have the *anticuchos*. That's shish-kebabs of beef heart, Mr. Cobb. Something your foreign palate might enjoy. And another drink, perhaps?"

He hadn't looked away from Sheba's gaze, confident that

she'd read none of his secrets in the practiced opaque of his own. "No, thank you. I have to eat, but I'm not being paid to dull my reflexes."

And with that blunt statement, he reminded them all of his purpose in South America. It wasn't to socialize or play tourist.

He was there to keep Paulo alive.

That knowledge effectively dampened the mood until another voice intruded.

"Little Sheba? Can this be you?"

Emotions clogging her throat, Sheba turned in her chair, her teary gaze filling with the bulky form of a woman nearly as wide as she was tall.

"Paulo promised me a surprise," she managed, her voice thick with crowding sentiments.

"It is a good one, no?" The woman grinned, opening up her arms.

Sheba rushed to fill them, losing herself in the fleshy hug and enveloping scent of gardenia and sunscreen. She allowed herself a moment of complete collapse, weeping unashamedly as a wealth of feelings and memories overwhelmed her.

Finally, the rotund elder woman patted her awkwardly and stepped back with the offer of a perfumed handkerchief. Sheba took the big, mannish calico square and noisily blew her nose.

"Better now?"

She nodded, wiping at wet cheeks and blinking away a fresh flood of tears.

"Some welcome. Watery eyes and a dripping nose."

Sheba took the mild chastisement with a weak smile. "I didn't expect to see you."

"You didn't think I'd come to welcome you home?"

Her smile wavered. *Home.* Filled with nervous energy, she turned to an unflappable Frank Cobb with introductions. "Rosa, this is Frank Cobb. Mr. Cobb, Rosa Kelly, one of the original protestors of anything politically incorrect."

"Now, child," Rosa chided. "You make me sound like an old hippy...which I guess is exactly what I am. Mr. Cobb, a pleasure."

He stood to politely offer his hand and was immediately engulfed by her hug. She kissed him loudly on either cheek then directly on the mouth. Sheba grinned at the sight of Frank Cobb totally nonplused.

"And Paulo Lemos, you handsome devil. Come give Aunt Rosa a kiss."

"You've changed your hair since I last saw you, Rosa. It's makes you look younger."

"It makes me look a fright, but I don't mind you lying to me just a little."

Paulo submitted to the same enthusiastic greeting then invited the big woman to join them. As he seated her in a protesting chair, Sheba leaned close to Cobb to tease, "Your mouth is open."

"She gave me tongue," Frank whispered back, sounding both shocked and horrified.

"Was that a first for you?"

"From a total stranger old enough to be my mother, yes." He then recovered himself enough to assist her into her seat, vowing to keep a close eye on the randy older woman. That was easy because she certainly was an eyeful. As big and bold and bright as the noisy jungle birds. Her refined features gave away a Mestizo lineage of both Indian and European; her flamboyant manner was definitely not rooted in some subdued Andean heritage. She wore gaudy American thrift shop clothing to clash with her carroty orange hair, a bad dye job that left it bristly and coarse as broom straws. But her deep skin tones and the heavy silver Spanish-influenced earrings she wore fashioned crudely in the shape of crosses, spoke of her local ties. That she had close ties to both Sheba and Paulo was obvious.

"Paulo told me you've come back for a visit," Rosa was saying. "Can I hope he was mistaken, that you've come back for good?"

Sheba's expression grew tense, her smile strained. "I'm afraid I can't stay long. I have another job waiting for me in the States."

Rosa waved a dismissing hand. "They waste your talents.

You are needed here, child. Your family is here."

She could have protested that she no longer had a family but that wasn't exactly true. These two people felt like family, if not by close blood ties, then by strength of affection. They couldn't be blamed for the past trauma that even now made her want to take the first avenue of escape before the jungle swallowed her whole. Could they be faulted for her wish to remain a long-distance relative? For tonight, at least, couldn't she surrender to the simple joy of being with those she loved and not think about the past?

Cobb was watching her through those inscrutable, all-seeing eyes. She determined not to give him a show.

"So, Rosa, what brings you away from your lobbying?"

"Besides the chance to see you again? Isn't that enough?"

Sheba scolded her with a look.

"All right. I'm going to see that wretched man, Paulo's uncle. Not to see him but rather to try to influence one or two of his guests."

"Uncle Sam isn't going to like that," Paulo cautioned.

"When have I ever cared what that man thought? And when have you known me to let anything get in the way of an opportunity? Never, that's when. And besides, I am a paying guest, and he would never turn away cold cash. He's still a bandit at heart, what little heart he can claim."

"I'm surprised you haven't been picketing to keep me out of the jungle. Or have you?" Paulo asked shrewdly.

She pinched his chin fondly. "You are one of us, Paulo. Even I am not so crazed by my cause that I can't see the good you are doing. Your heart is here in this place and your thoughts are for our people, not like Peyton Samuels with his fancy resort and clever schemes to rape the rainforest."

"Now, Aunt Rosa."

"Do not 'Aunt Rosa' me, boy."

"You'll have to excuse Rosa," Sheba told Cobb. "She's zealous."

"Don't go making any excuses for me, child. I never apologize for doing the right thing."

"And what is it that you're doing, Ms. Kelly?"

"She fancies herself as the guardian of the forest," Paulo drawled.

"Don't disrespect me, boy. Mr. Cobb will think I'm some kind of cuckoo tree-hugger."

"Well," Paulo challenged with a grin. "Aren't you?"

"Well...yes, I guess I am. But there's nothing wrong with that, is there? I mean, when there's nothing better to squeeze."

Frank grunted as she poked him in the ribs. He attempted a grim smile.

"Rosa lobbies for limits on oil and gas exploration in the jungle," Sheba explained to make her friend sound less eccentric. But there was little that was normal about Rosa Kelly.

Born of a Peruvian mother and a transient father working the lumber factories, she'd been able to escape her country's poverty, returning to the U.S. with her father to be educated in California. Rosa and Berkley in the '60s had been a beautiful match. When she brought that energy for change and revolution back to the rainforest, the government hadn't known what to make of her and her unorthodox methods of garnering attention to her cause. She was a hard woman to ignore, swaddling her amazing girth in bright woven patterns and her chubby wrist with a Rolex, calling down favors from influential friends who'd shared hashish with her in her squalid apartment and then chose not to be embarrassed by those reminders now that they held prestigious conservative positions of power. She'd done more single-handedly than any of the thirty-something native organizations pledged to defend the rights of the Peruvian Indians.

And she'd been Sheba's idol.

With Sheba's own modest and sheltered upbringing, Rosa had swept her imagination away with her ribald stories and endless enthusiasms. Against her conservative family's wishes, she'd snuck away to dress up in Rosa's silky scarves and bold cosmetics while a rapt audience for Rosa's instructions on life. A life far different from the one she'd seen firsthand. And a further cry from the one her parents had taught her was proper.

But it hadn't all been scandalous talk that would make most seasoned sailors blush. She'd fired in the young girl a desire to make a difference, a need to protect the innocent from exploitation. And she'd done her best to make Rosa proud of her successes the way a parent would be. The way her parents might have been. They'd always taught her to pick a cause and follow through. But would they have approved of the mission she'd chosen? A twinge of guilt always accompanied that question because, deep down, she knew the answer.

She was treading upon all they had held sacred.

"So, Mr. Cobb, what brings you to Peru?" Rosa drew a connecting glance between him and Sheba, supplying the innuendo with a lift of her heavily drawn-on brows.

"I represent the company that funds Paulo's work. I'm here in an observational capacity only." And he smiled disarmingly to convince the shrewd woman of his harmless intentions.

She wasn't buying it, but neither did she choose to challenge his claim. At least for the moment.

Their meals arrived and they ate with gusto, the trio reveling in their shared past and Cobb—grateful there was nothing hot contained in his food—content to listen and learn about his traveling companions.

Of the three of them, Paulo Lemos appeared the least complex. Highly educated, respected and purely motivated, he should have seemed the perfect match for the adventurous Sheba Reynard. Yet something about his interest in the ethnologist bothered him with the irritation of something wedged between tooth and gum that he couldn't leave alone. And it couldn't have been anything as basic as the sublime sexiness of Sheba's pouty lips.

No, Sheba Reynard was nothing he wanted to mess with. He'd learned his lesson in dealing with strong-willed females. They were best left to run their own course, be it one of self-destruction or self-fulfilling happiness. He had no time to participate in either path of discovery.

Her parents had been murdered when she was just a child.

How had that shaped the character of quixotic woman sitting beside him? He found himself wanting to know. Paulo had hinted at tragedy and unresolved pain. Was that what woke her screaming at night? And why was such a lovely, earthy female still single and seemingly oblivious to the signals Paulo flashed with every overly brilliant smile? What put such an edge to her manner, as if she were teetering on the brink of a scream?

Was it because these modern day murders mimicked the one that evaded her memory?

He liked to have his answers all neatly relegated before he chose to act, but he got the feeling that Sheba Reynard was going to deny him that pleasure, just as he planned to deny himself many others. Like discovering if those ripe lips tasted as sweet as they looked.

To distract himself from inroads best left untraveled, he turned his attention to Rosa Kelly. On the surface, she appeared to be an eccentric old kook with a thing for the environment, but he sensed there was more to this alarming eyeful.

And was there more, as well, to the timing that brought her here to this place to share their boat ride to Peyton Samuels' jungle retreat?

He ticked off those questions, aligning them according to priority and potential impact to his mission as he watched the three of them fondly reminisce. Their obvious closeness emphasized his estrangement from the scene. But being the odd wheel wasn't new to him. He'd spent his lifetime on the outside looking in and had long since stopped hungering for a way to fit into the picture of familial bliss. That's what made him so good at his job—his ability to alienate himself from the situation, to be a part but yet not belong. He'd almost forgotten himself on his last assignment and wore the reminder upon his cheek. No, it was far better to leave Dr. Reynard's intrigues alone and focus on what he was in Peru to accomplish, lest he come back with worse scars than those worn on the surface.

"So, Mr. Cobb," Rosa began, jerking him abruptly into the conversation. "What's a Fed like you doing here in this humble place?"

"Who said I was a Fed?"

Rosa chided him with her robust chuckle. "Only everything, honey. The way you sit, the way you watch the crowd, the way your smile never reaches your eyes. I rubbed elbows with my share of Bureau boys when I was doing subversive stuff in the '70s, but my guess is your branch of the government is a little bit further out on the limb. Am I right, or would you have to kill us if you told us?"

He supplied a thin-lipped smile that only served to chill his gaze further. "If that's the case, are you sure it's worth the price of knowing?"

"Humor me, hon. I'm an old lady. What do I have to live for if not a little excitement now and then? And I just bet you've had your share of excitement."

"I lead a dull life. Really. I'm working for Harper Research, just like I told you."

"Hmmmm. And what else aren't you telling us?"

"If I told you, I wouldn't be a very good secret agent, now would I?"

"So you admit it!"

"Did I?"

She laughed loudly, drawing looks from several of the tables closest to them. "Oh, you must be good at your job. You've got that doublespeak down to a science. But I don't give up easily. I'm going to worm your secrets out of you by the time we get to Peyton's."

And though she was grinning amicably, Frank felt a sudden shiver of threat in taking her words at face value. Paulo glared at him as if to say, "*Invisible, huh? Great job so far.*"

Great job, pal.

Time to gain a little of that objective distance.

"If you'll excuse me, I've got to find a phone."

Rosa smirked up at him as he stood. "Give J. Edgar our best."

He didn't mind Rosa's clever baiting, nor was he bothered by Paulo's obvious irritation. It was the way Sheba stared at him, expression perplexed and now suspicious, that made him want to wish the loud old woman would fall abruptly and inexplicably off the face of the earth.

Instead of searching out a telephone, he did his job quickly and efficiently, scouting the surrounding shops and cafes, noting the faces and postures of those sharing the quiet evening in proximity to the object of his attention. And he made himself invisible to those he protected, letting them talk and laugh with a careless abandon while he remained on the outside guaranteeing them their right to be oblivious to danger.

Until it came calling with a soft whisper.

"Cobb."

He spun about, still feeling the cool brush of his name breathed against the back of his neck where the hair now bristled in alarm. His hand went to the butt of his revolver.

No one was there.

His entire system tingled with the shock of surprise and helplessness. How had anyone gotten so close without his awareness? Who would know him by name?

The answer to both questions brought a rash of gooseflesh to his skin and a fierce tightening of determination to his gut.

He could have been dead, just like that, but that wasn't the way this particular villain liked to do things. This demon liked to play. And play for keeps.

"You won't catch me with my guard down again," he spoke aloud to the night, not knowing if he was heard, not caring if he let his quarry know he'd been recognized.

The game had begun.

SIX

The night was balmy, and once the two women shared it alone seated in Sheba's room and sipping tepid beer, their topic turned from the general to the pointedly and poignantly specific.

"I wanted to come visit you."

Sheba took that direct admission like an arrow to the heart. She winced. "Then why didn't you?"

"At first, they thought it best that you see no one who would remind you of what had happened. And then it was like you'd fallen off the face of the earth. That place would tell me nothing, and by then Sam and I were no longer exactly friends. In the last few years, I'd catch glimpses of your work in magazines, but by the time I'd track you down, you'd already be gone to some godforsaken place like Borneo or Brooklyn."

Sheba smiled, coaxed from the sense of abandonment she'd struggled under for far too long. "I never could put down roots. Too much bad influence from those stories you told, I guess."

"I finally got a hold of Paulo and I was so—thrilled and I'll admit, surprised—to learn you were coming home. I made my reservations that same day." Seeing the troubled puckering of Sheba's brow, she patted the younger woman's hand and asked, "What's wrong, hon? Is the past too painful now that you're back amongst all the memories?"

"That's just it, Rosa. I have no memories. None of that night at all."

"But I thought you were at a hospital."

"Hospitals can't cure every ill."

"So you don't remember?"

"Not any of it. Not going off that day to follow them into the jungle, not where we went, not what happened to them, not how I got back. Nothing."

"And you thought coming here would bring it all back?"

"I'd thought. I'd hoped."

"But?"

"Nothing so far." She sighed heavily in her frustration. "If I just knew what happened to them, I could live with the rest, no matter what it might be."

"Maybe you'll just have to learn to live without knowing, child. I know that's harsh, but you've got to face that possibility. Sheba, do you really want to face all that pain and sorrow again? The first time, it nearly–"

"It nearly drove me mad. You don't have to be afraid to say it. But I'm stronger now. I've been getting stronger all along."

"But can you ever be ready for what you might find? Even if it's nothing at all?"

She let Rosa take her up close in a loose embrace. How right her old friend was. Which was worrying her more: finding the truth or living with the knowledge that it would never be known?

Rosa held her back to study her wan features. "How are you, Sheba? How are you really?"

"I'm fine, Rosa."

Red lips pursed to refute that. "Hon, don't con me. You could never lie when you were a little girl, and the habit never stuck to you since then."

"It's hell being back here, Rosa," she finally admitted in a rush. And it felt good, so good, to purge that truth.

"Then why are you here, child?"

"Because I have to know."

"No matter how much it hurts? Or who it hurts?"

Who it hurts? What an odd way to put it. Who might be hurt by the solution to a two-decade-old mystery?

Unless the killer was someone she knew.

***

The only way to see the Amazon was from the river. The

natural highways cut through the rainforest in ever changing seasonal paths, transforming the landscape with their sinuous meanderings. At each bend, they undermined the forest, leaving a sheer mud and clay bank on one side and a broad beach of fine sand and silt on the other. When exposed to full sunlight, the banks became a colorful wall of climbing gourd vines whose large yellow, red and white flowers stood out in splashy contrast to the solid backdrop of green.

Stabilized by the fast-growing willow-like Tessera, the newly carved ground quickly spawned a crop of Cecropia trees which soared upward to form a canopy fifteen to eighteen meters over the Cana, a gap rapidly filled in by mahogany trees that would create a closed canopy at forty meters with a lush underscore of shade-loving Holocene and ginger.

Each twist of the river revealed something new and differed. Flooded forests where silk-cotton trees stood on giant buttressed roots with their straight stems poking up over thirty meters before splaying into an umbrella-like crown, gave way to seasonal oxbow lakes and floating meadows of herbaceous plants topped by passion fruit and morning glory vines. And everywhere there was life, from the sheep-sized capybara rodents drinking from the river's edge to small groups of spider monkeys performing lazy acrobatics in upper realms, leaving the lower level of epiphyte-clad trunks and branches to troops of saddle-backed and emperor tamarins foraging for blossoms, fruit and insects.

And amongst all the serene beauty, waiting patiently for opportunity to lend itself to a meal, were the predators: red-bellied piranhas with their lightning-speed attacks, the black caimans sunning themselves along the banks, and the huge coils of the anaconda ready to crush its prey into a more digestible form, reminding those who traveled the waterways not to get so caught up in the splendor that they ignored the darker elements.

And so Frank Cobb reminded himself as they puttered down the waterway in an ancient *pequepeques* river boat. Though he lounged in one of the deck hammocks strung beneath the stained and sagging overhead tarp, his attention rarely strayed from the woman seated on her big battered suitcase at the bow.

Her sun-bronzed features faced forward with a determined expression, belied by the way her arms wrapped about her in an almost consoling hug. Though she would try to appear the intrepid explorer, small clues betrayed her inner fears. Her eyes were shadowed by too little sleep. He'd been awake most of the night himself, listening to her restless thrashings once she'd returned to her room, just in case that invitation for a rescue came. The graceful line of her shoulders angled a bit too sharply to reflect anything but tension. Her quick breaths moved the open front of her khaki camp shirt in the faint, desperate rhythm of an animal cornered and faced with the deadly snap of an unavoidable trap. Slender fingers beat an expectant tattoo upon the curve of her thighs like the frantic flutter of a grounded bird unable to obtain flight. What was she so afraid of—what lay ahead or what she'd left behind?

Her past was unknown to him, but he had a pretty good idea what they were heading into, and it filled him with an anxious dread. If what he suspected awaited them, she had every reason for her fear. And he had every reason to question his ability to protect her.

He'd failed before, and that failure left its mark more harshly on his psyche than upon his scarred face. He hated failure, and this was one he meant to rectify fully and finally if Peyton Samuels' monster and his own were the same. And if his duty to Lemos clashed with his own need for revenge...he would work that out if and when the time came.

Lemos had been silent since they left the dock. Though he made every pretense of pouring over the books and papers that came with his latest shipment of goods, he too was preoccupied by the woman in the boat's bow. How much more did he know of the demons she traveled with? What part had he, her inseparable childhood friend, played in her past trauma? What was behind his insistence that her presence was the condition for allowing Cobb to protect him? A happy reunion? The chance to forge a romantic bond? Or something else, something less savory and stained by dark intentions?

Lemos was the job. Frank reminded himself of that. The man's motives, his shortcomings, his personality didn't enter into it. Frank was here to give his life if needs be to see that Paulo Lemos delivered. His own qualms and questions didn't play a part in that equation. And it didn't say much as to the value placed upon his own life. But that was the job.

He closed his eyes against the glare of the sun off the water, against the sight of the woman at the bow. And he tried to remember why the job superseded all else.

***

Sheba tried to see the beauty of the country she'd grown up in, but within the lush green tangle of forest, she was only aware of the shadows of threat and danger.

The last time she'd been in-country she'd been a child, protected by a child's innate sense of indestructibility and by the belief that nothing could rock the safety of the world in which her parents sheltered her. She'd known no fear, no prejudice, no uncertainties that her future would not continue, as contented and fulfilling, beyond the next golden sunset. She'd been a child of the forest, playing beneath its majestic canopy with the fearlessness of one of the squirrel monkeys leaping through its boughs. And she'd truly believed that nothing could harm her.

How wrong she'd been.

She would never look at anything through those innocent child's eyes again.

She blinked away the sting of memory, denying its power over her. She was here for Paulo, for the sake of their friendship. She glanced over her shoulder and smiled at the sight of him hunched over his studies. That much hadn't changed. Always the scholar. Beyond him, Rosa slumbered noisily in one of the hammocks and Cobb stretched out silently in another. She didn't know if he slept. She'd gotten used to the idea of him being like the armed forces: Always ready. Always prepared. And she felt safer for it.

Time was growing short. They would reach the Reserve by nightfall, and there was much she needed to learn if she was to be prepared herself.

Paulo looked up from his books as her shadow crossed the pages. His gaze warmed in welcome.

"Ah, there's my girl. Come for a lesson in botany?"

Her taut smile clued him in before the terse words followed. "We need to talk, Paulo. About the ruins."

Without comment, he cleared the crate beside him of its stack of periodicals and gestured for her to sit down. "You're wanting to know if they are the same ones."

Her nod was as jerky as her heartbeats.

"That, only you can answer, Sheba. You were the only one there."

"But I don't remember, Paulo. I don't remember any of it."

Even as she claimed that in a soft frustrated cry, she knew it wasn't the complete truth. She did remember some of it. Like having a handful of pieces to a puzzle, each with a different shape and color and none joining with the others to make any recognizable whole. She didn't know what she was looking at. All she had were those disjointed flashes that made no sense when taken alone.

She jumped slightly at the sudden pressure of Paulo's hand over hers, then she clung to it unashamedly.

"Perhaps, little Sheba, the memories will return when you look upon the site once more. Or is that what you're afraid of? Are you sure you want to know?"

"I have to know, Paulo. I've left this blank in my mind alone for too long. I've got to fill it in, if for no other reason than to honor my parents with the truth."

"But the truth will change nothing," he cautioned gently, telling her what she knew in her mind but couldn't accept within her heart.

"Or everything," came her fatalistic reply. "It depends upon what truth's been hiding out there for all these years waiting for a group of luckless fortune hunters to stumble over it." She met his compassionate stare, her own bright and glassy with purpose. "I'm afraid, Paulo, afraid to know, afraid not to. I've been living in fear of that truth since the night it happened, and I can't go on like this any more. I must know what my mind is trying so desperately to keep from me."

"Then I will help you uncover that truth. And together we will face whatever it reveals."

She embraced him then, overwhelmed with gratitude and relief not to be alone. Ignorant of the satisfied smile on his face as he held her close.

He hadn't planned to sleep. Awareness returned with the lethargic lurch of an overly warm afternoon nap. He shook off the sensation of sluggishness the moment he saw that the daylight was gone.

Good lord, he'd been sleeping for hours.

Disgusted with himself and embarrassed for his show of weakness, Cobb climbed out of the damningly comfortable hammock and went to join Sheba at the bow of the boat. Moonlight gleamed like quicksilver on the surface of the water and reflected in the darkness of her eyes, making them gleam like onyx.

"Have a nice nap?"

He winced at the slight chiding. "Did I miss anything?"

"If you do on the Amazon, it's too late to rectify the problem. You're usually someone's meal."

"Point taken. Where are we?"

"Almost there."

The anxiety in her tone was a palpable thing, as richly textured as the scent of butterscotch that permeated the air.

"What's that smell? Someone been baking Oatmeal Scotchies?"

That won a faint smile. She gestured toward the shore, where giant water lilies sprawled across the quiet backwaters on saucer-shaped leaves up to two meters wide. The flowers themselves floated like pale human heads peeling back into bloom at the same instant to emit their overpowering aroma to perfume the night. The effect was as gruesome as it was strangely beautiful. Like much of the Amazon itself. In tandem, an orchestra of up to fifteen different frog species began to tune for their evening serenade.

"So what's your connection to Peyton Samuels?"

There was no mistaking the sudden flat curtain of distance that came down over her shiny eyes.

"He's Paulo's uncle who made good. When I knew him, he was a bit of a schemer, always working some angle to get ahead. Apparently, he found that way. He's very respected amongst both the government and the people for the lengths he goes through to protect the environment."

"While bringing a non-stop influx of outsiders in, at great expense, I might add."

She shrugged philosophically. "You could argue that he balances that out with the money he raises off those wealthy guests to preserve the rainforest and educate those who might abuse the ecosystem out of ignorance. You won't find me saying bad words about him. It was through his generosity that I was able to go to school in the States. Otherwise, I don't know what might have become of me."

The shadows increased in her gaze until Cobb was moved to distract her from thoughts of the past.

"So who might have it out for this sainted jungle savior by wanting to close him down?"

Her features grew contemplative. "I really don't know. I've been away from the political arena for too long to know what toes he's stepped on. Paulo would be a better one to ask."

"Sammy's not to be trusted," came a sudden, intruding sentiment. "Don't ever forget where he came from or what he was, and you'll be fine. Just don't let yourself believe the sophisticated facade he's made for himself out here in the wilderness. The man who would be king." A snort. "He's a bandit, nothing more."

Then, there was a shifting of the boat as Rosa Kelly came up behind them, standing just a little too close to Cobb for comfort. He tensed, wondering what he should do if she made a grab for his butt. But her interest lay elsewhere, up river toward the shadow of a man emerging from the mists as if by magic to stand on water. But as they grew closer, Cobb could see he waited for them on the end of a dock.

"His majesty's lackey," Rosa drawled with obvious dislike.

Despite the fact that he moved on a partially crippled leg, the man on the dock made quick work of lashing the boat securely to the moorings before speaking to them. With the wide, flat features that claimed pure Indian descent, he was nevertheless dressed in Western fashion with modern, if shabby, outdoor wear right out of an L.L. Bean catalog. He spoke English the same way, well but sloppily.

"Good evening." There was a flash of bad teeth in the swarthy face. "I am Joaquin Cross. Welcome to Txukamayura. Mr. Samuels is expecting you."

He put down his hand to hoist first Sheba then a more reluctant Rosa up onto the dock beside him. Cobb and Paulo gathered up their gear, transferring it up before following themselves.

Their guide gestured to the stack of luggage and supplies. "Your things will be brought up to the Reserve. Don't concern yourselves with them. Come."

Contrarily, Cobb bent to pick up his duffle, his gaze colliding with Sheba's as she gripped her suitcase. He grinned to let her know that he was remembering her warning to keep his belongings close, and her sudden response was like those huge glowing flowers bursting into bloom. For a moment, Cobb forgot to breathe.

From the dock, they started up a wide cinder path that followed the bend of the river. It wasn't a long walk and, the minute they rounded the curve, Cobb could see it was purely for dramatic effect. Before them, illuminated in torchlight, was the Txukamayura Reserve.

It hunched down along the landscape like something constructed by the Swiss Family Robinson out of thatch, cane and natural materials. The main lodge building stood as a grand multi-storied parent followed by a brood of smaller hutches all interconnected by palm frond-roofed walkways. It looked frightfully rustic until one grew close enough to hear the hum of mechanization that meant civilization was at hand.

And on the main porch, a welcoming Mr. Rourke to his own Fantasy Island, stood Peyton Samuels, his white suit and silver hair gleaming in the darkness. While the rest of them waited at the foot of the stairs, Sheba raced up them and into the arms of her benefactor.

"Uncle Sam, I've missed you so!"

"And little Sheba, back home again where you belong."

And Cobb didn't have to see her expression to know how that observation hit her. The line of her shoulders squared as if to deflect a mortal blow.

And it was then he determined to find out all there was to know about Sheba Reynard's past.

SEVEN

After extending a stiff but not inhospitable welcome to Rosa Kelly, Peyton Samuels, with the forceful enthusiasm of someone who thought he had to explain and justify, showed them around the resort he'd carved out of the jungle.

Sheba had told Cobb that in his youth Samuels had been somewhat of a rogue. A kind understatement. He'd been a greedy adventurer, ready to strip the Amazon of its every available and profitable resource without the slightest remorse. And then he'd married a native woman, Paulo's father's sister and she died within the first year. Perhaps that shattering event changed him. Perhaps. Or, Sheba, wondered to herself, perhaps it had something to do with the missionary couple he should have guided into the jungle in search of a rumored cult.

Samuels hovered over Sheba with a grandfatherly air she found both touching and slightly suspicious. She didn't remember him well enough to hold more than a passing affection, not with the clarity she did Paulo and Rosa. He'd flitted in and out of her childhood, a handsome, colorful character who smelled of drink and smoke and spoke loudly with words her parents didn't approve of. He'd been her parents' guide on many occasions that took them into the deeper, unchartered and potentially dangerous areas of the forest, and he'd always brought them back safely. Along with a brilliant flower or two for their young daughter's hair. He was held as harmless, until after a long afternoon of drinking, he'd taught Sheba a song she'd proudly performed over dinner while her family entertained one of the sponsors of the Institute's program. Needless to say, the adults were more horrified than amused, and she didn't see Peyton Samuels for a long time after her recital. Her father had called him a reprobate, and that word had sounded ugly even spoken in his soft Alabama drawl.

Sheba remembered the wedding because she'd had to wear tights that were hot and constantly twisting, and pinching new shoes. Samuels married Paulo's petitely lovely aunt, Cipriana, which made him family in a roundabout way. Sam had smelled of hair oil and aftershave from then on, not of bad habits, at least until Sheba had to don the tights and shiny shoes again for the funeral. The lovely Cipriana Samuels died at the hands of a robber. It was Sheba's first brush with death. Not her last.

Samuels had been too drunk to take her parents on their last trek into the jungle. They hadn't come back safely. They never came back at all. Peyton never came right out and admitted his guilt, but then she did suspect he was behind the large donations that had kept her in a private school in the East on a generous allowance. He never said. She never asked. But before she left Peru, she would find out what kind of guilt caused a man to support a child not his own for twelve years of private schooling and undergraduate studies.

Unlike Rosa, whom she'd never seen again after her last day in Peru, Peyton kept in a loose sort of contact with her, always seeming to know where she was. He'd sent brief letters when she'd been well enough to receive them. His and Paulo's missives were the only things she'd had to look forward to for those first dark years. When she was at the university, exotic flowers would be delivered for her birthday. Then he'd sent a promotional video advertising the Lodge. But no invitation to visit. Never an invitation to return.

Because he knew she wouldn't or because he didn't want her to?

Samuels led their group on their tour from highlight to highlight within his eco-lodge. Paulo appeared proud, Cobb stoic and watchful, and Rosa seemed to be choking on her cynicism. Sheba reserved judgement.

How had he gotten the money together to front such an elaborate endeavor?

"There are no roads leading to Txukamayura, no direct

route to civilization. That way it has a harder time following us back here. While we provide necessities and more than a few luxuries, nothing we do here will upset the natural balance of the forest. Everything you see was built from traditional materials and techniques by native hands. Our staff are all area Indians who have grown up here and have a respect for the land and the environment."

"The same Indians that help carve through the mahogany forests?" Rosa interjected.

Samuels gave her a patient look. "When one is hungry, one takes whatever work is available. I think of this as a safe alternative to more harmful occupations."

"And how hungry were you, Sammy, back in the old days?"

"I devoured what I could." His mild blue eyes glittered briefly, then his smile returned as he patted his ample girth. "But as you see, I'm well fed now, as are our guests—on the finest of local cuisine." He turned away from her, returning to his promotional travelogue. "High quality meals and a comfortable rest are the key to our guests' enjoyment. We have thirty-two rooms, four rooms to a bungalow, each room with its own flush toilet and fresh sheets. We practice ecological waste management, no latrines or contamination of the river. Here, we think of ourselves as custodians of the jungle."

Rosa made a rude sound that he pointedly ignored.

They wound their way through the main lodge on floors of polished mahogany, where the roof was made of crisneja palm fronds and the dividing walls of cane and clay. Huge windows overlooked the river on one side and the jungle on the other. There was a small theater where films on ecology and the rainforest were shown to newcomers, along with a slick production promoting the Lodge and its role in investing in the health, education and financial stability of the nearby settlements. Upstairs were meeting spaces and an extensive library. The main lobby housed museum-quality artifacts as well as a stylish and expensive shop where tourists could purchase everything from cameras with .300 mm lenses or good binoculars to bathing suits, hiking boots with absorbent socks, head-to-ankle rain suits, guide books, insect repellent, digestive cures, and wildlife miniatures hand carved by a staff member. There was a tropical lounge with a bar and fireplace where guests could gather around low tables for cards at night or wait out the rain in bamboo chairs or rope hammocks. Opulent and exotic. Samuels knew how to entertain.

From there, they passed through the open air dining hall where fine netting kept out the pests but let sultry breezes filter through. He pointed out the research section where various ecologically-minded groups could host classes and studies. A group researching the feeding habits of the dusky-headed titi monkey had just left, and one studying the giant river otter would be arriving at week's end. A half dozen indigenous students were now waiting for Paulo's next forage into the forest for their first taste of field work.

And of particular interest to both scientists and tourists was the lodge's central focal point; a ten-story tower from which one could observe various levels of the forest then rise above the canopy for a spectacular view.

Of greater interest to Sheba were the bungalows where she could drop her weighty suitcase and change into fresh clothes. The four of them would share one of the quaint thatched huts that appeared rustic on the exterior but were made for relaxation and personal comfort inside with their private showers and netted beds.

"Dinner in an hour and cocktails afterwards," Samuels announced, obviously enjoying his role as genial host. "Mingle with our other guests and make free use of the hospitality of the lodge. If you have any particular needs that one of the staff can't provide for you, come see me. Enjoy your stay."

On that optimistic note, they were left to their own resources.

Sheba collapsed on her bed, releasing a huge sigh up into the darkness. The tension knotting through her shoulders eased with a leisurely stretch and roll. Well, here she was. So far, so good. She let her eyes close while she planned out the night ahead—a cool shower, dress for dinner, maybe a cocktail or two and a stroll in the fragrant night air. Her mind wandered to an improbable image of her and Frank Cobb, arm in arm. Smiling at that intriguing absurdity, she opened her eyes, sat up.

And screamed.

***

Invitation or no, Frank Cobb was through the doorway at the first raw cry. After sweeping the corners of the room for potential dangers, his focus returned to the woman on the bed. The sight of her brought the hair up on the back of his neck. She sat frozen, her expression stark and stiff with terror. Her face was as pale as one of the giant lilies floating on the river, her eyes saucer-wide. That blank, unblinking gaze seemed to stare right through him to some horror he couldn't see or recognize. She wasn't breathing.

"Dr. Reynard? Are you all right?"

He waited, releasing the grip of his pistol. Her response sank a shiver to his soul. It was a sound, a hoarse bleat of fear. He crossed to her in three quick strides, panicking now himself.

"Doc, what is it?"

The muscles of her face worked in jerky spasms, her mouth opening on a silent scream he didn't have to hear to grasp its desperation. A plea for help. For rescue. All the invitation he needed.

She didn't resist when he swept his arms around her quaking figure. In fact, he wasn't sure she was aware of him at all. Like a mannequin, she remained inanimate and unresponsive until he angled slightly to sit beside her on the bed.

And in doing so, turned her away from the object of her terror.

A shuddering breath ripped up from deep inside her and with it, a horrible, anguished weeping began, torn from memories past and bleeding with remembered pain. No images tormented her, just overwhelming, emotionally crippling sensations, so huge, so devastating, she couldn't defend against them as they ravaged her spirit and battered her mind.

What's happening to me?

She pressed her face into the sheltering lee of Cobb's

shoulder, her arms whipping about his neck in a circle the Jaw's of Life couldn't break. That was what he meant to her at the moment—life, safety, sanity—for those things wobbled in tenuous uncertainty as reality was pulled back toward the anchor he represented.

Save me, Frank! Save me!

From what? What threat had stunned and so petrified her that, even now, she couldn't grasp its enormity? Was she losing her mind? Nothing seemed real to her.

Except the solidity of Frank Cobb's embrace.

He was real. He was here and strong and perhaps capable of fighting back her demons. If he didn't think she was crazy.

As she was very afraid she was.

Her tremors lessened into an uncontrolled hitch of dry sobs. She used the rough nap of his shirt to dry her eyes. He smelled good, of warm cotton and heated male energy. He felt good, firm, reliable, unyielding to even the most unreasonable assault.

She let her fingers flex at the base of his neck, testing the corded power there that spread enticingly down his sturdy shoulders and well-defined upper arms, following that hard trail down to his rock-hard mid-section where taut tee shirt clung to the curve of his ribs and delineated abs. She traced the contours with her thumbs, lost in the sensual absorption of him because the very reality of him chased away all else.

Awareness became as basic and as primal as the forest beyond.

His arms were still about her, but if he realized the shift of her focus from fright to fascination, he didn't react to it. Was he unaware that her trembling now had more to do with him than with some abstract scare? Could he be that indifferent to her as a woman?

Or that dedicated to the job he was doing?

She drew a shuddering breath and turned her head slightly so that her nose was pressed against the warm flesh of his throat. She could taste the salt of his skin while riding his hard swallow. And suddenly, she wanted to taste more. If she were to drag her tongue up that firm neck, to chew his ear and eventually seek out his mouth, would he still be so unmoved by her? Would he still see her as a nervous scientist in need of careful coddling or as a needy woman desperate for the calming drug of passion?

How could her pride allow him to view her in either of those less than flattering roles? How could her fragile confidence as a woman endure it?

Resolutely, she let him go and leaned away. When she dared risk a look, she found him regarding her through an inscrutable stare. She couldn't bear the thought of pity or disdain behind that guarded gaze. She had to pull herself together, to present a halfway rational front. Not so easy when she had no logical means to explain away her actions.

And then he touched her, his thumb rubbing along the damp slope of her cheek in a gesture of heartbreaking tenderness so out of character with all she'd believed about him that she was startled and uncertain of how to respond.

"Another bad dream?"

His tone was as neutral and without judgment as his caress was rich with compassionate support. The contrast only confused her more.

"Yes...no," she stammered with the indecisiveness of a panicked child. Infuriated that she couldn't reply with more certainty, she cried, "I was awake. I closed my eyes for a moment, and when I opened them, I saw..." She stopped, unable to continue through the influx of gut-level fear square-knotting through her insides.

"Saw what?" he prompted softly. "Was there someone in your room? Doc, what did you see?"

"I– I don't know for sure. A figure through the netting. I can't seem to remember. Dammit, what's wrong with me?" She punched the heels of her hands against her temples, grinding them there as if she could clear away the maddening fog shrouding her subjective recall.

Again, he managed to shock her with the gentleness of his response. He covered her fists with his hands, squeezing lightly before coaxing them to lower while her watery gaze sought some sort of answer in the probing intensity of his.

Slowly, his fingertips moved down either side of her neck, gradually pushing back the collar of her shirt to expose the sculpted ridge of her collarbone. Her hand rose immediately to cover the medallion she wore, the gesture unconscious and protective.

"Was it a man you saw in your room, Doc?"

The subtle edge to his question alerted her to his motives for asking. It brought a flush of animation back to her face and a preserving indignation to her manner.

"If you're asking if I was entertaining someone, the answer is no."

He smiled slightly at the snap of her tone. "No, that's not what I was asking. I'm more concerned about someone entertaining unflattering thoughts about you."

"Oh." Her mood deflated with a sputter of embarrassment. She looked away from his patient expression, angered by his detachment and by the memory of her reaction to him. Her sigh was harsh and cleansing. "I don't know who or what I saw. Just a shape for a fleeting second."

"And what was it about that shape that threatened you?"

"You mean what reduced me into a puddle of useless gelatin?" Her cruel summation reflected her own assessment. He didn't jump to argue it. "I don't know, Mr. Cobb. I don't remember anything overtly threatening. It was instinctual. Is that a concept you can grasp?"

"Instinct keeps me alive, Dr. Reynard. It's nothing I ignore easily." He paused, then let the other shoe drop. "Has this happened to you before?"

What could she say? Oh, for about twenty years. I see things that aren't there. I wake up from dreams I don't remember without being certain that I'm no longer in a dream. I think I may have lost my mind. Could you help me find it?

She smiled tightly. "I'm sure it's nothing, Mr. Cobb. Just the product of any overly tired mind and an overly fertile atmosphere."

He regarded her unblinkingly, his steady stare not exactly calling her a liar, not in bold type anyway. Damn him. Why should she care what he thought?

He took another glance around and then went to the far wall. Upon it hung a native carving, a mask cut into rich, dark mahogany. He studied it for a moment then looked back to where she sat, still shaken and shaking.

"Could this be what you saw?"

"That hardly appears to be threatening, now does it, Mr. Cobb?"

"Through a filmy netting, with your eyes a little unfocused." He shrugged his conclusion.

"All right. Maybe it was. There. Are you happy?"

"Delirious."

She waved off his dry retort. It hadn't been some mask on the wall that yanked her up to the brink of hysteria. It hadn't. "Go away, Mr. Cobb. I have to get dressed for dinner and Sam's social mill afterwards."

Letting him leave her alone in that room was going to be one of the most difficult things she'd ever done. Letting him leave while smiling as if nothing was wrong, as if she believed his simple explanation, was close to impossible.

"I'll wait right outside," was his response to her attempt at bravery.

Part of her sagged in relief as another rebelled indignantly. "You'll do no such thing. As you can see, there is nothing in my room, and I am in no danger."

"And I'd like to keep it that way."

"Don't you have to get dressed too," she pointed out with a reasonable arch to one brow.

"I am not a guest here."

She waved her hand at him. "Just go. Guard the door if it makes you feel better."

He grinned. That sudden dazzle of charm threw her completely off balance.

"It will," he promised. With that, he was gone, leaving her almost more disturbed than she'd been when he'd arrived.

Good grief, she'd wanted to kiss him.

She was losing her mind, and all she could think of was the taste of Frank Cobb's kiss.

Maybe a sign that it was already gone.

***

She'd wanted him to kiss her.

That knowledge shook him nearly as much at the thought of her in danger. It made him pace the porch, desperately wishing for a cigarette.

He'd felt the instant her intent had shifted from seeking comfort to steeping desire. He'd felt it in the way her body went from inanimate to molten in a single luxurious movement. He'd been doing the noble thing in taking her into his arms. To console her like a child. Well, that child had grown up damn and disturbingly fast, and he'd found himself with a willing woman in his arms.

And himself with little will to resist.

He'd remained still while his imagination roamed every long and lithe degree of her, filling in what he didn't know from the feel of how she pressed against him. She was no fragile girl – probably from toting that hernia-popping suitcase of hers. She was tough and toned and yet still deliciously woman. He'd wanted to seek out soft spots with his hands, to taste sweet places with his mouth.

When her breath blew warm and seducing upon his neck, he'd been a shivering mass of lust right down to his cotton socks. If she'd lifted her head and he'd seen longing in her big brown eyes, it would have been all over for him. His nobility would have cracked wide open.

Thank God she had more control than he did at that precarious moment.

It wasn't him, of course. He wasn't fool enough to fall for that illusion. He'd been a ready substitute for safety and a handy male remedy for the loneliness that frightened her. If it had been Paulo Lemos at her door, she would have undoubtedly responded the same way. Not that the randy scientist would have resisted, he surmised with an odd tang of bitterness as uncharacteristic as it was unwise.

"What are you doing here, Cobb?"

Lemos's curt tone woke him from his musings. He regarded the man who saw him as a rival with a cool gaze and a crooked smile. "Just trying to fight off the desire for a smoke."

Lemos was impeccably dressed in an evening coat, his dark hair slicked back and gleaming, his dark eyes fierce and gleaming, as well. He assessed Cobb's appearance with a jaundiced eye. "If you plan to fit in invisibly this evening, you'd better change into something a little more...palatable."

Resisting the urge to sniff at his shirt for signs of offense, he held his ground, forcing Lemos to get right to the point of it.

"I'll escort Sheba to dinner, Cobb. It's not part of your job description, is it?"

He shook his head. None of his thoughts betrayed themselves to the possessive Peruvian. He didn't look offended or affected by the other man's rude summation. It wasn't personal. None of it was personal. It was a job. "No, it's not. Excuse me while I go to change into something more...respectable."

And as he disappeared into his own room, Frank wondered if Sheba would object to the last minute change in escorts. Or would she even notice?

Don't be stupid. Stick to the job.

That job wasn't to stick it to Paulo Lemos for having a condescending manner and irritating habit of looking right through him as if he truly were invisible.

Nor was it his job to stick it to Sheba Reynard, which was by far the more enticing prospect.

Something or someone had been in her room. Whether it was her imaginary demon or his very real one was the question he needed to concentrate upon. And until he knew for sure, whether Paulo Lemos liked it or not, he was going to stick to the pretty ethnologist like a new strain of flu.

All he could do was hope it wasn't something so contagious that he'd die from it.

EIGHT

Sheba realized her mistake the moment she stepped into the dining room.

She should have guessed when she saw Paulo in his sleek and shiny best, but she was so comfortable with her friend that she didn't make serious note of his appearance. And she'd been oddly disappointed to find him instead of Frank Cobb waiting outside her door. Paulo, being the consummate gentleman, never said anything to her and by the time she recognized her error, it was too late.

She was used to university and academic crowds where she was supposed to look the part of the ethnologist from the wilds. There, they were interested in her ideas and experiences. Not in her wardrobe.

What a surprise to come all the way to Peru to be shown the tremendous gap in her own social education.

The group gathered in the lodge's dining room could have been part of a photo shoot for some expensive liquor ad. In their tuxedos and glitter, the whole lot of them seemed transposed upon the scene from some New York penthouse party as they sipped champagne and indulged in polite chatter.

And there she stood like a jungle guide in her khaki shorts, hiking boots and dark green camp shirt, unadorned by makeup or jewelry and obviously bare, as well, of social instincts.

It was too late to back out before her disgrace was complete. Peyton Samuels, resplendent in his gleaming white evening wear, hailed her loudly and waved her over to his exclusive cadre of listeners. What could she do but swallow hard and obey the summons.

She was aware of the curious glances following her

through the elite company, but unlike Rosa in her bold floral kaftan who'd set up her own clique in a far corner, Sheba hated drawing attention to herself, and this scrutiny was like walking over hot coals.

"There you are, my dear." Peyton enveloped her in an embrace, then presented her like a prize to his other guests. "This is Dr. Sheba Reynard, whom I consider family."

The eccentric branch, obviously, she thought with a gritted smile as she nodded to each introduction. She didn't remember the names: a movie producer and his starlet prodigy, a billionaire commodities investor, several political lobbyists, a senator and his wife, a Peruvian television personality, and the president of a university. Only the last had heard of her or had the slightest clue what she was about. The rest greeted her with painfully indifferent smiles and continued with their conversations as if she were as invisible as Frank Cobb practiced to be.

There she stood, trapped at Samuels' side in the hell of social limbo. Looking about for rescue, she saw Paulo had been snagged by the research community. He already had them laughing at some clever observation, and his smile in her direction offered no invitation. Rosa, with her orange hair sticking up like a peacock's crest, her voice booming and equally loud persona commanding notice, presented no opportunity for a discrete retreat, either.

And then she saw Frank Cobb and hope flared eternal that he would come through for her with another spectacular, nick of time intervention.

But Cobb met her anxious glance with one of cool impenetrability. Not so much as a warming flicker of acknowledgment. On the job in his dark suit and buttoned up shirt, and invisible to the others in the room. If she were to cross over to him, bringing attention to his presence, she'd be compromising his effectiveness.

Grin and bear it, Sheba-darlin', her father would have said. His version of turn the other cheek.

Roll with the punches.

So she pasted on a stiff smile and managed to endure the

looks and whispers until she was able to escape to Paulo's side as they sought their tables for dinner.

"Why didn't you tell me it was formal dress?" she hissed up at him as he seated her.

He blinked in typical male oblivion. "You look lovely to me."

She sighed in resignation. "I look as though I should be serving the meal, not sitting down to it."

He laughed as if she'd meant it as a joke.

Feeling herself the joke, Sheba cast a look about for Cobb but, true to his word, he had become invisible. Wishing she could perform the same trick, she bared her grin and prepared for a long, painful evening.

***

From out on the wraparound porch, Cobb settled himself in for a long night of surveillance. For him, it was the worst part of the job, not because of the boring inactivity, but because it made him crave a smoke. Stakeouts would be much more pleasurable with a filter tip and a cold one, but both were no-nos. Each could potentially betray him in a very different way—the smoke by giving away his presence, and the beer by stealing his presence of mind. So he abstained. And he cursed.

Waiting was never a problem. He'd learned patience as a child. He'd learned to wait and not complain even if cold or weariness or hunger made him long to be inside familiar surroundings. He was none of those things now, so he had no reason to feel dissatisfied.

Except that Sheba was inside and all he could do was watch from an impersonal distance.

Such was the job.

He situated himself in his obscure vantage point and smiled wryly at the circumstance that would have him in the middle of a jungle observing what could have been a Manhattan party. He could say one thing for Peyton Samuels, besides knowing how to pull the right manipulative strings to get both him and Sheba to Peru, he knew how to schmooze. He had a room full of influential people dining on his food, sucking up his liquor, all ripe for the picking. Sheba had characterized him as a bit larcenous. Cobb couldn't fault him for that. He had a touch of the con man in his own soul. Samuels was a businessman, seeking to protect his investment, and it was up to Cobb to make sure he wasn't disappointed.

Not a particularly dirty job when he had Sheba Reynard to watch over.

The woman interested him. Not an easy feat. He was a hard man to distract with mere face and form. But there was so much more to Sheba. There was her quixotic nature. Sometimes the tough myth-buster, sometimes the wounded bird. And then there was the mystery. He was a sucker for intrigue. The obvious and proper never grabbed him up the way the incongruous and inconsistent did. Like the way the medallion she wore played peek-a-boo at the neckline of her shirt with just enough of a quick glimpse to stir the curiosity.

He watched her flounder in the midst of Samuels' elite, a daisy transplanted in a field of hothouse orchids. She wasn't elegant or eye-catching or even exotic, but there was an undeniable appeal to her simplicity. There was grace in her unrefined lines, a beauty without drama or artifice. Her very uniqueness made her stand out when she would seek to remain unnoticed.

And Paulo Lemos noticed, too.

Damn him.

Cobb had no reason to feel threatened by the suave scientist. Sheba was totally oblivious to his charms. It wasn't as if they were involved in a competition for the lovely Sheba's attention.

Were they?

Surprised by that thought, Cobb concentrated more fiercely upon his job. Courting Sheba Reynard wasn't part of it, not that he'd know how to go about the wooing of her anyway. He was about as naive and inexperienced as the blushing ethnologist when it came to romance. He didn't have the time, the temperament or the talent for it. While his peers had been coaxing their dates out of their panties in the back seat of the family car, he'd been learning to field strip automatic weapons in the dark. Though there were some similarities, an Uzi never asked if you'd still respect it in the morning. He had an ultimate respect for instruments of destruction and not a clue when it came to the opposite sex. Sex, he understood just fine. No problems there and no complaints. But the messy, emotional stuff that too often came along as baggage made him grateful he always traveled light. And alone.

He watched Lemos angle so he could drape his arm along the back of Sheba's chair. A nice, subtle move that allowed his fingertips to linger on her shoulder and play with strands of her hair. Perhaps Sheba's vision of him as a harmless friend would go against her in Lemos's game of seduction. She wouldn't expect such seemingly innocent touches to conceal ulterior motives. Until it was too late. Then Lemos would be tangled in her panties, and Cobb would be left holding his Glok.

The unfairness of that left a bad taste even though he had no business trying to nibble.

***

The minute they were excused from the dinner table, Sheba slipped from the crowd and hurried toward her bungalow. It had started to rain, one of the quick, drenching showers that came on in an instant. Protected by the thatched covering above the walkway, she slowed her pace to inhale the fresh bite of stagnant jungle revitalized by the downpour. The scent of wet greenery laced with fragrant blossoms was so crisp it almost hurt to inhale. That was the one thing she'd loved about the jungle, the way the rain made everything clean and pure again.

If only it could work the same miracle on her soul.

She let herself into her darkened room, switching on the light and glancing about cautiously before crossing to her wardrobe in hopes that time had managed to lessen the wrinkles in her clothes. Not great, but good enough. Good enough to blend with the group instead of standing out in glaring contrast. The last thing she wanted was to shame Paulo and her distant uncle.

She worked the transformation in record time, partly to get back before she was missed and partly because she didn't care to linger too long in the room alone so far away from the others.

The residue of her earlier scare still sat chill upon her nerves.

She made a face at the innocent looking mask upon her wall. It's hollow eyes seemed to mock her. *Well, let's see who has the last laugh, bub.* She snatched it down off the wall and stuffed it under the bed.

The rain had already stopped by the time she exited her little cabin. The day's heat steamed the newly fallen dampness to create a little fog where her bungalow was located away from the lights of the main building. Wisps of it crossed her path in thin tendrils and lay upon the grass like a foamy sea.

Perhaps it was the cloying dampness. Perhaps not. She began to walk faster, focusing on the welcoming doors to the Lodge. The closer she got, the quicker she moved until she'd broken into a brisk jog. Once inside, her pulse began to slow and she told herself she was being silly.

There was no one out there, watching her, following her.

It had been her imagination.

"She almost saw you, fool. You must be more careful."

"I thought the idea was to scare her."

"Subtly, discretely, yes. But so that no one else believes her. I want her doubting her mind, afraid to trust her senses. I don't want her alarming her bodyguard into suspecting she has a reason to be afraid."

"Cobb." The name spat out like something vile and bitter sitting upon the tongue. "I can handle Cobb."

"Can you? I wonder. He can spoil everything, so we must be careful."

"You worry too much. I know how to play the game. Just remember that, when the game is over, Cobb is mine."

"And you remember, it's not over until I've enjoyed my revenge and have my reward."

The vampire smiled, fangs gleaming in the darkness. "Until we've both had our revenge."

***

Cobb's stomach was growling by the time the tables were cleared and the pretty company filed into the soaring lobby area to appreciate native musicians on their flutes and drums. He glided along in the shadows, keeping watch, keeping his hormonal rumblings to himself.

"She's lovely, isn't she?"

Samuels' comment took him by surprise, not because it was true but because he'd managed to sneak up undetected to offer it. Concealing his startlement, Cobb played dumb.

"Who?"

"Sheba, of course. I've noticed you've had a difficult time keeping your eyes off her, but then, that's what I'd hoped for, after all. I want you to watch her, and watch her carefully. But for the right reasons."

"I thought I was here to chaperone your nephew." His bland remark in no way betrayed how Samuels' observation rattled him. Was he that obvious? No wonder Lemos was ready to demand his walking papers.

"Paulo, yes. But in most cases, my nephew can take care of himself. He's a man, after all. Sheba is different."

Cobb raised an eyebrow. Yeah, he'd noticed.

"I didn't want her to come back here. I did my best to talk Paulo out of making that condition. He thought it would be best for her, but I have doubts. Serious doubts. This trip may be disastrous for her. She needs someone to take care of her, Cobb. She won't let those of us who are close to her help."

Cobb's reply was dry as Lima dust. "It looks like your nephew is anxious to give it a try."

Samuels gave Paulo an indulgent look through fond eyes that also saw faults. "Paulo is a good boy. A smart boy. But he isn't always an astute boy. He doesn't understand the cruelties of the world the way you and I do, Cobb. The way Sheba does. He wouldn't be able to keep her safe because he couldn't recognize the danger. That's why she needs you."

"Why would you think she'd let me help her?"

"Because you have nothing at stake here. You're in it for the paycheck."

It was hard not to wince at that blunt summation. True,

though it might be.

"So, who am I protecting her from?"

"Herself."

NINE

At Cobb's perplexed look, Samuels began with purposeful vagueness.

"Sheba has known a difficult life."

"Paulo told me her parents were murdered."

Samuels nodded. "But even before that, she was like no other girl her age who grew up watching television, playing with Barbie dolls and gossiping about boys on the phone. Sheba grew up here, in the jungle, unspoiled and oblivious to the rest of the world."

As Samuels spoke of her, Cobb searched the room with his gaze and grew concerned when he couldn't find her amongst the other guests. Just as he was about to make a move inside, he saw her stop at the entrance to the Lodge. Her features were flushed as if she'd been hurrying. And she'd changed her clothes.

She'd gone from jungle guide to sleek, sophisticated guest in just the few minutes that she'd been missing. A colorful sarong was tied at one slender hip so that when she moved, a length of bronze thigh was tantalizingly displayed by the shift of silky fabric. She'd tamed her short curls with a scarf of the same exotic pattern. The gold-colored tank top she wore warmed the honeyed tan of her skin and made the most of her toned physique by baring her athletic shoulders and arms. She wore sandals, not heels, and as she crossed the room, she was as graceful as one of the river dolphins dodging between the other guests.

To go to Paulo's side.

Studying the lithe and now confident female tucked into Paulo's shadow, Cobb asked, "And that's a bad thing?"

"Yes and no. Living in Eden can be a wonderful thing until that first snake comes along. She wasn't prepared for the harshness of the real world from the rosy picture her missionary parents painted. She expected everyone to be like them. Generous, honest, giving and compassionate. They told her a lie and she believed it. You and I know one does not send a soldier into battle against evil with no weapons at hand, or at least without the knowledge of them."

"What kind of evil did she meet? What happened to her parents?"

Samuels' expression tightened, his gaze growing far away to some unknown place filled with guilt and grief. For a moment, Cobb didn't think he would answer. But when he did, the picture he drew horrified.

"No one knows but Sheba. Her parents were zealous in their desire to convert the native Indians over to Christianity, fearing for their souls, and all. They'd been particularly excited about a dark cult in the jungle, one that existed only in whispers. One that both my wife and Shari, Sheba's mother, were related to by blood. They'd asked me to guide them to a temple, but I couldn't take them. You see, I'd just lost my wife and I tended to drink a bit. A lot, really, and I was too hung over to go with them. They hired someone else and went off into the jungle. Sheba was told to stay at the village, but being the stubborn little monkey she was, she slipped away and followed them. When I found out she'd gone, I went after her to make sure she was safe."

He broke off then. Something dark and terrible played behind his eyes. Cobb almost stopped him then, but he didn't. He had to know the story if he was going to help Sheba.

"It was dark by the time I found her. She'd been wandering in the jungle for I don't know how long. She was in shock, close to catatonic, and covered in blood, none of it her own, thank goodness. I bundled her up and took her to the closest doctor, but he couldn't do anything to repair the injuries she'd received to her mind and soul. I don't know what she saw, Cobb, but her parents and the guide they hired were never seen again. She'd wake up screaming about some jungle tomb and some creature with fangs and glowing eyes. She said her parents were dead, but she claimed to have no memory of the deed."

Cobb had gone very still.

Fangs and glowing eyes.

"It took months for her to speak a coherent sentence. During that time, I went out every day, searching for some sign of them, for this mysterious temple. I found nothing. It was as if they'd vanished without a trace. And the answer was locked up tight in a little girl's mind."

"Why wasn't she sent to specialists?"

"We were in the middle of the jungle, Cobb. We don't exactly have psychiatrists clamoring to set up offices here. Most of the people in the basin still go to witch doctors. And then there was the money issue. There was no money, not for proper treatment or even to get Sheba to the States. Her parents were missionaries. They didn't believe they needed extra life insurance, if you know what I mean. Sheba had no one to look out for her interests. Neither the group her parents were affiliated with nor the government wanted to get involved in murder and potential scandal."

"Scandal? What do you mean?"

"A crazed girl found in the jungle covered in her parents' blood with no recall of what happened? There were some who were eager to blame her for the deaths just to put a neat end to it all."

"They thought she killed them?" Cobb's voice echoed his outrage and disbelief.

"They didn't know what to think. Sheba was no help. She was little more than a babbling vegetable."

A strange twist of sorrow and fury curled through Frank Cobb as he thought of the traumatized child no one would claim responsibility for. "So what happened to Sheba?"

"She was finally sent back to the States where she spent three years recovering."

Recovering. A cold shaft of meaning jabbed his belly. "Recovering?"

"In a mental hospital. She got better, eventually. The

quality of her treatment was improved, and she was finally released to attended a private girls' school. She graduated top of her class and went on to college, where she graduated at the top of her class. And she choose a profession that would debunk everything her parents believed in. A rather cruel irony, don't you think?"

He thought everything about the whole thing stank.

"No official investigation was done into her parents' disappearance?"

"By whom? The government in this country sometimes changes with the day of the week. It was even more unstable then. They were too busy worrying about coups and drug smugglers to care about the fate of two politically incorrect missionaries who some would say got what they deserved for interfering with the natural order of things."

"And what do you say, Mr. Samuels?"

"I think it's time someone found out the truth and set Sheba free."

And Frank got the idea that Samuels believed him to be that someone.

"So what does this have to do with the trouble your nephew is having?"

"Maybe nothing, maybe everything. It depends on why the Reynards were killed and by whom."

"And what's your opinion?"

Samuels sighed heavily. "It could have been animals. It could have been a greedy guide who took a fancy to Mrs. Reynard then killed them both and disappeared. Or they could have stumbled onto something they weren't supposed to see."

"Like what?"

"What kind of illegal activity doesn't go on down here? Drugs, smuggling or maybe some indigenous cult who resented the outside world butting into their beliefs."

Something about Samuels' expression told Cobb that he was leaning toward the latter explanation. "The same cult that's trying to keep your nephew out of the jungle? To preserve their way of life, or to keep him from finding out what happened to the Reynards?"

"I knew Harper would send someone clever. But are you clever enough to figure it out and still keep something bad from happening to my family? Paulo thinks the only way Sheba can get better is to confront her fears. I believe some things are better left alone. I don't know what she saw, but it stole almost four years of her life. A life that's never been whole since that tragedy. I don't want to lose her back to madness. Can you keep her safe, Mr. Cobb?"

Silence fell between them while Cobb pondered the question. Then Samuels pressed his shoulder.

"I must return to my guests. Let me say this last thing. I owe her family. I won't see them repaid by bringing her back here to succumb to their same fate."

Alone on the porch, Frank was startled by the screech of some nocturnal bird. He turned toward the solid green forest wall where no light penetrated the shadows and tried to imagine what it had been like for a young girl fighting her way through that blinding blackness with the knowledge of her parents' murder in terrifying pursuit.

Or her parents' murderer.

Looking back inside the lodge, his gaze sought Sheba in the milling crowd. He smiled to himself because she was no longer the timid wall flower. Several of the other scientists had latched onto her and were listening in rapt attention to whatever tales she was telling. Her face glowed with animation and energy. Her gestures punctuated her story like the graceful flutters of the forest macaws. And Frank Cobb, at that moment, was mesmerized.

He had a whisper of warning, a prickle of instinct bringing all his senses to immediate alert. Spinning to confront the jungle, he searched for whatever had tripped his self-preserving alarm. Nothing. Nothing seemed to move in that dense mat of green.

He thought it was a trick of the breeze at first. Until he realized there was no wind.

A ripple of sound played about him, soft, taunting. A chuckle filled with mockery and menace so close it made the hairs stand up on his forearms.

He waited, tense and ready. He didn't reach for his gun, knowing it would be useless against this particular threat. Instead, he loosened his tie and withdrew the small silver cross he never took off.

Silence steeped and thickened until he could almost believe he'd imagined it. Almost.

"Not much for the party scene, Mr. Cobb?"

Sheba watched him turn toward her. His wry smile couldn't waylay the message telegraphed from the tense set of his shoulders and hard glitter of his eyes. He looked like a man squaring off for a battle.

"Am I interrupting something?"

He bared his teeth. "Just communing with nature."

She made a negating sound. "You don't strike me as a nervous sort of guy. So what's got you spooked?"

She came closer and his eyes narrowed. His taut body posturing had her wondering if she spooked him. As amusing and flattering as that might be, it didn't answer the question. Something had his guard up, and if Cobb was wary, it wasn't without reason. She tried to appear nonchalant while her insides quivered.

His answer was an insult. "I'm just a city boy overwhelmed by the surroundings."

The noise she made grew ruder. "Oh please, Mr. Cobb. I doubt that anything overwhelms you."

Again the incremental slitting of his gaze. A gaze that briefly flickered up and down the length of her. The quivering within took on a different tempo, but before she could respond to it or to what his once-over suggested, his stare hardened like the sudden cooling of molten rock.

"That's because I don't take foolish chances. You should go back inside, Dr. Reynard."

Contrarily, she went to lean her forearms on one of the peeled wood porch rails. Instead of gazing into the forest, she kept her stare relegated to the neat, machete trimmed bushes that surrounded the lawn. "Why should I do that? I feel quite safe out here with you." And oddly, that was true.

"Maybe you shouldn't."

The cautioning rumble in his tone stirred a seismic response in Sheba. What exactly was he warning her away from? From the dangerous pull that drew her out into the night because she knew he was there? From the way her pulse beat a little faster when he joined her at the rail?

"Tell me about the work you do," she broached quietly.

"You mean babysitting?"

"Have you killed people, Mr. Cobb?"

After a brief pause, he said, "Not yet today, but the night is young."

His determined levity sobered her mood. "What kind of danger is Paulo in?"

"I'd say he's about to succumb to a deadly pair of big brown eyes."

She scowled at him, unwilling to be distracted by his teasing banter. "Why are you here, Cobb? Why did Sam call out the big guns? Or at least your big gun?"

"My big gun is my business, Doc. Let's keep it that way, okay?"

"Excuse me? I've faced down headhunters in Africa, supposed goat suckers from outerspace in Puerto Rico, cults in India and Malaysia that would curl your toes, and now I'm going out there." She gestured toward the forest without looking at it. "I want to know what I'm up against."

His stare was unblinking. "I think you know already, and that's what's got you scared to death."

The wind sapped from her argument and her lungs with the effectiveness of a blow to the mid-section. The remaining emptiness hurt more than the unexpected attack. She drew a tortured breath and hissed, "You're a bastard, Cobb."

She tried to spin away but he caught her arm, holding her fast, not so that he could protest her statement but simply so that she was forced to face him.

And the truth.

Her own defenses surged up on a tidal wave of anger and agitation.

"You don't know anything about me, Cobb. I don't care what you've heard."

She couldn't catch her breath. Panic and fury brought pindots of color to dance before her eyes. Behind them stood a stoic Frank Cobb, so smug in his assumptions, so cold in his summation.

"You asked, so I'll tell you. I think the biggest danger to Lemos is you."

Surprise and the absurdity of it shocked her back to a ragged sense of awareness. "Don't be ridiculous. It wasn't my idea to come here. What threat could I possibly be to Paulo? He's my oldest, dearest friend."

Then his question came with line drive directness right to left field.

"Are you crazy, Dr. Reynard?"

"W-what?"

"You know, crackers, loony tunes, nuts, bonkers. Are you insane? Is your instability going to put all of us in danger once we get out into the jungle? If it is, I need to know now. My job is to protect your oldest, dearest friend on his little hunting and gathering trek into the wilds. I have enough to worry about without waiting for you to go falling off the deep end."

"Don't you worry about me, Mr. Cobb." She chiseled out the words as if striking them in stone. "My problems are not your concern."

"You're wrong there, Doc. You are my problem. And I've got to decide on how to deal with you."

She drew herself up with a fiery indignity. "You don't get to decide anything. You're just the hired help here, along for the paycheck. You've got no stake whatsoever in this."

"That's right. I've got nothing invested except my life and, excuse me, but I do tend to place some value on that. And I do get to decide where I'm going to risk it. If I'm going to go out there and put it on the line for, as you so succinctly put it, the paycheck, I need to know if you can keep it together. If you have any doubts, you stay behind."

"I'll be fine, Cobb."

"Will you? Are you? Then tell me what you saw earlier tonight in your room. Can you do that?"

"A mask on the wall."

"Bull."

"I didn't see anything." His steady stare wouldn't let her leave it at that. "I didn't see anything real, okay. Is that what you wanted to hear? That I'm nuts, bonkers and all the rest? That I see things that aren't there? That I have a hole in my memories large enough to drive a mack truck through? That I can't trust myself to know what's real?"

"Trust me."

His sudden intensity dragged her back from the edge of hysteria.

"Why, Cobb? Why should I trust you?"

"Because I can protect you if you let me. Because I know you're not crazy."

"How do you know?" she whispered, fearing to believe it because she didn't believe it herself.

"Because I know what's out there, and it's real." He touched the scar on his face without being aware of the gesture.

"What's out there, Frank?"

A whisper. A plea.

"A nightmare that will suck you in and suck you dry if you let it. Don't let it, Doc. Stay close to me and tell me if anything strange happens to you, anything at all. I believe you, but you've got to learn to trust yourself and me if we're going to survive this little jungle walk. Can you do that for me, Doc?"

"Well, now, what's this? The party's inside, you two, or did you forget?"

Paulo's abrupt intrusion broke the tension between them and created a whole new arena of bristling confrontation between him and Cobb. Cobb smiled crookedly, the expression mocking more than it reassured.

"The doctor was just sharing a little jungle survival lore with me."

"I thought you were the survival expert, Mr. Cobb." The statement was more a sneer.

"It's a foolish man who thinks there's nothing more he can learn. Or obtain."

Paulo's dark gaze flared at the challenge. He extended his hand to Sheba. A claiming gesture. "Let's go in. Uncle Sam was asking for you."

Sheba wrested her attention away from Frank Cobb, but his incredible claim still beat fast and furious within her breast. *I believe you.*

Had more wonderful words ever been spoken to soothe a frantic mind? Inside herself she would hold onto that truth in a desperate attempt to save her sanity just as on the outside, she took the hand Paulo held out to her.

Cobb watched the Peruvian shepherd the lovely doctor away, but his thoughts weren't tied up to jealousies or macho posturing contests for her affection.

He was more interested in saving her life.

Red eyes and fangs.

Cobb confronted the jungle with a fearsome certainty.

"So this is where you've been hiding, you son of a bitch. I know your name and I know your game, and you're not going to have her. This time, I win for good."

TEN

The morning sun lifted above the tree line, striking the gray-pink clay bank on the opposite side of the river and awaking a rippling palette of red, blue, green and yellow as parrots vied for choice perches. Sounds that would have been ear piercing in a pet store, blended into the harmonious whole of the beat that was jungle life.

Though he'd only managed to snatch a few scant hours of sleep, the glorious cacophony of the rainforest waking with the sun renewed Frank Cobb's energy. He'd spent most of the night here on the porch, listening to the restless sounds of Sheba's nightmares. But with the daylight, his worries lessened a degree. What stalked Sheba Reynard moved in the night. Whether it was in dreams or in shadowed realities, he would soon find out.

"Breathtaking, isn't it?"

He answered Paulo Lemos's question with an affirming nod.

"There's nothing in the city that can humble you quite so completely as the sheer enormity of the jungle. Come with me, Cobb. I want to show you something." When Frank didn't respond, he smiled somewhat thinly. "She's all right now. She's sleeping."

Without any further argument, Cobb stepped away from the rail after snubbing out his cigarette. Lemos led him to the base of the canopy tower. Looking up the dizzying ten-stories as they disappeared into the trees, Cobb wondered perversely if Lemos planned to lure him up there to push him off to an 'accidental' death. Was he as big a threat to the botanist's budding romance as the unknown dangers Cobb was there to protect him from? Uncertain of the answer, Cobb began to climb.

He was in great physical shape, but after rounding the thirtieth turn or so, Cobb's knees began to protest Paulo's almost urgent upward pace. Was this to be a test of endurance, then? He sighed, cursing the decreased lung capacity from his two-decade old bad habit, and started up the final wooden ramp to the platform where Lemos waited.

And from that skyscraper-high perch, what was left of Frank's breath was snatched away.

Dawn rose over mist-covered trees that stretched for miles in every direction. High above the forest canopy, they saw a different world, where the brightness of the sky startled the eye and the jungle itself resembled bunches of broccoli. Out of those tight crowns of green burst birds of the most spectacular colors—iridescent fuchsia, daffodil yellow, brilliant viridian blue and tangerine—swooping and singing their welcome of the new day. As he admired the unspoiled view, he waited to hear what was on Paulo's mind. He got around to it, eventually.

"When I look at this amazing sight through a scientist's eyes, I see possibilities ripe for the picking. Cures for cancers, degenerative diseases, perhaps even life's longevity itself. But I look through different eyes as well, Mr. Cobb. I look through the eyes of my forefathers, those who would protect the forest and guard her secrets from the greed and indifference of the outside world."

"An interesting dilemma."

"Yes. How does one help the world without inviting the world to help itself?"

"You pick a forum that will respect what you're trying to preserve."

"And Harper isn't that forum?"

Cobb snorted. "Harper worships the god of bottom line. I've never known them to be overly concerned with anything other than results."

"Yet here you are, working for an employer you openly despise." Lemos sounded curious as well as ridiculing, so Cobb reeled out a little more of his story.

"I'm not here for Harper's benefit alone. What's going on out there, Lemos? What's preying on these people?"

"Sheba would say their superstitions."

"And you would say?"

"Oh, it's fear, all right. It's the fear of change. The fear of losing something you love, your way of life, your home, your culture, your beliefs."

"So you think that these attacks are the work of some radical protectionist group using native lore to keep outsiders away?"

"That's a simplistic view, Cobb, but essentially correct. That's why I've never felt myself to be in any real danger. I'm one of them, you see."

Cobb gave him the once over and smirked at the visual of the dapper scientist running about the forest in a loincloth "going native." "But is that how they see you, Mr. Wizard, with your college degrees and fancy gear?"

Paulo was silent for a moment, weighing the dichotomy of what he'd become by leaving the land of his birth behind. "They know I'd never do anything to harm my homeland."

"Who's they, Lemos? Who's behind this terrorizing of the people?"

"It started out mildly enough, just subtle warnings that got the Indians stirred up, and delaying mishaps like stolen supplies and sabotaged equipment. Irritating but harmless."

"And then it got ugly."

The Peruvian nodded. Something worked behind his bronzed features, something more than just the thought of working against one's heritage. Something more personal.

"Who's behind it?"

The reluctant silence stretched out another beat, then Paulo could contain his suspicions no longer. "I think it's my grandfather."

Cobb arced one brow. "And he would be?"

"Ruperto Lemos, a shaman, a powerful man with many followers. He was the one who taught me that the rainforest trees are the lungs of our planet, and without them we would be unable to breathe." Paulo looked out over the forest, his eyes clouding with pain as his memories played out before him. "We watched the rolling Amazon factory come like a fearsome monster on wheels two stories tall. It shot blue laser beams to slice down trees so they would fall on the conveyor belt that pulled them inside to be stripped, peeled and planked, leaving neat piles of lumber for the construction crews behind it. It ground up stumps, bulldozed the earth and laid down a smooth black road for more humans to follow, all in one neat, destructive pass. So efficient. So frightening.

"My grandfather, with all his powers, could not stop this hungry beast from coming, and coming and coming. He was angry and afraid and unable to strike back because he didn't know the white man's ways or words. He had to leave the fight to those like Rosa Kelly who could scream about deforestation and protest the oil company explorations. And still such a small percent of our lands are protected by parks and reserves. The northern rainforest continues to be destroyed by farmers who drain the ground of nutrients while lumber barons continue to cut away the cloud forest. The United States wants to spray a defoliant on the plantations that produce a 1.6 billion dollar a year cocaine trade and let that poison leech into the earth. Our heritage is stolen from us by tomb robbers, and our culture is stripped away by the well-intentioned missionaries who preach about a god who is not our own. Yes, my grandfather is angry and afraid for good reason.

"And when these invaders tried to include him in their blasphemous shamanistic tours, he was forced to retreat from the forests up into the hills near Cuzco, where he remains in hiding from the modern world."

"Hiding or plotting?"

"Perhaps both." Such sadness echoed in that simple claim, Cobb almost felt sorry enough for Paulo to let it go. But he felt more sorry for what someone was putting Sheba through.

"Would your grandfather be angry and afraid enough to resort to murder?"

Paulo wouldn't meet his gaze. "Not with his own hands, no. But he may have summoned up the means to have it done.

Means not of this world." Then the young scientist braced for the jaded mercenary's laughter. When it didn't come, he looked perplexed, and a bit grateful. "You're not going to call me ignorant for believing such things possible?"

This time, Cobb couldn't evade his curious stare. "I know there are such things as demons and monsters. You don't need to turn me into a believer."

Lemos studied the American for a long moment, then nodded. "*Bueno.* Then perhaps we can be some use to one another after all."

"I want to meet your grandfather."

Paulo pursed his lips. "That may not be possible. He is very wary of outsiders."

"Then I need to speak to anyone who's had close dealings with this creature no one will name. Know thy enemy, I always say."

"That I can arrange."

As Paulo turned to start down the ramps, Cobb gripped his arm.

"How much danger is she in if she goes into the jungle with us?"

Paulo's reply was carefully phrased and obviously well thought out. "Not as much as if she remains here in the dark alone."

"Do you think your grandfather was behind her parents' murder?"

A terrible guilt and grief colored his swarthy features. "I pray to God not."

Cobb didn't ask him exactly which god that might be.

***

What was waiting for her out in that impenetrable field of green?

The exhaustion of the past few near-sleepless nights caught up to her. As she stood sipping hot coffee on the porch overlooking the jungle, her brain felt bruised and beaten beyond the ability for clear thought. Traces of her dreams clung like oily film to the edge of her awareness, shaving the veneer of calm away until she was a raw nerve. When she heard a soft step behind her, she nearly vaulted out of her hiking boots.

"Sorry. Didn't mean to startle you."

Sheba glared at Frank Cobb while dashing the contents of her coffee cup from the right leg of her shorts. "Then you shouldn't have snuck up on me."

"A bit testy this morning, are we?"

"Only when you're around to test my patience."

"I love it when you talk dirty."

She made an exasperated sound. "What do you want, Cobb?"

He sobered so quickly, she was immediately wary.

"I need your help with something."

"Oh?"

"Your buddy Lemos gave me the names of a couple of people to question regarding the strange things that have been happening. Only I'm not exactly the sort to inspire confidence with the natives, if you know what I mean."

"You want me to prepare the way for you?"

"That would be greatly appreciated."

"Who do we need to see?"

"There's a woman who works in housekeeping whose husband was killed. And that guide, Cross. He discovered the body of Samuels' guest."

With tension seeping through her belly like ice over a winter pond, Sheba fought down the desire to beg off. Her eyes narrowed slightly. "This isn't some kind of cruel therapy you've come up with to make me face my fears, is it?"

Cobb blinked at her harmlessly. "Why is it that you doctor-types think everything revolves around you? I need someone who can speak Spanish better than my bumbling high school recall. If you don't want to help–"

She set the now empty coffee cup on the closest table. "Let's get this done."

Cobb had the decency not to grin.

***

Maria Ruis was busy thrusting armloads of table linens into the two huge industrial washing machines. Her face was florid from the exertion, but she paused to regard them politely.

"Is there something I can do for you? More towels for your rooms, perhaps?"

"Maria Ruis?"

She straightened at Sheba's gentle inquiry, one hand going unconsciously to her low back. "*Sí.*"

"Mrs. Ruis, I wonder if we might ask you a few questions about your husband."

A dazed, trapped look of loss dulled the dark eyes. Sheba, familiar with that glaze of pain, would have backed off, but Cobb gave her arm a slight nudge to proceed.

"I'm sorry if this subject is painful to you," she continued in Spanish. "But we must ask if we are to save others. What happened to your husband? How did he die?"

"My Paco was a good man," she began in a quavering voice, trying to convince both of them of that dubious fact. "It was my taking a job here that ruined him and stole his pride away. It is my fault that he took up the bottle."

Cobb frowned with impatience, understanding enough to know things weren't going full steam ahead. Sheba reproved him with a sideward glance.

"I'm sure you were only doing what you had to do," she soothed. "Tell me about Paco."

While Cobb chafed at the delay, Sheba listened as the woman poured out teary remembrances, past failures and regrets. And then, the tears were gone and the fear Sheba understood so well seeped into their stead.

"When he did not come back, I went out to find him. He was very drunk, so I knew he did not go far. I found him off the path, lying in the scattering of branches he was bringing back for our fire. He was dead. My Paco was dead."

Unable to wait any longer, Cobb asked, "How did he die, Mrs. Ruis?"

She stared at him through huge, luminous eyes, the image of her dead husband swimming there upon an eternally dark sea. "His throat had been cut."

"By a knife?"

She shook her head in quick jerky motions. "No. By teeth, two great teeth that bit him here." She tapped the side of her fleshy neck with two fingers.

"Have there been other attacks similar to this that you know of?"

"A few, mostly deeper in the jungle. One hears whispers and chooses not to listen. If I had listened, I never would have let my Paco go out there after dark."

Cobb didn't pause at the return of her weeping. His tone was quietly intense. "Was it an animal that killed your husband?"

"An animal on two legs but not a man," was her nonsensical reply. But watching Cobb's expression, Sheba could tell it made perfect sense to him. "All his blood was gone, *señior*. There was not a drop in his body or on the ground."

"You told this to the police?"

"There were no *policia*. I come tell Mr. Samuels and he take care of my Paco and see that he is buried like a Christian so no evil ones can disturb his rest. Mr. Sam, he take care of everything for me. He gives me a place to live here at the lodge, so I don't have to go back there into the forest again. But he can't give me back my husband." She scrubbed at her eyes with work-worn hands then bent to transfer the wet linens from washer to dryer. "Now, I must get back to my job. There is nothing else I can tell you."

Sheba thanked her for her honesty and commiserated with her pain before joining Cobb outside once more. She studied his set features for a moment, trying to read something, anything about what he was thinking upon those pleasant planes. No luck. In frustration, she had to ask.

"Well?"

He focused on her as if startled by her presence. "Well, what?"

"Your opinion on what we just heard?"

"No evidence that it's not an elaborate hoax. No evidence that it is. No body, no chance to examine the trace samples that could link this death to...other possibilities." If only he had the science at hand to prove the impossible to the disbelieving. He glanced away and sighed, "Doc, why do you have to be so far away?"

"I'm right here," Sheba objected. He stared right through her then blinked.

"I didn't mean you. Sorry."

It didn't take a great mental stretch for her to guess this other 'Doc' was a woman. The other woman in his life? Then she caught herself. Other woman? When had she started thinking of herself as Frank Cobb's woman? The idea surprised because of its ridiculousness.

Because of its sudden, unexpected appeal.

She'd never been anyone's woman before.

He was speaking to her, and she heard none of the words. With a sharp shake of her head to clear the nonsense away, Sheba asked him to repeat himself.

"The other man, Cross, will be here at dusk to lead the twilight tours. We'll have to wait until then to talk to him. Hopefully, he has something a little more useful for us to go on."

She was watching his mouth as he spoke, wondering again if he would have kissed her the previous night if she had taken the initiative to lean forward. Such a slight effort on her part to reap a tremendous reward. But would kissing Frank Cobb be reward or curse? She didn't want complications in her life. Her past contained a scary hole from which any number of demons could arise, and her future held little more than the same constantly mobile address she'd claimed for the past eight years. Not much to inspire thoughts of romance or permanence. As if a guy like Cobb understood either of those concepts.

"What are you smiling at?" he asked, suddenly suspicious.

"Just thinking how ironic that you and I must lead very similar lives."

"Yours that boring?"

"Just work and travel."

"Travel and work." His grin was cynical. "We're a pathetic pair, then, aren't we?"

"Are we?" she blurted out before thinking of the connotations of that question. *Are we a pair, Frank Cobb?*

"Most would say so. Isn't it a social abnormality to have attained an age of majority and not claim a mortgage, a 9-to-5 paycheck, a significant other, a dog and 2.6 kids produced under politically correct circumstance? Why don't we have those things? Or want them?"

He may have been teasing in his wry, Cobbesque way, but she was deadly serious when she replied, "Because we're smarter than the average bears. We can lead productive lives without hauling around all the baggage that's supposed to go with it."

"With a house and a spouse and kids?"

"Or with a mouse or in a box or with a fox. I could not, would not, Sam-I-am. I don't need that–" She broke off.

"That what?"

She was going to say "pain."

Instead, she waved her hand as if it was inconsequential.

But Frank could see it was anything but. He watched her expression close down, like a house of cards folding inward, flattening upon themselves when the bottom support was yanked away. What had turned this woman off so violently to the thought of a relationship? Funny, he wasn't musing over Paulo's disappointment. He was pondering his own.

"So, who is this 'Doc'?" she asked to shift the uncomfortable spotlight from herself to glare in his eyes. "Someone you worked with in the States?"

Well, he'd brought it up, hadn't he? Now, he'd have to tell her something.

"She was my last job."

"Under your protection or your scrutiny?"

His smile was as tight as the twist of his emotions. "A bit of both."

Her voice softened slightly, as if she'd read between the lines and found the story to be an unlikely romance. "And what happened?"

"I did my job. She did hers."

"And?"

"She's living happily ever after in some foreign palace with the man of her dreams."

"And you wish you were there?"

He winced away from her astuteness but didn't evade what was obvious. "Sometimes."

All the time, truth be told. Stacy Kimball had possessed his thoughts and dreams with her sassy mouth, lush body and sexy brain. She'd taken all his impossible wishes with her when she'd boarded the plane in Seattle to be with the man she loved. Talk about a Casablanca moment. He could have stopped her and kept her with him with a word but had remained silent. And perhaps, eventually, he could have won her love, even if he hadn't been the right man for her. Every time he breathed in, he could taste the scent of her hair. On every breeze, he was teased by the sound of her laugh. Until recently.

Until Sheba Reynard sucked up all his senses.

He sure knew how to pick 'em: a geneticist who'd had no future and an ethnologist who'd forgotten her past, so dissimilar in looks and attitude, so alike with their quick intelligence and the secrets they wore like armor to keep the world at bay. Alike, as well, in the dangers that stalked them?

That was what he had to find out.

***

"Money problem or man problem?"

Sheba glanced up from where she sat alone and smiled wryly at Rosa's observation. "Why would you think that?"

"Only two things I know that make a pretty girl's face so long." The large woman angled herself into one of the wicker chairs. It groaned under her weigh as she shifted to get comfortable. They had the dining room to themselves in the late afternoon hour. The heat made Sheba too lazy to move, and the confusion of heart had her open for any suggestion, even from such an unlikely source.

"And which do you think I have?"

"Since you inherited your dear ones' disdain for luxuries, I would guess it's a matter of romance."

"Men are so—" She couldn't find the right word, but Rosa nodded enthusiastically.

"That they are. And he's such a handsome fellow, your

Paulo."

"Paulo?"

Rosa reacted to the surprise in her voice with amazement then amusement. "Ah, so it is the other one who has your juices flowing."

"Rosa, I said no such thing!"

"No, but that rosy blush does. He is an interesting man, your Mr. Cobb. But such a man is not easily tamed to the leash of wedlock."

Sheba blinked, aghast at the other woman's assumptions. "Who said anything about marriage?"

Rosa chuckled. "You shock me, little Sheba, considering your upbringing. I thought your parents taught you to save yourself for the man you married."

"They did," she blurted out foolishly, then immediately regretted the confidence.

"You are a virgin?" Rosa leaned her beefy forearms on the tabletop and stared as if at some strange new species. "At how old?"

"Old enough to make my own choices without having to explain them," Sheba snapped, embarrassed and defensive, and wishing she'd never brought the subject up. But then she hadn't, had she. What made her mating habits, or the lack thereof, any of the other woman's business?

Then Rosa sighed and gave a sad smile. "Ah, child, there are many times I wished I had had your restraint. I was always too easy with my favors, and when I finally met the man I would have waited for, it was already too late. I admire you for your character."

Flushing hotly, she confessed, "It's not so much character as lack of interest and opportunity. If I had the interest, there was no opportunity. If I had the opportunity..." She shrugged philosophically. "Somehow, it just didn't seem worth the effort since I knew I wasn't going to stick around to see it through."

How strange to be having this conversation with the liberal Rosa Kelly. She'd always thought her first frank talk about sexuality would be with Shari Reynard, whose gentle ways and loving manner made it so easy to open up on any topic.

This was a mother-daughter talk she should have been able to share at the onset of puberty, but by that time, her mother was gone and no other had ever filled that void. Rosa was the closest anyone had ever come to a surrogate.

Though there had been no visits over the years, Rosa seemed to have followed her career with a nurturing interest, just as Sheba acknowledged the older woman's with an indulgent tolerance. And, if nothing else, Rosa Kelly was certainly a woman of the world.

"Am I being foolish to wait?"

"For the right man? Honey, if you've got the patience to wait, you'll have a treasure worth a stack of Inca gold. No matter how evolved the male species becomes, they still cling to that caveman attitude about being the first and only to conquer whatever they see."

"At over thirty, I was afraid they'd see me more as a joke than as a jewel."

Rosa shook her head at that cynical reflection. "No, dear. Hold on to that gift for the right time. You've no idea of its value."

Curious now, because Rosa always appeared to be more a free love advocate than an espouser of chastity, she asked, "Haven't you ever wanted to settle down with one man?"

"Oh, yes. There was a man, the only man for me."

"What happened?"

"Many things, but mostly another woman. By the time he was free again, the moment had passed. He was the only one I thought worth the effort. Silly me, for now we can barely tolerate one another. It would have made for a rocky romance, no?"

Peyton?

Had the love of her life been Peyton Samuels?

"Don't look so shocked, child. I was quite an eyeful back then and Sam, he was much like your Frank Cobb. He was quite the stud."

Sheba pinked at thinking of her quasi-uncle in such intimate terms...and at thinking of Frank Cobb at all.

Your Frank Cobb.

"Don't worry, Rosa. Frank Cobb has no interest in romancing me."

Rosa Kelly only smiled at the naivete of her claim. "His interest will last as long as the mystery does, but if he is able to learn all your secrets, he won't linger for long."

And Sheba knew she wasn't referring to the mysteries of her past.

The color in her cheeks grew hotter with indignation at the thought of his love 'em-and-leave 'em attitude. "The bastard," she grumbled, condemning without a trial.

"My advice, don't waste yourself on a flash of passion, honey. Get your money's worth, I always say. Frank Cobb would be a poor return."

Somehow, even though she believed Rosa was probably right, Sheba didn't think that was quite true.

A little flash of passion with Frank Cobb might be worth the investment.

ELEVEN

Joaquin Cross moved up the dock with all the awkward, ugly grace of the vultures that hobbled along the shoreline looking for an easy meal. A man of his circumstances should have evoked sympathy, but something about the arrogant, disdainful way he shouted at his subordinates precluded pity. He wasn't helpless nor was he interested in the least bit of charity, offered or implied. When Frank held down his hand to assist his step up onto the planked walk, he glared at that outstretched gesture in stony contempt until it was withdrawn. Only then did he drag himself up to head toward the lodge in his hitching but nonetheless speedy gait. He didn't ask any questions of the two who fell in beside him, assuming they would speak on their own.

"Mr. Cross, I understand you found Ambassador Kenyon's wife."

"I didn't have nothing to do with that," he snapped out defensively, hurrying his pace until he was hitching and rolling like a piston.

"No one suggested that you did," Cobb clarified. "But you were the first one on the scene, isn't that right?"

"You talk like a policeman." Suspicion colored his tone in angry shades.

"I assure you, I'm not the law."

Cross shot him a sidelong glance. "No, I guess not. You got a sneakier look to you. I already told my story. Why should I want to tell it again to you?"

"Twenty reasons."

The cash was gone from Cobb's hand in a greedy flash. "Don't expect much for twenty dollars."

"Give me the condensed version."

"I heard a scream and found her dead."

"Expand just a little bit more."

Ahead of them, the lights from the lodge glowed like tiny fireflies. Frog songs were nearly deafening as they serenaded the advancing cool of the evening. Cross paused to look from Cobb to a reluctant Sheba who had yet to say anything.

"You want me to get into it in front of the lady here? It's nothing she should hear...considering."

Sheba stiffened at the meaning then adapted a haughty posture. "You needn't worry about me. Nothing you can say could shock me."

"If you say so, ma'am." But his smirky smile said he thought otherwise. "Where do you want me to start? With the tight little short shorts she was wearing when she got off the boat, or the spray she wore on that teased up blonde hair to draw every bug within a half mile radius?"

"How about starting with the night you found her."

He shrugged as if to say your loss.

"She was a snotty bitch, that one, always accusing the staff of being in her room, snooping through her things. Always trying to catch someone in the act, you know."

"Did she have a lot of valuables?"

Cross smiled at Sheba's naivete. "Valuable to her, no doubt. She was fond of powder." He mimicked snorting cocaine. "She was always slipping out of her husband's fancy parties to grab a toot, thinking nobody'd be the wiser. But everybody knew."

"And somebody killed her," was Cobb's blunt conclusion. "For the blow?"

"For her blood."

Cobb passed over another twenty without being asked. "Keep going."

An enthusiastic and graphic storyteller, Cross plunged in, creating a vivid picture of supposition and fact that grabbed Cobb's attention and had Sheba staring out into the deepening night as if she could see the grisly scene enacted upon the solid green curtain of the jungle.

Suzanne Kenyon excused herself from her husband's fundraiser for ecological awareness saying she had to powder her nose. Literally. Anxious and edgy, she hurried to her bungalow to confront one of the house staff in the bathroom leaving the extra towels she'd requested. Suzanne had flown into a paranoiac rage, slapping the poor servant, accusing her of stealing and vowing to get her fired. After the young woman fled in tears, Suzanne proceeded to get gloriously stoned. After a few blissful minutes of enjoying her solitary high, she began to totter back to the party, her nose still red and weepy from abuse and her senses none too reliable.

Alone in the night.

Easy prey.

"I heard her scream. At first, I thought a caiman had gotten some luckless water bird. Then I saw her foot sticking up on the deck. She wore this silly little bracelet around her ankle that was all sparkly, so I knew it was her before I even looked down into the bushes."

He went on to describe Suzanne Kenyon as she'd looked in death, with wide eyes reflecting the moon and another silenced scream contorting her features. In the darkness, the blood on her throat gleamed black and oily.

"It was then I heard something moving just at the edge of the trees. Moving so fast, it was just a blur. I yelled out and it stopped for just a second to glare at me with its red eyes, and then it was gone."

"What was gone?"

"That what got her."

"What did you see, Mr. Cross?" Sheba's question, though softly asked, bit like a blade.

"You know, Missy. You seen it once yourself, long ago. The old one, him what guards the jungle."

"Nonsense." Sheba whirled away angrily, her arms hugging tight about herself. "Silly superstition and nonsense. It wasn't a chupacabra or some creature out of your ancient legends. It was a drug theft gone wrong and disguised to frighten everyone from asking too many questions."

Cross smiled blandly. "If you say so, Miss."

"Did she have drugs on her?" Cobb demanded, glancing

distractedly at Sheba, who paced the path like one of the jungle panthers.

"Enough to draw a Federal rap for intent to distribute."

Cobb gauged the Indian narrowly. "Now you sound like a cop."

"Starsky and Hutch reruns. I used to love those guys when I lived in the city. No cable out here. A pity."

"So why does a hip and savvy guy like yourself believe in superstitions?"

"I know what I saw. And I know what I believe. Greedy folks got to poking around where they didn't belong. Something got woken up out there in the jungle, and it's hungry. Ask her. She knows. And if I was you, I wouldn't go out there 'less I had already made my funeral plans. It's out there and it don't like strangers. That's all you get for your money. I got work to do."

Pale as the moon overhead, Sheba watched the guide continue to the lodge. She could feel Cobb's stare, his questions stabbing at her like needles in her nerves.

"Well," he drawled at last, "what do you think?"

"About what?" she snapped, looking ready to snap, herself. "Ignorance? I could smell the stink of lying all over him. Do you know how many times I've heard those same silly stories repeated and repeated until they're believed? I know an urban legend when I hear one."

"And I know fear when I see it. Why are you so angry, Doc? If there's nothing to what he's saying, what's got you all worked up?"

"I'm not–" She broke off, realizing her voice quavered on a shriek. More calmly, she continued, "I'm not worked up. I'm irritated. Superstition irritates me because it excites the ignorant into believing lies, then you have to work that much harder to find the truth."

"And what's the truth, here, Doc? He said you knew. What do you know?"

"I know I've had about enough of this."

She started for the lodge in great, fierce strides. For a moment, she'd begun to hope Cobb wouldn't follow, but then she heard his soft tread and knew he wasn't about to let it go. Cobb was a bulldog when he got something between his jaws. He came up beside her and before she had the chance to shoot him a warning glare, he sunk his teeth in and gave her a shake.

"What did you see, Sheba?"

"Nothing," she hissed. "Nothing. I don't know what he's talking about."

His hand on her elbow forced her pace to slow, but her heart continued its frantic race.

"Then why are you so upset?"

She faced him, seething with fury and panic. "Because I don't like people trying to stick memories in my head. I don't know what he's talking about. How would he know what I saw or didn't see? He made it up to weasel an extra twenty from you. You know why there are so many myths and scary legends told decade after decade? Because there's a buck to be made out of it. There's always some sucker willing and waiting to buy in and be taken for a ride."

"Where's this ride taking us, Doc?"

"Out there." She pointed into the jungle. "Out there where the stories can seem so real..."

"What? So real, what?"

"That you begin to believe them." She continued to challenge him with her stare, with her aggressive stance that dared him to make more of it. Finally, she relented with a heavy sigh. "Leave it alone, Cobb. I've got packing to do if I'm going to be ready to leave in the morning."

"We wouldn't want to keep Paulo waiting, would we?"

She searched for some ulterior meaning in his quiet claim and, finding none, she simply pulled away. This time, he didn't follow.

***

Dammit, what had she seen?

Cobb watched her break into a coltish run in her hurry to escape him and the provoking questions he might ask.

Tomorrow they were going into the jungle. If she was this fragile here, where they were still surrounded by at least the vestiges of civilization, what was going to happen when they were swallowed up in the primitive abyss? Would she crack wide open or just go quietly insane?

Cross's story had touched a raw nerve. Had the man done it on purpose, just to play with her head, or was there fact behind what she steadfastly called fiction?

Lemos believed it would be therapeutic for her to confront her fears. Samuels was worried.

Cobb was afraid it would be suicidal.

He started toward the lodge, his steps slow to suit the ponderous turn of his thoughts. Why wasn't anything ever easy? Why couldn't Suzanne Kenyon have been killed for the drugs she was so fond of, or maybe by a disgruntled employee tired of her abuse? Why couldn't it have been wild animals that tore the throat from Paco Ruis as he gathered wood for his fire? Why did he have to care if Sheba Reynard's mental status shivered like fine crystal about to shatter?

All part of the job. Part of the damn job. A job he'd begun to hate because it was the only thing he was good at. Concealing emotions. Playing games. Sneaking. Lying. Even stealing. Great qualities suitable for no decent job he knew of. Except for being a spook. Except for working for places like Harper who didn't care how the job was done as long as the results were favorable.

Perhaps it was time to tell Sheba Reynard what he was really after.

Perhaps, for once, the truth should start with him.

She was standing on the wrap-around porch, her long, lean form silhouetted by the faint light coming from inside her room. He allowed himself a moment of sheer lustful indulgence, picturing her waiting there in the shadows for him in nothing but lace and fantasies. No, she wasn't Stacy Kimball with her sinful curves and aura of sensuality that drove a man into hormonal overload. Sheba was like glimpsing at a dream—basic, simple in its necessity, yet still just out of reach.

Travel and work. What a pair they were. He wondered fleetingly how she would react if he suggested they chuck all their independence for a shot at the suburban ideal. Mortgage, dog, kids and all. Would that be so bad?

Surprisingly, his usual skittishness failed to save him from further musings.

A home, a hearth and a bed with Sheba Reynard in it. Not exactly hell on Earth.

Now that he was close enough for her to see his face, he made sure none of his thoughts were apparent. He smiled thinly and was ready to let loose some irreverent banter when she spoke one word.

"Frank."

Alert in every fiber, he bolted up onto the porch beside her. God, she was as white as those water lilies.

"Doc, what's wrong?"

She stepped silently aside, and he strode past her into her room.

The light in the bathroom was on, sending out just enough brightness to catch in sparkly flashes on the diamonds set in the bracelet on her bed.

Suzanne Kenyon's ankle bracelet.

TWELVE

There was really no doubt.

The second he saw it glittering there, a mocking obscenity, Cobb knew it had to have come off the ankle of the dead woman. And he was just as certain about who had put it there for Sheba to find. He backed out of the room and shut the door. Sheba's wide doe-in-the-headlights eyes lifted to his when he took her a bit too roughly by the arm.

"Come on."

She didn't ask where. She just went with him. That docility was more troubling than her temper of moments before. He steered her inside his room and told her sternly to wait there. The luminescent blankness of her stare made him hesitate a fraction of a second before leaving her alone.

He did a quick yet thorough sweep of her room. No sign of forced entry, nothing else out of place. No surprises. He knew the MO. The bracelet he lifted carefully and bagged, planning to take prints off it later. The eventual results would be no surprise either, he was willing to wager.

And just as he was about to leave, he paused. Sheba's big suitcase was open.

Wondering if it, indeed, held the kitchen sink, he drew closer. Someone had ransacked it. Wondering what else it might contain? He glanced in and frowned in surprise.

Bibles. Bibles, hymnals and prayer books.

It was her father's suitcase.

These were his books, his lessons, his notes. And as much as she might protest against their beliefs, still she carried them with her everywhere she went.

A bittersweet pang shot through his heart because he had

nothing to carry to remind him of the past.

He closed the lid and snapped the latches, letting his palm linger on the lid.

"I'll take care of her, Reverend Reynard."

After turning off the light and snatching up a big fluffy robe he found hanging on the bathroom door, he went next door, not sure what kind of shape he'd find his guest in.

The shower was running.

Okay, that was good.

He locked his door, checked the windows with professional paranoia then, satisfied, went to stand by the closed bathroom door.

Steam curled out from beneath the door.

He knocked softly.

"Doc?"

No reply.

He knocked louder, keeping the worry from his tone as he called, "Doc, you need anything?"

Just the sound of the running water.

He gave her a few more minutes, just for propriety's sake, pacing all the while as a bad feeling curled in the pit of his stomach. Finally, he gave in.

With a loud rap on the door, he bellowed, "I'm coming in," and did so.

The small bathroom was filled with mist. It billowed over the top of the fern-patterned shower curtain like a volcano about to blow.

No more time for modesty, his or hers.

He pulled back the curtain and was momentarily taken aback to find no one standing beneath the forceful stream of water. Where the hell was she?

Then a soft, snuffling sound directed his attention downward.

She was sitting on the floor of the shower, naked, hugging updrawn knees, shaking like a wet kitten. Her fixed stare never lifted as he reached to turn off the faucets.

"Save any hot water for me?" he asked casually as he draped a towel about her quaking shoulders. "Nothing worse than an inconsiderate guest. Up you go."

He tended to her as if she were a child, ignoring her nudity and keeping up the gently chiding chatter because it distracted her from it, too. While she stood there, breathing in quick snatches, dripping and shivering, he fetched her robe and bundled her inside it. Only then did he pat her dry with brisk, impersonal efficiency. The discarded towel he wrapped turban-like about her hair.

"Okay, that's a sauna and a rub down. Sorry, I don't do pedicures."

She blinked, focusing on him somewhat dully at first then with increasing awareness. She sucked a shuddering breath.

"You saw it, too."

"Yes, I did."

"I'm not crazy."

"No, you're not."

She went limp against him. "Thank God. Thank God."

With Sheba hanging off him like sagging wallpaper, Cobb returned to the main room, leading her over to the edge of the bed. He'd hoped to deposit her there, but instead of releasing him, she pulled him down onto the coverlet beside her. He surrendered with only a tiny voice of caution whispering in the back of his brain.

This is not a good idea.

Because she was still shivering like a Chihuahua, he kept her tucked close against his side and reached across her to pull the lightweight bedspread over the both of them. Her arms were about his neck like a choke chain and her breaths tickled against his neck in quick snatches, but when she spoke, her voice was almost steady.

"The first thing I remembered was waking up to bright lights and unfamiliar faces. Imagine my surprise to find I was no longer in Peru but in Pennsylvania amongst strangers. They told me it was a private hospital, conveniently leaving out the word 'mental.'"

"Doc, you don't have to."

She ignored his quiet protest. "They wouldn't tell me anything, not where my parents were, not what I was doing a world away from everyone and everything I knew. Everyone was just so...nice about avoiding the subject. I never heard the word crazy. They called it more polite things, like traumatized, repressed memory, but not what it was. Nuts. Looney Tunes, isn't that what you said?"

"Shh," he whispered against her brow as his hand stroked the towel from her damp hair. His fingers threaded through the curling locks to anchor her head to his shoulder. But she didn't want to be soothed or subdued. She'd had years of that kind of helpful smothering. Her tone grew stronger.

"Then when I'd ask about my parents, they'd answer with questions. What did I remember? Why didn't I tell them? I thought they were the insane ones. What was I supposed to tell them? I didn't know. I had no idea. Eventually, I learned that my parents had disappeared and were presumed dead. I thought they were lying to me at first. I don't know if I ever accepted it. I just pushed it deep down inside and focused on finding a way to escape the questions. Those questions, the same ones over and over. I learned to give them the answers they wanted to hear. And then I learned to act normal." She smiled against his shoulder, the gesture small and grim.

"I made it my goal to fool people into thinking I was normal, that nothing terrible had happened in my past, that past I couldn't remember. For a while, it worked. If I didn't get too close, if they didn't get to know me too well, if I kept on the move. But that meant I was always alone except for the calls and letters I'd get from Paulo and the occasional gifts from Sam. But the loneliness was better than being different, than the whispering once they knew. Once they knew, I couldn't pretend to fit in any more. Then it was time to move on. I guess that would be kind of hard for you to understand."

She rode the vibration of his quiet chuckle.

"Not hard at all. In fact, I understand better than you know." When she started to lift her head, questions at ready, he pressed her damp curls back into the protective lee of his shoulder, saying, "But that's a story for another time."

"Another time," she echoed softly, sealing that promise to heart.

For a moment they lay together, sharing heartbeats and even breaths while their secrets held them apart.

"So," he prompted at last, "what made you decide to become a myth-buster?"

"The dreams started. I guess I'd had them all along but I started to remember them."

How to describe their true terror to him when they had no real substance? The dark, the sweaty heat and drumbeats that she soon realized were from her own heart thundering in her ears. The smell of the dank, rotting jungle and that subtle metallic scent mingling vilely just beneath it. And the panic, rising like a tide, stirring up a drowning whirlpool of fear and desperation. Running but never escaping. Hiding, praying the horror would pass her by. The pain in her palm, the surprise of finding it was from the medallion cutting into her fingers from the pressure of her grip.

And the eyes, glowing hot and red, penetrating the darkness like twin laser beams. Closer, closer to finding her tucked back beneath the fronds, with insects swarming the blood that coated her clothing and skin.

"What are you running from, Sheba?" he asked gently.

"For the longest time, I thought it was just symbolic, that I was running away from my fear of the unknown. My father told me there were no monsters, that the godless made them up to explain away their fears. How could I explain away what I believe I saw that night? So I spent the rest of my life trying to strike down those myths, trying to prove the monsters weren't real. Until I'd close my eyes at night and they'd be there waiting."

She had tried therapy, drugs, even hypnosis but what she'd buried, she'd buried too deep to be reached by mortal or medical means. What she'd buried was like the jungle, layer upon layer upon layer until there was no sense of solid ground.

"It was easier to think it was madness," she said at last. "It was easier to attack the very thing I was afraid of because every victory made me feel stronger, more ready."

"For what?"

"For this. All my earlier work was leading up to this, to

confronting the one monster I could never explain away. Until I do, until I meet it head on, I'll never be truly strong."

He was silent for a time, his hand moving absently through her hair while he mulled his silent thoughts with the same restless repetitions.

"What if the monster's real, Doc?"

"Of course it's real. I know that now. It's someone hiding behind those legends Cross spins so well. And that someone killed my parents." Her tone toughened at that last claim, becoming hard as steel.

"Sheba, what if the monster is real?"

She did lift her head then in order to meet his gaze directly. Hers expressed her scorn and disbelief. And yet there were shadows lurking behind the bravado. Shadows he hated like hell to bring out into the open.

"It's real," he repeated.

She reacted with a snorting laugh. "Real, as in the Fanged Deity the Indians worshiped before the Incas? Oh come on, Cobb, you can do better than that."

But his expression remained somber and his stare unblinkingly sincere. "Sheba, there are monsters, and I know this one by name."

She tried to laugh it off but the attempt at humor lodged in her throat, a hard, choking lump of horrible truth. Because she knew Cobb was not lying to her. But to say she believed him was to let her own personal demons loose. And she wasn't ready for that yet.

"I've heard a lot of different names, Cobb. Which one are you picking?"

"Vampire."

THIRTEEN

She was silent for a long beat, and he thought she was actually considering it.

"Vampire," she mused. "I haven't heard that one for a while." Then her tone went dry as Lima's desert. "Really, Frank, I would have thought you'd be more original."

"How's this for originality?"

He seized her hand, his grip far from gentle as he placed her fingertips upon his savagely scarred cheek. He pulled her hand along that angled wound so she could feel how very real every stitch had been.

"A myth didn't do that, Sheba. A man didn't do that. A vampire did. His name is Quinton Alexander, and he's in Peru. You asked me what I was doing here. I came to do my own monster hunting." He paused. "You're speechless. I believe that's a first."

Sheba sat up, pulling her hand away from his warm, yet so obviously damaged face. Tugging the covers about her as if they'd shield her from the truth he was trying to force upon her, she shook her head.

"There are no such things."

Cobb came up on his elbow to regard her with a wry smile. "Oh, I would have been the first to agree with you there. Once upon a time."

"Talk to me, Cobb. And make it damned convincing."

So he told her about his previous job, that of spying upon a brilliant geneticist by the name of Stacy Kimball whose work for Harper Research was being funded by a reclusive Seattle billionaire and studied by the U.S. government for potential military application. Her field was genetic alteration and repair.

And her test subject was Louis Redman, billionaire vampire. Both had a keen interest in the results—Redman to find a cure for his preternatural ailment, Stacy for a more deadly disease, that of cancer.

And in spite of herself, Sheba was fascinated, drawn into the tale, suspending disbelief as Frank Cobb presented it with all the factual blandness of reading a police report. That was what made it so frighteningly real.

"There'd been a series of attacks on women along the waterfront, attacks that escalated into murders. It was from a study of their DNA patterns that the Doc got on the trail of possible blood chemistry repair. I'm not a scientist, so I can't give you all the whys and wherefores, but the sample she found led her to suspect Redman was the killer...a five-hundred-year-old killer. They made a business arrangement. If Stacy could study him for the potential good of mankind, she would try to cure him."

"So where did you fit in?"

"It was my job to keep her alive long enough to do it. You see, the real killer took a shine to the Doc and started leaving her little tokens from each of his victims."

Sheba shivered at the significance. "Like the ankle bracelet."

"To that point, I thought I was dealing with a flesh and blood wacko. Imagine my surprise when this monster nearly put me through a wall. His strength was...unimaginable." He traced the scar with the pad of his thumb. "I knew I was way out of my league."

"So it was Redman who saved the day and got the girl."

He grimaced at Sheba's condensed version. "Pretty much, yeah. But by this time, Harper got wind of what was going on and got to thinking about the potential of having a serum that would grant virtual immortality. Think of it. Indestructible soldiers."

Her eyes narrowed, that suspension of disbelief becoming an impossible cavern.

Cobb rolled to his other side, fishing in the drawer of his night table to draw out two objects, his revolver and a cigar case. He left the gun on the night stand and opened the silver case to withdraw one of two blood vials, each packed with a syringe.

"Go ask Alice," he murmured. "I saw an injection from this cure Stacy Kimball's cancer. And a shot from the other one made Louis Redman into a man again. Harper sent me down here to protect their investment in Lemos. And to bring back a vampire for further study. A study not for the good of mankind, I can guarantee."

She stared at the ruby-colored vial, mesmerized, horrified by what he suggested. "You'd give that kind of power to the military?"

"That's my job."

Her features reflected her disgust with that claim. "That's a poor excuse, Cobb. And it's a dirty job."

He shrugged without comment.

Her gaze returned to the gleaming vial. "So why didn't you give them those samples to start with?"

"That's my insurance policy. My job security, so to speak." He replaced the vial and the case in the drawer. Then he looked to Sheba to see if any trace of acceptance showed in those expressive dark eyes.

"Now I'm beginning to wonder if we're both crazy," was her pronouncement.

"He's here, Sheba," Cobb told her flatly, allowing for no misinterpretations. "He's preying upon these people and playing at being a god."

"What does he want with me? And what does he have to do with my parents?"

With those two simple questions, she was close to accepting all that he said as truth.

"He likes games, and he likes you. From what the Doc told me, he fancies himself a romantic hero, and I'm his arch rival. He's taunting me."

"Because you came after him, or because you couldn't protect her?"

How that cut to the core. Cobb refused to react. "He took me by surprise. That won't happen again."

"You can keep me safe." Her statement was edged with a whisper of doubt that slashed to Cobb's soul.

"I'll see that both of us are vindicated," was his stalwart vow. "Lemos is taking us to see his grandfather, and then we'll go pay a visit to this tomb he thinks might be the one your parents were going to when they...disappeared."

"When they died, Cobb. They died." She released a savage sigh and sank back upon the mattress to stare at the netting over head. "Someone or something killed them, and I have to know who and why. I don't know if it's your vampire or my demon or just some greedy fool who got in over his head and had to resort to murder. But I have to know. Help me, Frank." She turned her head to gaze at him in entreaty.

"We'll help each other."

She nodded. And after staring into his impenetrable gaze for a long moment, Sheba decided it was now or never if she wanted to help herself. There had to be some reward worth all the danger she'd be facing. Without weighing the consequences, she palmed the back of his head and pulled him toward her.

His breath sucked in between his teeth. For a moment, his mouth was thin and immobile against hers as he weighed those consequences she was determined to toss aside. Fearing she had made a dreadful mistake but forging on because her only option would be to draw back with an apology, she touched the tip of her tongue to the firm seal of his lips.

And unlocked his passions.

With a fierce exhalation, he slanted his mouth upon hers, twisting, tasting, satisfying all the curiosity and want he'd suffered since first charting those lush lips with his imagination. She was glorious. Soft, supple, and so sweetly urgent in her need to respond to his every nuance. The moaning sound she made in her throat was liquid with pent up longing. Again, he wasn't stupid enough to think it had anything to do with him. It was reassurance she was after, validation of her womanhood, of the fact that she was alive. At the moment, he didn't care if it was just sex. In fact, it was better if that was all it was. He understood sex a lot better than he could comprehend or fulfill the complexity of Sheba's demands upon his emotions.

So he kissed her, making it a simple response and exploration instead of anything that might get messy or meaningful. He fed off the pliant luxury of her lips while refusing to indulge the sudden sense of starvation that urged him to take more, to delve deeper, to meet any demands Sheba might make.

And when she opened her eyes to stare up at him, it was with perplexity, not passion. And then with injured pride.

"I'm sorry. I know that's not part of your job."

How prickly she sounded, the spines of insult surrounding any possible vulnerability. He grinned, impressed by her porcupine toughness despite the barbs he'd just received.

"Tonight it is," he answered. "And I'm sorry it wasn't my best work. Maybe later we can try it again, when there isn't so much at stake."

"Don't flatter yourself, Cobb."

Chuckling softly, he drew her up against him. For a moment, she was stiff with resistence. Then when she realized his motives were protective not seductive, she relaxed an increment at a time, until only her embarrassment separated them.

"Go to sleep, Doc. I'll take this watch."

Too tired to argue for the sake of personal vanity, Sheba closed her eyes and let exhaustion overcome her. So, she'd made a fool of herself with Frank Cobb. Surely she wasn't the first woman to throw an incomplete pass his way. Work and travel. A man with no time or interest in fun along the way. She, of all people, could relate to that. But at this point in time, in this place of hidden terrors, she'd wanted to relate to another person in a very personal way. And silly her, she'd wanted that someone to be the wily mercenary.

There was something about Frank Cobb that touched a kindred chord in her. Something about his dedication, his drive, and the loneliness he accepted because of those two things. And he believed her, believed in her. Perhaps that was all it was. Just a pathetic gratitude. And the sudden, inexplicable desire for intimacy.

She'd wanted that kiss to sizzle with enough heat to burn down the surrounding jungle. She'd wanted fireworks, and she'd gotten a flick from a Bic. A nice steady flame, but hardly a forest fire.

He'd been humoring her. Perhaps that's all he'd been doing all along as part of his precious job. Keep the crazy girl happy and out of the way. Tell her what she needs to hear, and she'll follow you anywhere. Humiliation blended with hurt to make a nearly fatal cocktail of disappointment that was more than a little bitter to swallow.

Why had she ever thought she could trust a man who made his living lying?

But liar or not, it felt too good being near him to allow pride to have its way. The calming cadence of his breathing in the darkened room held a mesmerizing effect, quieting her need for anything but sleep.

It wasn't his fault, after all, that she'd been looking for signals that he'd never sent. Tomorrow, when she was rested and on top of her mental form, she would rehash what Cobb had told her. Right now, tangled emotions and weariness prevented serious thought.

Vampires, he'd said.

Nonsense, of course. Just a way to distract her.

There were no monsters, her father had told her. And hadn't she proved it over and over again?

But look what had happened to him.

From the deep shadows of the porch, Paulo Lemos watched the door to Frank Cobb's room. As he waited, his hope that Sheba would emerge and return to her own quarters faded.

Fury and endless pain twisted through his soul.

She was his. That was the way they'd planned it. The way it was meant to be from the time they were children. He'd never considered any other possible scenario. He'd never considered...that she'd fall prey to a man like Cobb.

He sat and mulled over the two options before him. He could burst into the room and drag her out. His hot Latin blood demanded action. How satisfying to reclaim the woman he loved from the arms of a villain. But the thought of finding her tangled intimately with another man...thinking about it and being confronted with it were two very different things. Would he ever be able to look at her the same way again? His heart ached with indecision.

Or he could do nothing.

He could return to his room and pretend he'd never seen the two of them disappear behind Cobb's door. A man like Cobb wasn't a permanent interference in the future scheme of things. He didn't want Sheba for anything long term. And when he cast her aside, Paulo would be there to pick up the pieces of her broken heart and put them back together.

And then she would turn to him as she always did, for comfort, for understanding, for love.

Yes, he liked that idea very much. Much more than the thought of direct confrontation, which made his stomach go queasy. He could beat Cobb in an IQ test but probably not in a test of strength.

But doing nothing meant spending the evening knowing exactly what was going on in the other room between the man hired to protect him and the woman who was to be his wife.

"An awkward situation."

The voice, coming from so close to him and speaking so personally to what plagued his thoughts, startled Paulo, but he smiled ruefully at the speaker. Why bother to deny the very painfully obvious truth?

"Yes, isn't it? I have no idea how to act without acting the fool."

"Ah, what man hasn't acted the fool over a woman? And this one, such a prize."

"Yes," Paulo said again, this time with a tang of bitterness. "He knew she was mine, and he took her anyway."

"Then he should be punished, am I not right?"

Punished. Yes. How good that sounded.

"But how?"

"I have the perfect solution for how you can strike back at Mr. Cobb."

Paulo turned toward the speaker, a question forming on his lips. His answer came without words, in the shape of horror so unbelievable, so sudden and terrifying, he had no time to object or resist as fangs sank into his throat.

The vampire drank, not until full but until satisfied. Then Lemos was released to totter on weak legs, his mind a blur until a strong suggestion filled it.

"Go back to your room and sleep. Wait for my instructions. Together we will have our revenge upon Frank Cobb."

FOURTEEN

Frank Cobb awoke surrounded by hedonistic luxury. Silken heat curled around him. A warm scent that could only mean woman toyed with his senses. And woman could only mean—

Sheba.

He was instantly alert, but true to his training, didn't move until the situation was fully assessed. His room, daylight, Sheba in a bathrobe beneath his covers, twined about him in the most inviting manner. No threat, except to his resolve to stay emotionally detached from the woman in question.

Except the robe had come undone.

During the night with her restless twists and turns, she'd managed to slip the belt and wiggle herself almost completely free of the binding chenille.

Her very naked self.

She lay nose to nose with him, one long, lithe leg tossed carelessly over his hips, one arm wound possessively about his middle. Her tousled head tucked in neatly beneath his chin, tickling him with a riot of gold-tinted curls. If he'd been able to look down, he could have seen what his senses sucked up so greedily—her small, taut breasts pressing to his shirtfront, puckered and pointed from exposure to the lazy stir of the ceiling fan. No more than a glorious handful.

But his hands were already full, one with a mass of those untamed locks and the other with the sleek curve of her bare flank.

In all his years of having to wriggle out of dangerous and potentially lethal situations, this one provided no easy out. Probably because he felt no immediate desire to escape.

Lord, she smelled good, of his soap and traces of body lotion that clung to the robe. Beneath his palm, her skin was as supple and firm as glove leather. He ached to follow that tempting contour, over and under, where other pleasures were unexpectedly open to him.

Exerting tremendous control, he wrestled his focus up from certain disaster and took a slow, deep breath, inhaling the smell of her herbal shampoo. He nuzzled into that fragrant cloud, finding her streaked hair as soft as spun silk, and suddenly he was unbearably curious to discover its true color since the opportunity presented itself. All he had to do was disengage the wrap of her limbs and roll her gradually onto her back and glance down, down—

"Are you trying to cop a feel, Mr. Cobb?"

Caught by the tart demand, in thought if not yet in deed, he did the only thing possible. He lied.

"No, ma'am. That's the farthest thing from my mind."

In truth, it was only a little bit farther than the urge to get that good, unrestricted look at her. Groping couldn't come close to what he had in mind. He wanted her tangled around him with those long arms and legs and himself buried in her. But discretion was sometimes the better part of getting out of a sticky circumstance alive.

So he lied again.

"I was trying to decide the best route for causing the least embarrassment."

A perfect choice of words. Thoughts of romance and passion were slapped out of her head.

"Well, why don't you cover your eyes so you won't be morally compromised."

He shut his eyes, pinching his lips together to restrain the grin that wanted to break loose. Now was not the time to take amusement in the situation.

In a flash, she was out of his arms and off the bed, dashing his desires but hardly stamping out the flames they'd started. He couldn't remember ever wanting a woman as desperately as he did the slender scientist who stood wrapped up in her robe as if it were armored dignity.

"Thank you for taking me in last night," she stated with an icy civility. "If we're to get an early start this morning, I've got packing to do." Her gaze raked over him as he stretched out leisurely on the rumpled bedcovers. "No, don't get up. I can handle things perfectly well myself."

Not as well as he'd wanted to handle them.

His smile slipped free in slow, sly increments as she slammed the door.

***

She'd been naked in his arms, in his bed, and he hadn't even tried anything!

The humiliation was devastating.

Sheba struck the betraying dampness from her cheeks and continued stuffing her belongings into a rugged backpack.

What was wrong with him?

What was wrong with her?

Was he that much of a saint, or did he find her so unappealing that he wasn't even tempted by the availability of her beneath his covers?

Men! Hang them all! Unpredictable, unreliable and totally undecipherable.

What was it about this one man that had her spinning in circles like a hound chasing its own tail when the rest of the species were so easily ignored? She'd had no trouble relegating them into something to be studied for sociological and cultural significance rather than as having any personal significance within her own exclusive realm. Until Cobb pushed his way into that previously impervious focus with his crafty smile, competent manner and disarming claim of "I believe you."

What a bastard!

And now after he'd gotten her all worked up into a hormonal lather, he expected her to rinse off in the cold shower of his indifference.

It wasn't that she'd been hungry for sex...well, she was, but it was more than that. She'd wanted...oh, hell, she didn't know what she'd wanted.

No. That wasn't true. She did know. She wanted Frank Cobb, as a man, as a mate, as a friend and confidante. But the feeling obviously wasn't mutual.

Well, she'd disgraced herself enough for one lifetime. Time to stop acting like a moonstruck teenager and comport herself like the professional she was. She'd given romance her best shot, and it had deflected her punch. Time to move on to the grim purpose of the trip. The jungle awaited, and whether it held the key to her past or the vampire of Cobb's imagination, they would find out soon enough.

***

"Good morning, Paulo." She bent to press a quick kiss upon his oddly unshaven cheek. Instead of studying his usual periodicals, he was lost in the examination of his coffee cup. He didn't look up at her.

"Sleep well?"

The smooth stab of that question had her frowning as she sat next to him at the breakfast table.

Why did he sound so angry?

"Yes, actually I did. And you? You look like you spent the night cramming for a university final." She meant to bring some levity to his obviously dark mood, but he preferred to remain sullen.

"Sorry my looks don't appeal to you as much as some others I might name."

"What?"

He glanced at her then, just a quick flicker of red-rimmed eyes up to accuse her of something she—

He'd seen her with Frank.

That explained his surly temper. Though why he should react to the details of her personal life with such an angry extreme was beyond her.

Unless...

No, this was Paulo, her lifelong friend of childhood.

A child no longer.

Understanding struck like a downtown bus.

Paulo was in love with her. What had been a boyish crush had developed into a man's desire. Looking back with unfortunately clear hindsight, she recognized the clues he'd thrown at her like darts into a board, if only she hadn't been too dense to realize what bull's eye he was aiming for. Paulo wanted her as much as Frank Cobb did not.

And he'd seen her with Frank.

She started to explain that nothing had happened, if only to put her friend's mind at ease. But that wouldn't be the absolute truth. She'd kissed Frank Cobb. If nothing had happened, it wasn't for her lack of trying, and Paulo would see right through any comforting lie she tried to tell. And that would make matters ten times worse.

The three of them were about to head out into the forest together. They could go as companions or as rivals. With what they might be facing, she would just as soon it be in partnership. They would need to be able to depend upon one another.

So she decided to do what she did best—tell it like it was.

She sighed. "Oh, Paulo, I've made the most dreadful fool of myself over that beastly Frank Cobb."

She had his attention now. "How so?"

"I had a bit of a scare last night, and he took me to his room until I could calm down."

She could almost hear her friend's molars creaking as his jaw ground down on that image. So she laughed bitterly at herself and continued.

"I thought he had romance on his mind, and he was only interested in his paycheck. I feel so stupid. Thank goodness he was gentlemanly enough to set me straight the second he saw where I was heading...down the wrong road, obviously."

Enough of her humiliation seeped out to color both her admission and her cheeks. Paulo sat back, restraining a satisfied smile as he asked, "So nothing—"

"Nothing at all, unless you want to count my self-confidence taking a nose dive."

Paulo's arm stole about her shoulders, tugging her up close against him. She felt his kiss against her brow and tried to whip up some of the delightfully confusing sensations she experienced when Frank had held her near.

But there was nothing.

"The man's obviously a moron not to realize what he was

throwing away. But thank goodness for that, right? I mean really. Think about it. What future could such a relationship hold? You have nothing in common. What place in your life would there be for a man like Cobb?"

"May I join you?"

Cobb's cool interjection had Sheba jumping free of Paulo's embrace. Had Frank heard Paulo's snide summation? She couldn't tell from the bland front the other man presented if the words had hurt, or indeed pierced his thick skin. With Cobb, one would never know unless he chose to reveal it. This morning, he was a blank slate and Paulo was writing cruel things upon it without fear of reprisal. Sheba bit down on her annoyance with him. When had Paulo developed such a mean streak? She remembered him as a shy, kind boy who would trap a creature to release it unharmed outside rather than step on it. With Frank, he was grinding his heel without mercy. And she didn't find this trait at all attractive.

She gestured to an available chair. "Help yourself."

"Not that it will do you any good," Paulo muttered under his breath.

Sheba wanted to smack him but instead she bestowed her sunniest smile on their third wheel. "Have you got everything ready to go?"

"Tooth brush and bug spray," he drawled out. "What more do I need? How many are going on this little safari with us?"

"I've got a group of five research interns going with me and a guide."

Sheba covered Paulo's hand for a squeeze. "Like you need someone to show you around in your backyard."

"Our backyard, Sheba. You know it as well as I do."

Her smile thinned. "Not anymore.

"It'll all come back to you," he assured her.

Wasn't that what she was so afraid of? Her teeth clamped together. Paulo lifted her hand to kiss her knuckles, totally missing the anxiety behind her pinched smile, but she could feel Cobb's all-too-knowing gaze upon her, gauging her weakness, wondering if she could tow the line.

She'd show him.

"I can't wait," she proclaimed, to convince herself as well as the others. "I've been away too long. It's time to get back to the things I know and love."

"Yes," Paulo all but purred. "About time."

Cobb may have been clearing his throat, but to Sheba it sounded like a comment. A raspberry.

"If we start off at once, we should be able to reach the highlands by late tomorrow. Then we'll see my grandfather and put an end to your suspense, Sheba."

"Yes." Was her response as faint as her heart at the thought of that confrontation with the past.

"If he has something to tell us, that is," Cobb amended with a dampening reason. "Or if he'll tell us anything."

Paulo turned on him, eyes blazing. "You think we waste our time?"

"It's your time," he drawled.

"Our time and our money, and don't you forget that. My priority is getting Sheba well. What's yours, Cobb?"

Cobb's gaze never faltered as he met the other's fierce glare. "My priorities are bought and paid for."

That's not what Sheba wanted to hear. She wanted him to make some grand declaration in the face of Paulo's antagonism. She wanted him to damn his duties and take up her cause. But then, that wouldn't be the truth and she knew it. And that truth hurt.

Wanting to strike back, she smiled sweetly at Cobb and said, "Mr. Cobb is here on a vampire hunt."

There was no accusing stare of a confidence betrayed. Cobb looked right through her with a stoicism that blamed worse than any words could.

Paulo crowed incredulously. "Really? How delightfully colorful, Mr. Cobb. I wouldn't have thought of you as a true believer in such things even though you'd admitted to it. You seem so...grounded in reality."

"Realities change, as do perceptions," was Cobb's cool rejoinder. "I'm here on Harper Research's dime to protect you from whatever threats are waiting."

"And you are very good at that, aren't you, Frank? What's

your success rate in keeping your clients safe?" Trying to pry an honest reaction from him, Sheba goaded where she knew she shouldn't go. "Ninety-nine percent? But it's that one percent failure that always gets you, right?"

"One learns from one's failures and moves on."

"And moving on is what you're best at, isn't it?"

"You should know, Dr. Reynard."

His quiet parry and attack effectively quelled her own rather childish offensive. Ashamed of her unworthy attempt to wound the impervious Frank Cobb, Sheba stood and faced the inevitability.

"I'm going to say good-bye to Sam."

"We leave in an hour, Sheba."

She nodded glumly at that news.

In an hour, she would confront her greatest fear, the fear that lived inside her, as big and dank and smothering as the rainforest.

Would she be strong enough to face it?

***

Sheba heard voices as she approached Peyton Samuels' office. She paused, not wanting to interrupt some business wheeling dealing and then, just as she recognized the other speaker, she heard the words.

"What are you going to tell her when she finds out the truth?"

Sheba crept closer to the closed door. What were Peyton and Rosa Kelly discussing with such fierce intensity? Usually, their meetings involved tones raised high in heated and opposing opinion, but this morning, they were prophetically hushed, almost conspirational.

They were talking about her.

"She won't find out." That was Samuels. His words were forceful. And fearful.

Find out what?

"How are you going to prevent it now that she's here? Considering where she's going?"

"You worry too much, Rosa. I've already taken care of that."

"How? Like you took care of the other problem?"

Sheba barely heard the sneering sarcasm in that demand. She was reading between the lines.

She was a problem to be dealt with. Like her parents? Was that the other problem the two of them discussed so passionately? She clapped a hand over her mouth to silence the agony of that possible discovery.

Peyton Samuels, her benefactor and Rosa Kelly, her mentor. Had they schemed together to hide the fact that they were involved in the death of the Reynards? By seeing she was taken care of? By pretending to be like family? Because they were guilty of destroying the family she once had?

No, it was too awful to consider.

She leaned against the wall, pain surging inside upon a brutal sea of suspicion. How could matters get any worse than to doubt the love and nurturing of those who'd known her since the cradle?

"This time, I've turned it over to a professional," Samuels continued, firm in his reassurance. "Frank Cobb came highly recommended. He'll see she stays in the dark while salvaging our interests at the same time."

She was going to be sick. Bile boiled up in the back of her throat as her knees went weak.

And then she saw the doorknob turn.

They were coming.

They couldn't know what she'd overheard.

She managed to straighten and paste on an expectant smile just as Peyton pulled open the door. Damn him, his features registered only pleasure at seeing her standing there.

"Sheba, there you are. I was hoping you'd stop by before heading out with Paulo on your expedition. Like old times, eh, the two of you?"

She couldn't respond. She could barely breathe. Then Rosa enveloped her in her fleshy, scented embrace. Her head swam with the smell of gardenias.

"Oh, sweet child, how I envy you the adventure...and the company of those two lusty young men. Do I detect a little jungle romance for our little girl? Ah, to be thirty years younger and have knees that would support such a hike. In my youth, I would have given you a run for your money."

Sheba's eyes squeezed tight to hold in the tears of anguish and betrayal as she listened through new ears to the familiar bawdy talk. This was not the playful banter of a dear, oft-emulated friend. It was the clever spinning of lies to create a web of deceit and self-preservation. And Cobb was tangled up in it, too. The one person she'd wanted so desperately to trust.

"We won't be gone long," she finally managed in a voice that was almost normal. "I'll keep them both on their best behavior, don't you worry."

She stepped out of Rosa's smothering hug to confront the tenderness in Peyton's gaze. Oh, the misery of seeing through that benevolent care.

"But I do worry, my dear."

How kindly and sincere he sounded, how genuinely emotional over her well-being.

Liar!

"I'll be careful, Sam. I'm a survivor, remember?"

And she would survive this, too. If for no other reason that to see her family and her shattered trust avenged.

FIFTEEN

They followed the river by boat for the better part of the day. In the soggy heat of twilight, they turned up a silty tributary and around the first bend, were confronted by bright slashes of blue and yellow tarp roofs where mining dredges labored between canyons of solid green. Wooden shacks on steel pontoons rode the lazy current, lashed together to form a community of noise and lights. Rafts cluttered with pumps and sluice boxes provided homes for miners, drilling platforms for endless lengths of pipe, a gas station, restaurant, cabaret and even a powder blue whorehouse that sagged in the middle like most of its patronesses.

"They're dragas," Paulo explained in answer to Cobb's curiosity. "Primitive factories that work around the clock to strip minerals from the river bottom." He made a scathing noise that voiced his opinion even without words. "Gold miners are like an AIDs epidemic. When they leave the area, there'll be nothing alive on the land or in the water."

They approached the floating city cautiously. Shirtless men, their shoulders heaving like pneumatic drill operators, worked long-handled electric mixers to churn the mercury, silt and hopefully gold. As the outsiders drew notice, the frantic activity slowed then stopped all together as they were assessed as a possible threat.

"No need to worry," their Indian guide Manolito assured as he stood at the bow of their boat, waving his arms. "My brother-in-law and his family run the restaurant. Just keep your eyes and your tongues still, and there'll be no trouble."

"Trouble?" Cobb posed casually. "Is this an illegal operation?"

Manolito pretended not to hear the question.

Paulo shrugged. “The government has lost control over such endeavors. For every ton of gold mined legally, four are smuggled out. Environmentalists are constantly protesting about the water and air damaged by mercury pollution. Many of these dragas launder cocaine money. Do you want to go up and ask them if they have a permit?”

“I’ll pass. None of my business.”

A sinewy Indian with an apron and a half dozen children of varying ages swarmed the edge of the nearest platform, waving and shouting to Manolito in the language of their people. Manolito turned to them with a grin.

“We’ve been offered a free meal and a place to sleep for the night. I guarantee you’ve never had cooking so good.”

Paulo sighed impatiently, glancing at Sheba to gage her response. “We really should push on. We’ve got lots of ground to cover.”

Manolito listened to a rather urgent entreaty from his brother-in-law, then passed the information on in English. “He says we would be fools to go into the jungle after dark and bids us to stay here in the lights where we’ll be safe.”

“Safe from what?”

After a moment’s pause, Manolito translated his question. A long, tense silence followed. Finally, the wiry Indian on the platform shooed his children away and faced them nervously. He spoke briefly, fearfully.

“The Ancient One,” Sheba interpreted, speaking up for the first time since they’d left the lodge that morning.

“Native superstition,” Paulo scoffed. “Right, Sheba?” When she didn’t answer, he looked in turn to the others on their boat. All nervously evaded his gaze. “I say we continue on. We’ve another hour of good travel time.”

A ripple of anxious muttering swept through Paulo’s indigenous students. Cobb glanced from them to Sheba’s still features then announced, “Thank your brother-in-law for his hospitality, Manolito. We’ll be staying.”

Paulo turned on him in a fury. “And just what gives you the right to make that decision?”

"Common sense. And if you had any, you'd agree without any further tantrums."

Sheba stepped in to halt the potential battle of wills. She quieted Paulo with a hand on his arm. "We should stay. I'd like to speak to Manolito's relatives and find out why they're so afraid, if it's nothing but superstition."

"All right, Sheba," the scientist relented at last. "You win. But we leave at first light." With that command to make him seem still in charge, he tossed a mooring rope to Manolito's brother-in-law. His students were quick to scramble off the boat and into the welcoming pools of light.

Cobb turned to Sheba, offering his hand. "After you."

She ignored the help and the man with a brusque, "I don't need a babysitter."

Cobb dropped his hand and watched her climb out of the boat, appreciating as she did the way her khakis hugged her slim hips and rounded bottom. As much as he would have liked to give her a boost, he restrained himself. Wisely.

The restaurant was little more than a square of corrugated metal walls with uneven planks for tables and wire spools and kegs for chairs. Insects droned about the naked bulbs strung overhead, but to the credit of Eddie Chala's family, the place was scrupulously clean. From out of the back kitchen, deliciously spicy scents emerged. Their party was quickly seated and served by a youthful staff that was always ready to bring piping hot estofado stew—with its mainstay of chicken, corn, carrots and tomatoes—along with chicha morada, the white corn beer that helped cut travel exhaustion and the tension after the second glass.

Since they were between shifts, Eddie was able to join them at their table, bringing a large pitcher of beer and a near-toothless smile, along with his bevy of children. It was with pride that he ticked off their names and ages as well as their culinary specialties. While the others ate the mild and filling fare, Eddie and Manolito exchanged familial news. But when the children were sent back to the kitchen with empty plates and compliments, talk turned to serious topics once more.

"Safe from what?" Cobb repeated. "Have you been having

problems out here?"

In broken and labored English, Eddie explained, "It come at night, taking ones who leave the light."

"What comes? Has anyone seen it?"

"My daughter, Phillippa she saw this thing take one of the working girls up into the sky."

"Up into the sky," Sheba interrupted in her cool, clinical tone. "How do you mean?"

"This woman was standing on the platform outside the...the—" He broke off, looking embarrassed.

"Yes, we know where you mean," Sheba said impatiently. She switched to Spanish to hurry the story along and so as not to miss any subtle nuances of the tale in telling. Cobb could pick up what he could follow, and she would translate the rest later. "Go on."

"One minute, she was smoking a cigarette and the next, she was gone, lifted straight up into the air without any sound. My Phillippa ran to tell us what she had seen. She was very frightened."

Sheba nodded empathetically, well imagining the child's terror. "And was this woman ever found?"

"No, *senorita.* No trace of her. The bosses, they say she was a restless girl and that she simply ran away. Ran away to where? To what? There is nothing within a day's journey a-foot. They said my Phillippa was making up stories so that we would have more customers. What child creates nightmares for herself? All she can talk about is the red eyes glowing in the night coming after her. She cannot sleep alone at night. She has been in my bed between me and my wife since it happened."

"And when was this?"

"Two months ago."

Two months ago. Shortly after the tomb robbers uncovered death in the jungle, opening the way for what to escape? Red eyes. Cobb's vampire, or legend's Ancient One?

Or were they one in the same?

"Have there been other attacks?"

"Several of the women who entertain the workers have

been found wandering as if in a dream. They have strange marks on their necks and no memory of what happened to them. We are to believe that one of the miners has particular habits." Eddie snorted. "That's not what we believe at all."

"What do you believe?"

"We believe that the Ancient One was made uneasy in his rest. He hunts the night, devouring the unwary and will continue to do so unless he is put back where he belongs."

"And where is that?"

"In his temple. Only the sacrifice of a royal one can make him return to his home to sleep for another generation."

"A royal one?"

"One of the old family, of the old ways. Only they have the pure blood to ensure his sleep."

"And you believe this?" Her tone lacked its usual incredulity, drawing Cobb's notice.

"Not only me. We have lost almost a third of our workers. No amount of money could make them stay. To keep up production, the bosses have to run shifts all night long, then they have to pay those who work at night an extra bonus. They threaten and they bribe, but they cannot make the fear go away. Only an *altomisayoq* can put those fears to rest."

"A what?" Cobb interrupted.

"A ritual specialist. A *curandero* or shaman who cleanses and appeases the spirits."

"And do we know of any of these specialists?"

"My grandfather is one," Paulo stated quietly.

"I need to meet this man."

Paulo gave him a hard look. "But will he want to meet you, *civilizado*? He has no love of the white man or the outsider. You have nothing to offer that will interest him."

"Oh, I think I do," was Cobb's mysterious reply. Then he looked toward their host. "May I see your daughter, Phillippa?" At the man's first sign of hesitance, Frank added, "Don't worry. I won't ask her any questions."

A lithe, pretty child emerged from the kitchen at her father's call. She was all liquid eyes and timid manner as she came to stand before the strange American. From out of his pocket, Frank drew one of the delicate silver crosses he'd purchased at the market in Lima. The child's gaze followed the bright metal as Cobb lifted it and draped the chain about her neck. She touched the fragile necklace with awe and delight, looking first to Frank then to her father.

"Wear this and sleep well," Cobb told her.

To this, her father nodded.

And at that simple, compassionate gesture from a man she believed held no agenda but his own selfish one, Sheba's emotions took another traitorous turn.

Hang him for showing that he had a heart and making it that much harder to hate him.

***

They slept on makeshift beds in the restaurant's dining room with the noise and throbbing pulse of industry all around them. Though they were wrapped up in their own separate blankets, Sheba was achingly aware that Frank Cobb was close by. Surprisingly, Sheba found it easy to slumber in the midst of that chaos. Or perhaps not so surprisingly. She woke before dawn, refreshed and eager to put down some of her impressions from the night before into one of the notebooks she was never without.

And that was how Cobb found her, at one of the far tables, hunched over one of her spirals she toted in her weighty backpack, scribbling down notes and observations.

"Looking for a logical explanation?" he asked as he settled onto an opposing seat, literally and figuratively. She didn't spare him a glance.

"It's an old story. Use a well-known myth to frighten workers and progress away."

"And you think that's what this is? A pretty simplistic answer."

"Sometimes things are simple unless you go out of your way to make them complex. I find the obvious is most likely the right answer and the obscure is an excuse to justify an unnecessary expense."

He was smiling. "Such as?"

"Your salary."

His chuckle was as warm and inviting as the cup of coffee he pushed toward her. "Since you're not paying it, why are you so annoyed?"

"I just don't like to see people taken advantage of."

"Neither do I. Which is why I want to find out who's behind this, whether it be real or elaborate deception. Isn't that what you want, too, Doc?"

"It depends upon who's misleading whom, wouldn't you say, Mr. Cobb? Isn't that one of your specialities, too?"

"Goodness, but we've woken up on the wrong side of the hostility bed this morning."

She looked up at him then, glare cutting right through the pleasant looks and sultry gaze to the cold intent that motivated him. "You might just say I'm seeing things in a clearer light these days."

"Good. One should always go into situations with eyes wide open."

She grabbed up her books and papers, irritated beyond the scope of their conversation. "Excuse me. I think I need some air."

She could feel his penetrating stare on her until she was safely out of the building and out of sight. Only then did she expel her breath and vent her frustration by throwing her materials down onto the dirty deck. She dropped beside them, not caring if the seat of her dungarees was hopelessly stained. Appearances didn't count for anything anymore. Only truth mattered.

And what was the truth?

That she'd been lied to and mislead by those she thought cared about her? Samuels, Rosa Kelly, Frank Cobb—all grand deceivers, playing her for their benefit.

No more. She'd be no one's pawn. She knew the rules of this game they were playing. It was called intimidation through fear. She'd seen it in countless countries, had been a victim of it herself. Well, she'd be no one's victim again.

Who was manipulating the area myths to make a profit? And for how long? Who stood to gain if production shut down on this rig? If Paulo was kept from the jungle's interior? If

Peyton was forced to close down his lodge? Or was the wily Peyton Samuels just trying to misdirect suspicion by pretending to be a victim, too? How she wished she had someone to bounce her theories off. But Paulo was too close to the matter, and Cobb was to be trusted about as much as the caiman's lounging with supposed indifference along the shore's edge. But let her jump into the water and see how indifferent they were. She'd be a meal in minutes, no mistake about it.

Frank Cobb was not going to feast upon her ignorance any longer.

It was just as it had always been, Sheba Reynard on her own, pursuing her own opinions, proving her own hunches.

"Good morning."

She smiled up at Paulo, happy to see that his pasty color of the day before was back to its healthy bronze. His dark eyes gleamed with excitement and adventure, a duo she'd always found irresistible.

"Are you ready, Sheba? There are great things out there, waiting to be discovered."

"And you are the man to do it."

He lifted her up by the forearm then held her just a little too close for comfort while he adored her with his gaze. How had she been so blind not to see his very male interest in her? And why wasn't she able to respond to it? Things would be so much simpler then.

But simplicity wasn't always the answer.

"There's a truck going in our direction. That should cut about a half day off our travels. From there, it's on foot, I'm afraid."

"Gone soft on me, have you?" Sheba goaded. Her teasing provoked a very different response.

"No danger of that, *novia*."

Sweetheart. The endearment and the husky way it was spoken alarmed her almost as much as the sudden possessive power in his grip.

It was Frank Cobb to the rescue with the brusque intrusion of his Jersey Shore accent. "I've had my coffee. I'm ready to roll."

Paulo's grip eased and Sheba was quick to step back, unintentionally making a statement with that withdrawal that neither man missed. The Peruvian's eyes narrowed at the presentation of a challenge, then nodded.

"Let's go. But remember, Mr. Cobb, there are many dangers in the jungle if one is not careful."

"Always prepared. That's my motto."

Paulo grimaced at his flippant reply. "We shall see."

***

The truck Eddie arranged for them bruised kidneys on a barely visible two-track for the better part of the morning as it carried them deeper and deeper out of civilization's reach. Until the road and their ride ended as abruptly as it had begun. On foot, they surveyed what lay ahead as the roar of the departing truck was swallowed up by the cadence of the jungle.

They entered a world of reduced light. Leaves shaped like fingers, hearts, arrows and blinds covered the spongy ground. Beneath the dense canopy soaring some 150 feet overhead, life on the jungle floor struggled to survive by climbing upward. A complexity of forest vines twisted like serpents around buttressed trunks with the girth of redwoods, squirming toward the light from the cool, ferny darkness of the forest floor. The sound of insects upon the wet, heavy air was overpowering as millions of them called to one another in the greenery up above. Light changed with elevation, becoming brighter but diffused midway up on the shade-loving trees then bursting into blinding halos where the crowns were hit by direct sunlight. Patterns of that jewel-like brilliance filtered down in startling flashes with the tiniest sway of the ten-story bower as monkeys leapt between trees, barking to each other in quick, hoarse snatches.

Mysterious alleyways and false paths led off through the brush and struggling saplings, a mass of confusing details to the untrained eye. Once inside it, the forest contained all the secrets and shadows of a witches' wood where the trees assumed writhing shapes and the streaks of light created an eerie aura upon the backdrop of textured green. Life stretched up toward the sun, and in death dropped away from it, leaving a graveyard of decay at human level.

Shouldering her pack, Sheba drew a shuddering breath.

Here was the doorway to terror. The Green Hell from which she might never emerge.

SIXTEEN

He tried to think of it like a Boy Scout outing.

Frank had never been a Boy Scout, but this was how he imagined it. A comradic tramp through the woods...with lots of bugs. In fact, if this was indicative of the Scouting experience, he was heartily glad he'd missed it. There was nothing adventurous about sweating, stumbling, swatting and swearing. The only thing that made it halfway interesting was wondering how Sheba Reynard endured the discomfort without complaint.

She was a trooper, a true pioneer spirit. She conquered the miles without comment, her Amazonian stride never faltering while Lemos's students, most of them indigenous to the jungle, were struggling to keep pace. Her stamina was a marvel, but what really impressed him was his awareness of just how difficult each of those steps was for her to take.

She had to be terrified, but one would never guess by looking at her. She kept her dark bogeymen to herself.

Something had changed. He couldn't quite put his finger on it. She paid him as much attention as one of the vine-choked trees. Gone was the adversarial tension along with its frustrating side of sexual temptation. Since they'd left the lodge, she'd acted as if her Peruvian buddy had succeeded in making him invisible.

Was it something he'd said?

Or something he hadn't done?

Women were enigmas at best, but the brainy ones were worse. More comfortable with business than burgeoning passions, they were a confusion of mixed signals and scrambled emotions. Was she embarrassed because they'd kissed, or pissed off because they hadn't made love? Clueless, he could only suffer her silence with inadequate second guesses.

She had to know that intimacy between them would have changed everything.

And, as Lemos had put it so brutally, he had nothing a woman like her would want.

Her attitude should have made his job all the easier.

Should have.

But while scanning the endless backdrop of green for possible threat, watching where he put his feet and she put hers, the gears of his mind ground upon the reason for her disaffection. He couldn't let it go, nor could he ask for an explanation.

And those two things made for poor trailmates as they hiked toward their first sunset.

***

Sheba wasn't thinking about Frank Cobb.

She was trying not to think about anything as she allowed her experience and training to take over on the trail. Just routine, like any other expedition. Be alert, be ready, and gather every possible scrap of information on the way. This was a job, like any other. There were victims, and somewhere there was a manipulator behind their pain and sorrow. Someone was trading upon fear for profit. And that someone had to be stopped. Keep it simple, keep it impersonal. This wasn't about her.

That last was a hard mantra to repeat when every step she took, every breath she drew reminded her that it had everything to do with her.

But how?

And why?

That's what kept her going when her inner instincts were shouting, *Run! Run away! Hide before he finds you!*

Before who finds her?

One of the great mysteries she had to solve.

Because she'd resolved to dismiss Frank Cobb from mind, Sheba concentrated on Paulo to give her thoughts a much needed respite from worry. He loved his work. It was in every gesture, every word, even in the spring of his stride. This was his world, his element, and here, he was king. And every frequent glance he sent her way reminded her that he would have her as his queen.

Why did she rebel against that notion?

Paulo Lemos had been her one friend, her soul mate, so why was it so difficult to picture him as a lifemate? They understood and enjoyed the same things. They shared the same history. Perhaps it was that familiarity that bred her mild contempt. Or was it a lack of familiarity? What did she really know about the man he'd become? She seen some very unappealing samples since their reunion. Where she'd wanted him to be selfless, he was self-absorbed. Where she'd needed him to be compassionate, he'd been petty in his beliefs. Where once he'd been so giving and full of charity to all, he seemed stingy with it now.

Did she really like the man the boy had become?

Perhaps she was being unfair. No one could attain the pedestal she'd placed him on. Was it his fault that she'd never allowed him to grow within the realm of her childhood memories? He'd always be the Paulo of her wild days—her companion, her rock, her salvation, the image she clung to for sanity when nothing else was real. Now that image was no longer reality, and she could either accept the change or surrender the ties.

And be all alone with her treasured virginity.

They paused on the trail while Paulo took samples. She watched him investigate a trellis of vines, lean toward the trunk that supported them to sniff like a perfumer, to check the pattern of veins on the underside of the leaves, separating potential cure from possible poison. A brilliant man, a handsome man.

But not the man for her.

She knew, right then, with a certainty. She would never be capable of the answering passion he deserved in a wife. It would be unfair of her to lead him on.

So where did that leave her? Work and travel, chasing

other people's monsters as a substitute for her own.

No.

Not any longer. Her monsters were here, waiting. And they knew her name.

***

The deeper they went into the jungle, the more nervous the students and their guide became. Sheba, contrarily, seemed the soul of calm determination. Frank had to admit that he was surprised by her, just as he had to admit he was hopelessly lost. He felt like an explorer expecting hungry cannibals and a stewpot around the next bend.

And then it started to get dark.

Shadows began to lengthen, filling in the filigree of foliage into a solid tapestry of green. Every rustling of sound took on sinister echoes as the jungle closed in upon them.

"We'll set up camp here," Paulo announced to everyone's relief.

While the light held, they made quick work of erecting a trio of tents. Paulo, Sheba and Cobb would share one, and the others would divvy up the other two. There was very little conversation as they waited for their meal to cook, perhaps the toll of exhaustion, or perhaps the weight of their fears increasing with the darkness. The others were quick to seek their rest, but Sheba lingered at the fire, putting it off as long as possible. She wasn't convinced it was rest that awaited her. Her gaze leapt up as Frank stood.

"I'm going to check the perimeter."

"Watch your step," Paulo offered generously, eager for him to be gone so he could have Sheba to himself.

Glancing between the two of them, Frank gave a wry smile. "I always do."

Sheba tried not to recognize her own panic the minute Frank left the fire. She could see the high beam of his flashlight dancing through the night. He hadn't gone far.

The sudden touch of Paulo's fingertips upon her shoulder made her rapidly beating heart lunge up into her throat. She forced a smile as he settled close and fought the urge to sidle away to place some breathing room between them.

"How are you holding up?"

"I'm doing fine, Paulo."

"I'm very proud of you, you know. It took courage to come back here and face your fears."

Her smile thinned. She didn't feel particularly courageous cowering within the circle of light.

"Have any of the memories begun to return?"

"No. Not yet."

The massage of his fingertips upon her tense muscles grew more intimate in their caressing. "I've dreamed of this, Sheba, of the two of us out here, exploring the boundaries of our world together. And I was hoping..."

Unwilling to hear the rest of that desire, Sheba bolted up to her feet. "It's getting late." She glanced rather desperately through the trees, searching for the bobbing beam of light. "I don't see Frank."

"Cobb is a big boy quite used to taking care of himself. Forget about him."

Paulo stood beside her, as symbiotically close as a clinging rope of ginger to an anchoring tree trunk. His palms rubbed her arms, her hips in long, aggressive strokes.

"I want you to think about us, Sheba. About our future once you put this nonsense behind you."

Nonsense.

"Nonsense?" The meaning of that one word quivered through her.

"You know what I mean, *novia.* You must let go of this obsession with the past so that we can move on together. It's unhealthy, Sheba, the way you let it consume you. You bring on your own nightmares and fears by refusing to accept and let go. I'd hoped that once your were here, you'd realize the foolishness of your quest and get on with life."

"Foolishness?" She turned toward him. "Is that what you think it is to want to find out what happened to my parents, to me?"

"Sheba, be logical. That was twenty years ago. No one remembers. No one wants to know. You are the only one keeping questions alive and until you face the fact that there are no answers, you'll never be free of them."

"So we can get on with your plans?"

He shouldn't have missed the ice creeping into that claim, but he did.

"Yes. The plans I've made for the two of us."

"How good of you to decide my future for me as if I were incapable of doing it for myself. Poor little Sheba, so confused and in need of direction."

"That's not what I meant."

"Isn't it? Hasn't it always been? Haven't you just been humoring me all along?"

"Sheba, it's not like that."

"Of course it is, Paulo. It's just like that. You wanted to bring me here so I'd fall apart and you could get me to admit that I'm helpless. Then you'd be the strong one, the hero, and take care of everything for me. Isn't that why you resent Frank Cobb?"

"Don't bring him into this," Paulo growled, his bristly attitude confirming her summation.

"I didn't have to. You did."

"Sheba."

And there it was in his tone.

"Don't patronize me, Paulo. I am not a little girl anymore. I'm not helpless and I'm not crazy. And I am not in love with you."

That wasn't how she'd meant to say it, blurting it out with an amputating slash, but she was glad it was said. It had to be said.

Paulo stared at her for a long moment. Varying emotions swept across his dark gaze like clouds scudding ominously across the moon. His jaw worked upon his pride and disappointment. And finally the pride, that overpowering Latin pride, won out.

"You are wrong, Sheba. We are meant for one another. Once we put your past to rest, you will see. You will love me."

In a flat, somber tone that left no room for question or hope, she told him, "No, Paulo, I won't."

She gasped as he grabbed her forearms and yanked her hard against him. She angled her head away from his attempt to kiss her, and his bruised pride evolved into anger. He pushed her from him, not caring that she nearly fell or that he'd left darkening circles upon her arms from the possessive bite of his fingers. He glared at her, seething with fury and injury.

"You will regret this, you and your Americano lover."

"Frank's not my–"

He waved a hand to cut off her protest. In his mind, that could be the only excuse for her rejection. As if afraid he'd come to violence if he remained, Paulo stalked away from the fire and into the night. At first Sheba felt relief, then concern. He hadn't taken a light.

"Paulo. Paulo, come back."

"Don't you dare consider running after him."

She whirled to face Frank Cobb who had very probably witnessed the whole sordid affair and was probably snickering over his supposed part in it. She struck out at him in her frustration and embarrassment.

"Don't presume to tell me what to do."

"Then don't try to make your problems my fault."

She was angry at him, irrationally, illogically furious and all without cause. Or perhaps because she had no cause. She wished Paulo's accusations were true. She wished she could claim Frank Cobb was her lover. She wished, foolishly, that he'd made those same declarations about a future and plans and hopes. But he hadn't and he wouldn't and that's why she was so mad.

That wasn't his fault.

But it didn't stop her from being angry.

"No, of course not, Mr. Cobb. None of this is your doing. Your job is to sneak around in the shadows, to manipulate and lie to get things to go your way. Or rather your employer's way."

"I haven't lied to you."

Said so calmly, with such bland sincerity, was rubbing salt into her wounded ego.

"You're lying right now. Maybe you're just so used to it,

you don't even realize you're doing it."

Still, he remained unruffled in the face of her tirade. "What have I told you that's not true?"

"That you were here to help me."

"That's not what I said, Doc. I told you why I was here. I'm here because Harper sent me to do a job."

That's exactly what he'd told her. Over and over. Just a job. Work and travel.

"And I'm just a job to you? That's not what you let me think."

"I didn't lead you on, Sheba. I never let you think there was anything personal going on."

No, he hadn't. Damn him.

There were tears on her cheeks. Her voice shivered like a petulant child's.

"But you said you believed me. You told me to trust you. And all along, all along, it was just a lie to keep me happy, to keep me out of the way, to keep me from poking around where Peyton Samuels doesn't want me."

"Why would you think that, Doc?"

"Because I heard them talking. Sam and Rosa. I heard him saying that he'd hired the best to make sure I didn't get out of line."

"To make sure you didn't get hurt," he corrected quietly. "That's why he hired me."

She took a great hitching breath, blinking against the burn in her eyes. "What?" She swallowed hard, struggling to rein in her runaway emotions. "You mean you weren't trying to placate me with what you said?"

"What I said was the truth. I told you I believed you because I do. It's not personal, Doc. The job is never personal. I can't afford to let it be more than a job."

"I see." She sniffed up her tears and frantic feelings, trying to look as though that truth wasn't almost as bad as the lie.

He smiled, a thin cocky smile that lifted one corner of his mouth and crinkled the scar upon his cheek. An indulgent gesture. "No. You don't see. It's more than just the job, Doc. That's the hell of it."

She wasn't sure which of them made the first move, but suddenly their arms were entwined, their lips wildly slanting, their tongues tangling in a forest fire kiss that singed all the way to her toes. She grabbed at his head, clenching her fingers in the short nap of his hair while his combed through her unruly curls. And there was nothing the least bit impersonal in the way he sought to acquaint himself with her tonsils.

All hot and cold and shivery inside, she gave her all to that kiss, all the loneliness, the longing, the hunger, the need, not just for anyone. For him. And if he didn't realize that by the time they broke apart to grab for breath, then he wasn't such a smart guy after all.

His eyes blazed, rich, green-gold fire. Burning for her and her alone. And his smile, that crooked, smug smile made her feel like laughing out loud over how foolish she'd been to think he wasn't interested. A mistake she wouldn't make again.

But what to do about it?

She stroked through his hair and let her fingertips trail down to the sides of his mulish jaw.

"Is this a good thing, Frank? It feels like a very good thing."

"It could be, Doc. Right now I'd lay odds on it."

Her eyes closed languidly and she leaned back into his kiss, this time sampling him fully with a thoroughness that wrung a groan of restless complaint from him. For that moment, the world and all its problems ceased to exist. There was only the delicious taste of Frank Cobb made doubly sweet by the drizzling of her own pent up desires.

"Let's get a room," he whispered huskily against her provoking lips.

"I'm afraid the accommodations are rather primitive out here."

"I'm feeling rather primitive at the moment."

He was feeling huge and urgent where his hips ground into hers. A giddy sense of excitement rippled through her, of a wondrous discovery about to be made.

Until Frank stepped back from her with a suddenness that left her gasping. Fumbling to gather her wayward senses the way she'd put together disheveled clothing if they'd had time to go that far, she followed the intensity of his stare to the edge of camp.

To where Paulo Lemos stumbled into the light, his eyes glazed.

His throat black with blood.

SEVENTEEN

"What are we going to do?"

Frank looked at the pale figure tossing restlessly on the cot. His response was grim. "We go back. We have no choice now. He's lost too much blood. He needs a hospital, a transfusion, care we can't give him out here."

Sheba tried to look upon Paulo's deathly white features without tearing up. Panic beat in her breast. She would have thought she'd jump at Cobb's suggestion of retreat. Why she didn't was a mystery to her.

"What...what attacked him?"

Cobb peeled back the crude bandage from his neck to reveal the twin puncture wounds. "My guess would be a myth. What would yours be?"

A vampire.

He was saying it was a vampire.

But at least he wasn't saying I told you so. Raking her fingers through the chaos of her rumpled hair, blocking her mind to the remembrance of Frank Cobb doing the same thing only an hour before, Sheba tried to think logically. An explanation. There had to be one. Something other than a preternatural creature from the late show. Something that wouldn't defy the rationale she followed when casting doubt upon fiction and poking holes through fantasy. But those avenues failed her when confronted by this truth. Something had attacked Paulo Lemos and drained him nearly dry in a matter of minutes, without a sound, without raising any suspicion or alarm.

While she and Frank Cobb were lip-locked only yards away and oblivious to his peril.

And if Paulo died, he would be on her conscience, too.

She closed her eyes, breathing deep, struggling to separate fright from reason. Failing.

Outside, the rest of their group muttered in increasingly vocal anxiety. Sheba's cry upon seeing Paulo had pulled them out of their tents but Cobb, quick-thinking Cobb, had covered the source of the attack.

"What are we going to tell them?" Sheba asked, referring to the others who waited for some word.

Cobb's smile took a cynical turn. "That he was bitten by something potentially fatal. No sense causing a panic and no sense trying anything before daybreak. Going out into the forest at night would be...suicide."

"So we wait."

"And we watch."

And Sheba watched as Frank took another from his collection of silver crosses and fastened it about Paulo's neck, just below the patch that covered his contamination. By what? A vampire? Vampire bat, perhaps. That would explain the mark. But she had the feeling that Frank Cobb wouldn't go for that explanation. And beside, how big would a bat have to be to consume such a quantity of human blood? Man-sized. Sheba shuddered as the trap of logic closed tighter about her. A logic that said Cobb was right, had been right all along.

There *were* monsters.

Her gaze followed Cobb as he rose to his feet and approached her. The awareness of how he'd tasted, how he'd felt, so hard and strong against her, momentarily swamped her senses. Then the fact that they'd been enjoying one another while Paulo's life was being drained away sucked all the passion from her memories. She went cold inside.

"Here."

Cobb hooked one of the small crucifixes about her neck as well. The metal quickly warmed to the heat of her skin.

"Don't take that off."

"Shouldn't I wear a necklace of garlic, too?"

Cobb didn't smile at her slightly frayed attempt at humor. "If I had one, you'd be wearing it. You need to take extra precautions. When he wakes up, he might be...different."

She fingered the cross and looked back to where Paulo tossed and turned in a fever of possession. "Different? Different, how?"

"He belongs to Alexander now. He'll be his master's eyes and ears during the day and his puppet during the night."

"Isn't that a bit dramatic?" she asked, wishing it was, knowing it wasn't.

"Believe what you want, Doc, if the evidence isn't enough to convince you."

She took a shaky breath. "If this creature is after you, why attack Paulo?"

"To make us go back. He'll know it's too dangerous to travel with him, for Lemos' sake and ours. That was the whole idea, wasn't it? To sabotage this trip. To keep us out of the jungle."

"Why? What's out here that's more important than the lives already lost?"

"The lives of an indigenous tribe. A way of life and the means to support it. I don't know. I'm not a philosopher or an ethnologist. This is more your area than mine. With Alexander, there doesn't have to be a reason."

"Other than to get back at you. It would seem that you're our problem, Cobb."

"Now who's being overly simplistic. The problem was here before I was, but I can be the solution. I know the enemy—"

"And he's gotten the upper hand on you again."

Cobb's features closed down tight.

With a sigh, Sheba rubbed her aching brow. "I'm sorry. I'm being an idiot. We've got enough to worry about without tearing at each other."

Cobb accepted her apology without a blink. "I'll go tell the others that we're leaving in the morning."

After he'd slipped out of the tent, Sheba went to kneel next to Paulo. His terrible white skin and shallow breathing brought tears of anxiousness and frustration at last. This was her fault. If she hadn't been so brutal in her rejection of him, he wouldn't have placed himself in jeopardy, alone in the jungle. If she had been a true friend, she would have been watching out for him instead of pursuing her own selfish desires. She'd come all this way, back into the shadow of her nightmares because he'd called and when he needed her the most, she'd failed him.

"I'm sorry, Paulo. I should have been stronger for you."

Lifting his alarmingly cold hand in hers, she pressed her cheek against the back of it and let sorrow shake through her shoulders. When she felt the faint stir of his fingers, she leaned back to anxiously search his ghostly features for signs of awareness.

His eyes opened, burning like dark coals. Though he stared at her, there was no recognition.

"You have the key, Sheba." His words rasped out, dry and cracked, the voice not his own. "How many must die before you find the courage to use it."

Chill fingers closed about her hand with a strength both crushing and dominating. Sheba lunged back, pulling free.

"What's going on?"

She turned to Cobb, teetering on the edge of a scream. "Nothing."

His narrowed gaze said, *Yeah, right. Looks like nothing,* but he didn't challenge her directly. He had an uncanny ability to recognize when the time was right to keep his mouth shut.

And maybe it was time for her to show a little courage.

***

Neither she nor Cobb slept that night. Paulo grew weaker and, finally, as daybreak approached, his thrashings stilled. He lay close to death.

It was then that courage came to Sheba.

She said nothing to Cobb. He had his own job to do. This was hers.

And when Paulo was strapped down on a makeshift litter and everyone was anxious and ready to start back, she let them know her plans.

"I'm not going with you."

Cobb's stare came up with an intensity that nearly knocked

her backward. “Yes, you are.”

She took a breath. She’d come up against difficult obstacles before. She wasn’t about to let Frank Cobb intimidate her.

But she could see why he was so good at what he did even as she put her best argument forward.

“I’ve come too far to give up now. If I go back, I’ll never find the answers I need. That’s why Paulo brought me here, to put the past to rest.”

“And I was brought here to make sure the both of you survived this little expedition. There’s no way I’m going to let you wander off by yourself.”

“I won’t be wandering. I know this jungle inside out. I was raised here, remember.” Her smile was thin, almost condescending. “There’s no way you can stop me, Frank. This isn’t about you or Paulo or Sam. It’s about me and the things I have to know. If Paulo’s grandfather has the answers, I have to ask the questions. I have to know. I can’t go back without knowing.”

He studied her for a long, stoic moment then pronounced, “Bull. You’re going with us if I have to carry you the whole way.”

She shook her head, still smiling the enigmatic smile. “No you won’t, Frank. You’ll let me go. Your job is to stay with Paulo, and I’m trusting you to do that job, to keep him alive and safe. Earn that paycheck.”

For a minute, she thought he might actually say to hell with it and go against his duty for her sake. But being Cobb, she should have known better. He gestured to the others to pick up their gear and to her, he had a terse suggestion.

“Watch your back, Doc.”

Swallowing down the sense of disappointment, she nodded. “Do the same.”

With one last look at Paulo, who was critical at best, she turned and continued on. She didn’t look back as she heard Cobb give brusque orders for them to move out in a judicious hurry. Without her.

Cobb would see that Paulo was safe. He’d earn that big

paycheck.

And she would continue on to confront her demons. And earn her self-respect.

***

By late day, she started climbing. Shaded by the jungle canopy, it wasn't bad at first. Then the foliage thinned, and the sun's intensity increased, beating down on her shoulders like the heavy yoke of her thoughts. Spongy ground gave way to hard-packed earth and the path, as well as the going, got rocky. That was good. Having to concentrate on the step-by-step of her travel kept her from ruminating over the whole of it. It was too late to second guess her choice. She'd never catch the others before darkness fell, and there was no way she was going back into that forest alone after nightfall.

Besides, what could they do to protect her from the fears that lived in her mind?

What could Cobb do to protect her from his monster?

What to believe? Was his creature the same entity that stalked her in her dreams? How could that be? And how did the one or the both tie into the death of her parents? And why? The why had always been the worst. The not knowing. The wondering why she alone survived.

And what had she done with the precious life that had been spared? She'd continued to live it in the shadows, alone and afraid. Was that the kind of testimony her parents would have wanted from her? Had their fate meant so little that she'd hidden from the truth of it for twenty years? She'd convinced herself that she was doing the good and right thing, destroying the illusions that preyed upon people's lives through fear and ignorance. And yet while conquering their demons, she'd let her own go unchecked. Wasn't it time she stopped challenging the symbolic dragon and confronted the real one which scorched her dreams in flames of dread and mocked her from the empty corners of her mind? She'd always known the answer was here, and yet she's chosen to avoid seeking out that truth.

In the pristine hours that followed dawn and led into the scorch of late afternoon, those were the realities that came to her to shape the course of her actions. No more hiding. No more pretending that defeating substitute monsters was the same as dealing with her own. Watching Paulo suffer for the sins of her fright and denial brought it home with the abruptness of a slap. How many more need die before she found the courage? Paulo? Cobb?

She drew an agonized breath as her thoughts touched upon the cocky mercenary. It was the man, not the altitude making her light-headed. A man she'd begun to believe she could love and live with for the rest of her life.

If only he felt the same way.

He'd made no secret of his agenda. Protect Paulo. To redeem himself in the eyes of the other woman he'd loved. The woman she knew nothing about, the one who'd had his heart and soul and had yet turned away to give herself to another.

Obviously a stupid woman.

For those two things Frank Cobb would risk his life. He considered them worthy endeavors. But he'd done nothing to stop her from going off on her own to face certain peril whether imagined or dangerously real. How that wounded, and yet she'd known Cobb wasn't a hero. He was a realist – hard-bitten, scarred by harsh experience and totally dedicated to the job at hand. He was in the jungle for revenge not romance. And yet, as she'd turned away from him to start out in her own direction, a part of her longed for him to surrender all that he had been to be by her side.

A silly yearning.

Paulo was the important one. Within his brilliant mind lay the possible betterment of mankind. What could she offer that would compare to that? Frank had done the right thing and she admired him for his resolve.

But oh, his kiss had been magnificent. She could taste it even now as she climbed ever upward toward the unknowns of her future. And she smiled to herself as she considered how different things might have been had they been other than who they were.

But if they were, would the attraction be as strong? Wasn't

it the very impossibility of their union that made it so irresistible?

As soon as she faced this nightmare, she'd be free to pursue that dream.

Nothing was impossible if one had faith, her father had told her. Though her faith in the things he'd believed in had fallen off over the years, her faith in herself had undergone a wondrous renewal. Determination replaced the crippling dread. If Ruperto Lemos didn't know the answers, perhaps he could help open her tightly locked mind to free the secrets it had guarded for these past twenty years. She was finally strong enough to learn them, to accept them whatever they might be.

And then she could get on with her life instead of being held prisoner by it.

***

While tourists flocked to the Inca Trial at Machu Picchu to endure the three day climb and explore the remains of a civilization, when Ruperto Lemos went into seclusion to avoid the modern age, he sought out a more ancient and mysterious world from which he had descended. His people, like the Quechuas, founded Peru, only as the Quechuas expanded to form the Inca empire, his own remained isolated and unchanging, content to continue worshiping in the old ways and contemptuous of all that was progress. Because of that choice to scorn expansion, it doomed itself to ever-shrinking numbers and an increasing battle to retain its purity.

The Reynards had convinced Ruperto that in order to preserve his people's past, it needed to be documented. To do that meant developing a written language to interpret the centuries-old dialect. Afraid that his rich culture would fade and be forgotten, Ruperto had agreed to let the Reynards live amongst his following, learning their language and translating it into a symbolic form. After all, what did he have to fear from Shari Reynard, who was of their own blood? But the exchange was far from one-sided. As the Reynards studied his people, so did they observe the strange *civilizados.* And among those who were tempted and lured away by what they learned were Ruperto's only daughter and his grandson, Paulo.

Perhaps Ruperto had never forgiven that defection. Perhaps he blamed his own naivete and that of the Reynards. But had he blamed them enough to wish them dead? That's what Sheba would find out. If she could find the elusive shaman amongst the ruins of his past.

She paused upon one of the terraced slopes to take a long drink of tepid water from her canteen. She dampened her neckerchief and, after blotting her face and nape, looped it about her neck to offer a vaguely cooling relief. She was close. She knew it. Perhaps even now she was under the surveillance of Ruperto's clan. Would they show themselves, or would she be forced to laboriously search for them? Either way, she was not leaving until contact was made.

A slight trickling of stones from on the path behind her alerted Sheba to the fact that she was not alone. Taking a firm grip on the walking staff she'd fashioned to aid her climb, she turned abruptly, ready to face any foe.

But not her heart's desire.

"I thought you were going to watch your back."

Relief filtered through her in tiny shivers. Contrarily, she weighed her staff and arched a haughty brow. "You came very close to having what few brains you possess seriously rattled. What do you mean sneaking up on me like that?"

"Sneaking? I've been stomping around behind you for the last two hours. You must be deaf not to have heard me."

"I wasn't expecting anyone to be skulking in the bushes. Why didn't you just tell me you were there?"

"I would have...if I could have caught up to you. Woman, you've got one hell of a stride."

A foolish grin struggled to escape, but she fought it back to demand, "What are you doing here, Cobb?"

"Watching your back."

"And what about your duty to Paulo?"

"I know, and to my paycheck. Got it covered. We ran into a convoy of trucks that are going to get him to the river, and from there the others will see he reaches the hospital."

"Oh. Good."

"So, with that taken care of, I found myself without any

gainful employment. I figured I'd just go and see what kind of trouble you'd gotten yourself into."

"As you can see, I'm not in any kind of trouble at all."

He smiled grimly in response to her claim. "Then who are these fellows surrounding us, and why do I feel we're about to become the main course at their evening meal?"

EIGHTEEN

Ruperto Lemos was hardly a figure to inspire terror or legend. He sat upon an ancient stone step, a mantle of crudely spun cloth about his shoulders, his sickly, stick-thin legs poking from beneath a huge, swollen belly. From out of a face as withered as a winter apple, he regarded them with sightless eyes. He appeared much like the majority of the indigenous people of Peru, in ill-health, starving and desperately clinging to a sense of the past. Or so she would have believed had she not noticed the way the others deferred to him. Or the way his hunched shoulders straightened, dragging him up into a posture of pride and power. A big, rich voice burst from the shriveled frame.

"Daughter of the missionaries, why have you come?"

Out of respect, she answered in the same ancient tongue. "I've come to ask you to cast a mesa so that you might show me the truth about how my parents died."

"What can you learn from me, child? You have lost the beliefs of your family and deny the power of this land. The spirits cannot speak to you through the wall of doubts about her mind and soul."

Though she winced at the barb of that surprisingly accurate truth, she kept her tone calm and reverent. "I ask that they speak to you, *altomisayoq*. Your power can overcome my weakness of heart."

"And the one with you, what does he believe?"

"In the truth, Great One. He has sworn to protect your grandson but cannot do so without the knowledge I seek. Paulo is ill, perhaps dying. We have little time to listen and learn. Will you help us? Will you give us the wisdom to save his soul from the ancient evil?"

"He of whom you speak has been long dead to me."

It was not going well. There was so little time to charm an old man with sentiments of family and loyalty. And even though he was blind, Sheba guessed that Ruperto Lemos would see right through any lie. So, she stuck to the truth, hoping it could melt some of the icy indifference about the shaman's embittered heart.

"Paulo is of your blood, of your people. He has done nothing to harm you or the spirit of the land. He only seeks to help others by tapping into the strength of the jungle, much in the same way you and your fathers before you have always done. He deserves your respect, not your contempt."

"Yet it is contempt he shows for his heritage. I may not have eyes, but I see. I see him in his fancy clothes, speaking with his educated tongue. He is of another world now. He does not belong."

"In his heart beats the soul of the forest. In his blood, flows the strength of his ancestors. He hasn't turned from you, Great One. You are the one who drove him away with your refusal to accept his curiosity about the world around you, just as you did your own daughter, Cipriana, and your niece Shari, my mother."

"They were contaminated by the knowledge and greed of the outsiders." A hint of angry querulousness crept into his tone. Their defection had hurt him deeply.

So there was still hope.

"No. They sought to protect their past by giving it the means to survive in the modern world. They did so out of hearts of love, not disrespect. It is you who disrespects their memories by hardening your heart to the good things they have done."

Ruperto sat unmoving for a long moment, and Sheba feared she'd said too much. She couldn't afford to alienate this one link she had left to her own past, her own memories. But before she could apologize, the old man chuckled softly.

"You speak well, child. You do those before you honor."

"Thank you." The humility in her voice was not pretended

and he nodded, feeling her sincerity.

"You wish to hear of things long past. What do these things have to do with my grandson?"

"I was hoping you could tell me."

"Come sit, child." He patted the blanket-covered rock beside him. "I would like to get a better look at you. I do not like speaking to strangers."

When she took a step forward, Cobb's hand went instinctively to her arm to halt her, to keep her close to his side. An immediate bristle of crude spears arose from the circle of men around them. With their nut-brown bodies bared except for a loincloth and their black eyes bright with suspicion, they didn't look helpless in the least. Sheba placed her hand gently over Cobb's, lifting it so she could move forward. If he chose to act rashly, their lives could end in a moment. But he did nothing, trusting her the way he'd once asked her to trust him.

She glanced up at him, taking just a fraction of a second to convey with that warm look how much his faith meant to her.

Sheba sat and remained unmoving while Ruperto explored her features with surprisingly dexterous fingers. He expression softened fondly.

"You have your mother's beauty. And her gentle temperament as well?"

"I'm afraid not."

His fingertips lingered over her self-castigating smile. "Still, I feel her spirit in you. And that of your father. He was a good, honest man. You honor them both." His exploration stilled when touched by the warmth of her tears. Slowly, he followed along her arms so he could pick her hands up in his, feeling their shape, stroking her palms.

And then his manner changed as his dry fingers investigated her open palm. The endless creases forming caverns in his ancient face seemed to fill and firm. His eyes came alive with a blaze of strength and knowledge. His hand closed over hers, his grip startlingly powerful.

"Who has sent you to me?"

"No, one. I came on my own."

"After all these years of silence, why now?"

"Paulo asked for me to come."

"Paulo did? Paulo, not Samuels?"

Suspicion sharpened her question. "Why do you ask? What does it matter?"

"The motive makes all the difference if you still have the key."

The key. There it was again. "I don't understand, Great One. If I am the key, what knowledge do I have? I don't remember what happened the night my parents died. All I've heard is rumors."

"What rumors?"

She took a breath and glanced toward Cobb. Though he didn't understand their conversation, he guessed at its content. He shook his head slightly, warning her to tread carefully. But she forged ahead with a giant, reckless step.

"That perhaps you arranged it to keep progress from your people."

The old man didn't appear shocked or surprised. Or guilty. A partial smile crooked his thin lips. "And who spread these rumors? Samuels?"

"Mostly."

"I do not deny that I have done what I can to keep civilization away, but those steps have not included murder. If I had the ability to defeat those who strip our forest, would I be hiding here in this inhospitable place while outsiders enjoy the legacy of plenty our land provides? I think not, child. I think not."

"Paulo told me that you were asked to speak at their councils and you refused."

He made a disparaging noise. "Who among them would listen to my voice?"

"More than you know. But you'll never know if you continue to hide up here, hoarding the old ways to yourself instead of sharing them with the world."

He smiled again, and some of the fierceness left his sightless eyes. "Now, you sound like your mother, too."

"She was right. You should have listened."

He appeared thoughtful then worried despite his feigned indifference. “Paulo is ill, you said. What has happened to him?”

Sheba didn’t try to soft pedal it. Her response was as quick and as instinctively merciless as the creature that had left Paulo near death. “He was attacked by something in the jungle. Something that pierced his neck and drained his blood.”

And all the blood left the old man’s face. “It cannot be. Someone has used the key.”

A mix of frustration and confusion shortened her tone as she demanded, “What key?”

He held up her palm so she could inspect the outline of scars upon it. Scars made twenty years ago when a frightened child had made a fist about a medallion until her hand bled.

“This key,” he told her. “Do you know where it is?”

Contrarily, she demanded, “What does it do? What does it open?”

“The secrets of our past. The evils we laid to rest. Who has released them? Who has the key?”

“I do.”

“Where did you get it, child? Who gave it to you?”

“I don’t know. I found it in my hand on the night my parents disappeared. On the night they were killed. What does it mean? Tell me!”

“It unlocks the treasures and the terrors of my people’s past,” came his innocuous reply. “In each generation, a member of the royal family is entrusted with its safekeeping. My daughter, Cipriana was that guardian, but when her...body was found, the key was missing. All these years, we have rested without ease, fearing it had found its way into the wrong hands. And all this time, we needn’t have worried.”

He closed her hand into a ball and held it tightly between his own.

“A new guardian has been found.”

She tried to pull back, alarmed by what he insinuated, but his grip was amazingly strong. “What do you mean?”

“You are of your mother’s blood, and that is shared with me and the royal families of centuries past. You honor your people by protecting the key from those who would use its power unwisely."

Sheba relaxed her struggle, knowing she couldn't prevail. Now was not the time to protest her unworthiness. She was close, so close, to all that she needed to know. She leaned forward, pressing her other hand over his imprisoning one. "What power, Great One? What does it do?"

But he evaded her question. "You must be hungry after your long journey, and I am being a bad host. You and your friend will dine with us and then we will talk more."

After waiting twenty years, the possibility of all her answers lay just hours away. Anticipation shivered beneath her outward display of resolve.

But Frank Cobb had less patience than she did.

"What was all that about?" he demanded as they were led back to a small village of crudely constructed huts.

She gave him a play-by-play to the best of her recollection then waited to hear his conclusion. He lifted her hand and studied the marks on her palm somberly, tracing them with his thumb. His grip was warm, the feel now familiar. Much of her jumpy anxiousness ebbed away beneath that calming touch.

"These scars are from the medallion you wear."

"Yes. And I think Cipriana Lemos—Samuels was killed for it."

He was staring at her bosom, at the spot where the medallion lay cradled between her breasts. Unexpectedly, embarrassingly, her nipples tightened at the attention, craving his touch there, as well. There'd been no time to address the tension between them, and it boiled like whatever hung over Lemos' fire. Until Cobb's brusque tone called her back to business.

"Does anyone know that you have it?"

"No. No one but you. And now Ruperto."

"I wonder who else would be interested in finding out?" he murmured.

Though he'd mused that more or less to himself, Sheba latched onto the direction of his thoughts. "Like bait for a trap?"

"We'll see. And only as a last resort." He looked ahead at the old man they followed and nodded. "What's your take on him?" He still hadn't released her hand.

"He admits to wanting outsiders to leave the forest, but I don't think he's had anything to do with what's been going on. Or with my parents. I peg him as more a pacifist."

Cobb made a doubtful noise. "Yeah, but I bet in his heyday he could stir up a lot of rowdy stuff. A reluctant pacifist, maybe, but if you ask me, I'd guess there's still some fire in the old guy."

"I feel sorry for him. He's such an old man who's lost so much."

"That would be your mistake. An old warrior is still a warrior."

"Like you're going to be when you're seventy?"

He smiled slightly, glancing at their armed escort. "If I live that long."

Around the fire, they shared a flavorful, if watery stew with a dozen of Ruperto's extended family members. Wary eyes regarded them with suspicion, but taking a cue from their leader, none challenged them overtly. The meal was a time to take sustenance not make conversation, so Sheba hurriedly scooped up the last of her broth, eager to continue their talk. This close to her goal, she was surprisingly free of apprehension. But the sense of expectation zinged through her, leaving her nerve endings humming like electrically charged wires.

The truth was here with this old man, and she would finally know an end to her anguished quest.

When the meal was cleared away the others disappeared, leaving the three of them before the fire. Across the flames, reflected embers danced in the old man's sightless eyes, giving them the illusion of some magical power to see beyond what was before them. Perhaps into the past, when an ancient medallion opened a doorway—either by accident or on purpose—to release an incredible evil.

"Tell me about the medallion," Sheba urged, translating

her words and the reply so Cobb could follow the conversation.

"In the days of our ancestors, when our people ruled a great empire—before the time of the Inca, before the coming of the Spanish—we worshiped a powerful god who protected and provided for us. But as with man, this god grew greedy, and soon our offerings of tribute no longer satisfied. The people rebelled against his demand for blood sacrifice, and they went from being the chosen to the victims of his wrath. Many were slain before they trapped this divine evil in a tomb. They were then safe from him, but vulnerable to other tribes without his fearsome strength to keep them away.

"So this wise and selfless leader struck a bargain with their blood-thirsty deity. He would remain asleep until called forth to defend the people. Then he would return to his rest when appeased by the offering of royal blood and sleep until called upon again."

"So the royal family made a sacrifice from among them for the sake of their people."

"Only they could release the demon god and then call him back to his rest. It was an awesome responsibility, but one that was borne proudly, humbly and—if the situation demanded it—bravely."

Sheba listened the way she would to any myth being spun, with the indulgent disbelief of one chronicling the fables of the past. But Cobb leaned forward, his expression alert, his gaze sharply intense, as if the old man was revealing the secrets behind the origin of man.

"This god," he asked at last, urging Sheba to translate his words when she would hesitate. "What was he?"

"A supreme being, one of power and darkness."

Cobb made an impatient gesture that was lost on the speaker. "Yes, but if you strip away all the fairytale trappings and the cultural mumbo-jumbo, is what you have left what we would call a vampire?"

The old man thought a moment. "Perhaps to your over-simplified thinking he might be called that. The Fanged Deity, the Ancient One who only wakes by night and demands payment in blood. There is more I have not told you. It is said that if a member of the royal family, a virgin, is given to the Great One as his bride, he will reward the giver with faithful service for the lifetime of his mate."

After he heard the translation, Cobb made a noise. "It's a good thing there are so few royal virgin brides to be had these days, or we might have to worry."

"Frank."

Sheba's tone warned him that he wouldn't like what was coming.

She looked him in the eye, her calm demeanor belied by the bright, embarrassed color warming her cheeks.

"We'd better start worrying."

NINETEEN

Cobb stared as Ruperto waited for a translation.

"Don't tell me. You're royalty."

She nodded, the heat rising, color seeping up into her cheeks in a determined tide.

"And the other thing, too?"

He looked so insultingly incredulous. Her temper bristled in spiny defensiveness.

"Chastity isn't a disease, Cobb."

His mouth shut with an audible clack. She waited dispassionately for him to regain his wits. His recovery was far from stellar.

"I never said it was."

Her glare could have made him into a eunuch. Clinging to the last of her dignity, she turned her attention to Ruperto to inform him of the rather humiliating circumstance. He saw no humor in it. Only horror.

"This is a disaster," he exclaimed.

"Well, it hasn't been great on my social life, either. Something about a thirty-year-old virgin makes men run for the hills." Even a man like Frank Cobb, if his pole-axed expression was any indication. Usually such a master of his emotions, he was clearly struggling with them now. Probably between astonishment and laughter. At this moment, she didn't think she could survive his mockery. But true to form, he surprised her by pulling his composure together and remaining silent behind his stoic facade.

"Who knows of this besides us?" Ruperto wanted to know. His urgent manner left no more room for shame.

"Just a friend," she admitted at last, then more wryly, "It's not something I discuss over dinner."

But was Rosa Kelly her friend? She'd thought so once...before all her realities were discovered to be as deceptive as her dreams. She didn't know what or whom to believe in any more. Nor did she want to believe the shaman's incredible story. Superstition and nonsense. Sacrificial virgins and vengeful gods, indeed.

"Your disbelief is plain in your silence," Ruperto intuited without accusation. "Such doubts are dangerous to you, child. It's not necessary for you to believe if there are others who do. I would suggest you find the means to alter your circumstance, and the sooner the better."

He was advising her to chase down a man to end her unfortunate state of grace. And where in the jungle was she to find such a martyr?

Slowly, her gaze slid to Frank Cobb.

It wasn't the worst solution she could think of.

But she'd rather take her chances at the sacrificial altar than beg that favor from a reluctant suitor.

Or would he be reluctant?

His kiss in the camp said no, even if all his actions leading up to it disagreed.

To distract herself from the shivery hots and colds of anticipation, she emotionally pinched herself. "Ruperto, what happened to my parents? Who killed them and why? And why was I left alive?"

"These are questions you alone have the answer to. You and whoever was there in the jungle with you. Whoever even now seeks to silence you." He sighed. The wheezy sound of sorrow rattled from his sunken chest. "I should have been watching. I should have been on my guard, but I was mourning the loss of my daughter. I did not expect evil to strike so quickly at the heart of my family after taking my child away from me."

"Peyton says you blame him for what happened."

How ancient and tired he suddenly looked, as if all the fight left him with only his loss. "I blame him for being handsome and young and charming, for tempting my sweet

Cipriana with a glimpse of a world she'd never known. She was such an innocent, much like your mother was."

And she, herself, was.

Who could so cruelly take advantage of that trusting naivete? And why? Over some ancient lore? Over promises of power made by some mythical god? Logic told her to find another reason.

But since when had logic held a place in the jungle? It was a place to believe in ancient demons and the wrath of a legend scorned. A place where the impossible was the ordinary.

A place where a virgin could still be given over to wed a god to earn his favor and good fortune.

She was in big trouble.

And the answer to her peril sat beside her.

"Child, there is a way to unlock your memories. The way is dangerous and not always clear even once revealed."

"What is the way?"

"By taking the vine of the dead, you can learn the truth in the spirit world from those who went before you. It is not a path to be walked lightly. The way is dark and sometimes deadly and should not be walked alone. Have someone you trust to safely guide you if you decide to find your answers there."

Impatience conquered any reluctance.

"I'm ready."

The old man smiled. "You are too eager, child. Think about the risk and prepare yourself for the journey. At dawn, if you still want to take the path, I will guide you. And then, you must leave this place quickly. I would like to think that all my people are above the temptation of trading upon our past for a profitable future. But sadly, that would be foolish of me and dangerous for you. Reflect upon the path you will choose, and I will see you in the morning."

Two of the younger tribe members helped their leader to his feet and led him away from the fire. Then, Sheba was faced with an impatient Cobb who waited to hear what had transpired. She gave him the abbreviated version, the one that didn't involve the urgent need to lose her virginity.

"Vine of death," he mused. "What the hell is that? Peru's answer to magic mushrooms?"

She found his brusque anxiety touching. "Shamans have been using psychoactive plants for centuries to take spirit journeys. On the coast, they use the San Pedro cactus which produces a form of mescaline. In the highlands, they chew coca leaves. But in the forest, they take the ayahuasca vine. It's a powerful hallucinogenic drug that allows the user to see and interact with the spirit world."

"And you're seriously thinking of going on one of these psychedelic mystery tours? I don't think so."

Again, there was that blunt and erroneous assumption that she would blindly obey.

"It's not your choice to make, Frank."

And that said, she left him at the fire, needing to be alone to consider the step she was about to take, be it enlightening or deadly.

***

Virgin sacrifice, mind-altering drugs. What next?

Cobb knew what next. He had to get Sheba out of this godforsaken jungle and back to the States where she'd be safe from all the mystic mumbo-jumbo.

But that would mean abandoning his job.

Face it, his job was over. He'd been hired to protect Paulo Lemos and if, by some miracle, the scientist was still alive, he was hardly going to give a glowing recommendation. Cobb was batting zero for two on that score.

And what about Quinton Alexander? Could he just walk away knowing that Alexander's evil would go unchecked? What guarantee did he have that the vengeful vampire wouldn't follow him, if not immediately, then whenever the quirky mood struck him. He couldn't picture a spoiled and dapper fellow like Alexander living in the jungle for long, even pretending to be a god. Then he'd be responsible for whatever maniac deeds were done and, knowing the crazed killer, Sheba would be his first target.

She'd be no safer in the States than here. At least from Alexander's threat. Better to deal with it here and now than wait for it to catch up later when they were unaware and unexpecting.

That left all the pre-Columbian crap to take care of.

He didn't know if he believed in the spiel Ruperto Lemos was reeling out. Hell, months ago he hadn't believed in neck-biting blood-suckers either. The best bet was to treat it as a real and very present danger.

And that meant sticking to Sheba like glue.

Sheba, his warrior virgin princess.

His...

"Mr. Cobb?"

Frank looked up into the expectant face of one of Lemos's great nephews. What was his name? Josef.

"Yes? What is it?"

"My uncle would like to speak to you."

Frank's gaze jumped immediately to the rocky surround in search of Sheba.

"Do not worry. We will watch out for her. Come, please."

Humor the old guy. Frank followed, ducking into a wretched little shack only to jerk up in surprise.

"Holy shit! What's all this?"

There was wall-to-wall short wave equipment, new and undeniably expensive, hooked up to a generator.

Josef grinned. "We are isolated, not ignorant, Americano. I learned how to handle this stuff in the military. You can get it cheap, if you know where to shop."

"And I bet you're not referring to K Mart."

"Not on your life, Jack. My uncle wants Sheba out of here in the morning. We're arranging for a pick up, so be ready at 0800."

"Ready for what?"

"Anything, *civilizado*. Anything."

"Can I place a call on that thing?"

"It'll cost you, bro."

Ruperto issued a sharp bark of words, and Josef looked chagrined.

"Uncle tells me not to haggle, so you may make your call. If it's to the States, it may take about an hour to get the relay through."

"It's not like I was watching the game on TV. Unless you have a big screen around here someplace."

"Sorry, man. This is our one and only piece of the twenty-first century."

"Nice piece."

"I would say the same about your companion...if she weren't family."

Cobb grinned then grew serious. "Why does he want to talk to me?"

"It's about Sheba."

"Are you going to ask me my intentions?"

"I know what my intentions would be if I were you. Sit." Josef gestured to a blanket covered floor and Frank sat, waiting for the old man to address him. Instead, Ruperto reached into a clay pot on the floor beside him and threw a handful of dried herbs upon the fire. Quickly, a pungent smell permeated the small space.

Cobb's brows soared as he took a sniff.

"Am I going to have to arrest myself for inhaling?"

"Relax and enjoy," Josef suggested with a grin. "It's spiritual medicine, and Uncle thinks your spirit is wound too tight." For a moment, Ruperto talked, then Josef translated. "He feels much darkness in your past. You have done things you regret."

"Haven't we all."

Josef ignored that wry interjection. "You feel a bond to Sheba because you understand the shadow she walks in. You think by saving her, you will save yourself."

"Is this Cracker Jack Psychology 101?" Beginning to feel light-headed and uncomfortable with the personal turn of conversation, Cobb tried to stand but found his legs would not cooperate. A worm of panic wriggled in his belly. "I need some air."

Josef speared him with a authoritative stare. "You need to listen, bro. Open your mind and heart and hear what my uncle is saying. You only feel fear because you are thinking of your mother."

"What? What!" He struggled fiercely, angrily, commanding his rebellious limbs to move.

"Let that go, brother. You and she do not share the same fate or the same spirit. She chose her path, and you cannot change that. Nor do you have to walk it."

"What the hell are you talking about?"

But he knew. Somehow, the old man had looked into his soul and seen his anguished past as if watching it on that non-existent big screen.

"Her guilt is her own," Josef continued in his relay of the old man's words. "It's not for you to apologize or atone for it. If you want to help Sheba, you must let go of that pain so you can see your own way."

Frank couldn't breathe. The air seemed to thicken, to take on bright swirling colors that became patterns then pictures from his own memories, re-running the horrors of his own past in grisly Technicolor. His mother's face, wan and wasted, twisted by her last scream.

"No!"

He fought against the images, kicking at the fire. A shower of sparks rose, each ember carrying that frozen snapshot fixed in his mind for the past eighteen years. He sat back, gulping for a saving sanity as, one by one, those images disappeared, filtering back into the fire as ash. Then there was silence as his breathing rasped loud and raw.

"I couldn't save her," he said at last, his confession little more than a whisper.

"No one could. She didn't want to be saved, Frank. Let it go. She forgives you."

He closed his eyes and wiped the sheen of cold sweat from his brow.

"But you can save Sheba if it's for the right reasons. Look into your heart."

Cobb shook his head slowly. "I'm not what she needs."

"You're exactly what she needs, *hermano*. But you must put her first, above the past, above your duties. And for you, that will not be easy."

Cobb sat silently, blinking as he stared into the firelight.

Josef pressed a large, ancient goblet into his hands.

"Drink."

When Cobb recoiled suspiciously, the young man laughed.

"It's only water, *amigo*. Drink and let your head and heart focus upon what's important."

He drank, long and greedily, with an endless, unquenchable thirst. And as he lowered the cup, he stared at the intricately detailed engravings, blinking, looking closer. They were startlingly graphic depictions of sexual activity. And not much had changed since pre-Columbian times. The various and innovative positions put the *Kama Sutra* to shame.

"It's a Moche drinking vessel," Josef explained. "Our answer to pornography."

Cobb didn't respond to the other's lusty amusement. Because as he stared and studied, the face of the female on the cup altered from flat, simple lines, becoming more detailed. More recognizable. Becoming Sheba's. It was her lithe form writhing and twisting beneath the hugely endowed Man-Animal god of pagan lore.

A god with long, sharp fangs and eyes that momentarily gleamed red.

Josef deftly caught the cup as it fell from Cobb's numb fingers. "Easy, bro. You need some fresh air. Let me help you, man."

Only after he had dragged in great lungs' full of crisp twilight air, did his head begin to clear and his anxious thoughts turn to Sheba.

Where was she?

As if he'd read the direction of his thoughts, Josef said, "Look for her among the ruins." He pointed upward, toward what looked to be an impossible climb. "I'll put through that call to the States for you. What number are you trying to reach, so I can try to link you up through some of my *compadres*?"

Cobb scrawled out the number but his attention was elsewhere and the moment he was able, he began to hurry along the rocky path, stumbling at first then moving faster, easier as the effects of the smoke cleared from his mind. How could he ever forgive himself if something had happened to

Sheba while he was getting high with the natives?

How could he find room in his conscience for one more life lost because he hadn't been ready?

His heart pounded. He labored to get a decent fill of air in the thinning higher altitude. Fear and culpability fueled his rush up the nearly impassable slope.

And then he reached the top, and seeing Sheba there made his heart beat hard and fast for an entirely different reason.

The stone slabs were old, some toppled and broken, all worn down by the weather. Sheba sat atop one of them, leaning back on her palms, her knees updrawn and head dropped back as if soaking up the silver rays of the rising moon. Or as if offering herself to its embrace. She wore baggy hiking shorts and heavy boots with a skinny little white tank top that hugged her lean curves in loving relief. The silver of the cross he'd given her glittered at the hollow of her throat, and the key to her people's past lay exposed between her breasts.

It was suddenly clear to Frank Cobb.

He was in love—wildly, irrationally and perhaps for the first time.

And surprisingly, it didn't scare the hell out of him.

"Moon bathing?"

She turned her head toward him at the sound of his voice and smiled. It was as if the sun rose in a blaze of warmth and brilliant glory.

"You shouldn't be out here alone."

She grinned at his scolding. "I'm not. I'm perfectly safe. You're here." Serenely, she turned her face back up toward the heavens.

A massive weight of emotion flip-flopped in his chest.

He was in big trouble.

He waited, but all the warning bells and whistles that had saved him from taking any kind of committed step in the past remained silent. There was just Sheba and the moon and the crazy tightness around his heart that just kept building. She was a heart attack and he ignored all the cautioning signs as he approached her in the soft glow of evening.

"Ruperto has arranged for some kind of transportation to

take us out of here in the morning."

"Fine. I've been worried about Paulo."

Cobb scowled slightly. He hadn't been thinking about Lemos at all.

"And hopefully by then, I'll know everything I've come here to learn."

Apprehension soured his appreciation of the taut curve of her tanned calves and thighs. "Sheba, maybe you should just let it go." Ruperto's suggestion rang in the back of his brain, reminding him of those same words directed toward his ceaseless quest.

"Let it go?" She stared at him, the look accusing and slightly wounded. "I can't, Frank. I've come too far and waited too long. It's a risk I'm willing to take to put the past to rest."

But he wasn't willing.

He wanted to shout that at her, to shake her and forbid her to take ridiculous and dangerous liberties with her life. But he had no right to impose his unspoken feelings upon her. He could only attempt to make her see reason.

"You're talking about taking a potentially lethal drug, that's illegal as well as unstable. It's not like having your palm read or looking at Tarot cards. You're going to be putting a mind-altering narcotic into your body without knowing the results."

"Ruperto knows what he's doing."

"Ruperto's not the one taking the risk."

"Yes, he is. He's risking everything he holds sacred by telling me what he's told me tonight. He's counting on me being honorable and brave, and I won't disappoint him."

"Think of what you might be sacrificing, Sheba."

She ignored his challenge by purposefully changing the subject. "They used to sacrifice to the gods in this place to receive bountiful crops and beneficent weather. Some gods were satisfied with grains and small domestic animals, some with gold and precious stones, but others who were more powerful and therefore less content with trivial gifts, demanded offerings in blood and human life. When they excavated the tomb of the Lord of Sipan, they found not only treasures but the bodies of young women buried with their lord, sacrificed to provide him with service in the afterlife."

"Sounds like quite the deal for the lord but not so good for the ladies."

"More than likely they were honored to surrender themselves to the cause of his peaceful rest, but I, for one, could not go so docilely and with so little reward."

He'd come to stand at the end of the stone upon which she was half-reclined before him. "And what kind of reward would you require, princess?"

"This sacrificial virgin thing sucks big time. I wouldn't be content to go with my innocence intact. That would be grossly unfair."

"To you or to those who would line up for miles for the chance to deflower you?"

"Miles? Really? You think so?"

"From here to Chile and back," he assured her. His tone had grown husky, the playful banter shifting by increments into more serious and sultry territory. He was thinking of that Moche goblet and the engraved image of Sheba arched in ecstacy upon it. "And I'd be first in line."

She went still for a long moment, just looking at him through studious eyes as the silver of the moon cast mysterious lights within that intense stare. "Would you, Frank? If this was my altar, would you pay homage to me upon it? Upon me?"

Now it was his turn to go still in reflection. When once she might have chosen that time to withdraw behind shyness and insecurity, she advanced boldly. The toe of her boot nudged at his hip then rubbed over the strained material at his groin, the pressure only adding to the tension already nearing meltdown inside him.

"Sheba," he warned half-heartedly, catching her ankle to plant her boot firmly on the stone. But his hand wouldn't remain still. His palm slid upward to the taut length of her calf, sampling the heat and firm texture of her with a slow, plying motion. Her eyes grew heavy-lidded as she moistened her lips.

"If you're still waiting for an invitation, Mr. Cobb, this is it."

Her legs were slightly spraddled. When he moved his hands from ankles to knees, from strong revolutions there into a leisurely descent along beautifully toned thighs, her knees dropped open as she lay back upon the stone, offering an invitation impossible to refuse.

Her breath escaped in a shuddering sigh as he stroked down her inner thighs to their apex. His hands stole inside the loose fabric of her shorts to caress over the increasingly damp cotton of her panties. She made a sound halfway between a moan and a wordless demand and closed her eyes. His thumbs worked their way under the elastic of either leg opening, touching for the first time upon unexplored terrain, parting, probing gently until her hips rose up in welcome, reaching for him in tiny, instinctive thrusts. She was hot with anticipation, and the shorts had become an intolerable restraint. With trembling hands, she undid them, lifting so he could slide them and the unnecessary shield of her underwear down her long legs and out of the way.

It was dark, her natural hair color, a soft curling mat of it centered between bronzed legs and belly upon a delicately pale bikini triangle of protected skin that opened to ripe secrets in hues of glistening coral. He bent, tracing his tongue along one firm inner thigh as he coaxed her knees to grip either side of his shoulders for stability. Her breathing fell into a broken rhythm of anxious expectation until he finally reached his destination. Then it stopped altogether as he tasted her for the first time, lightly so that her nerve endings shivered with want, then aggressively so that she would want for nothing.

She exhaled explosively and began gulping for air.

And when he inserted his forefinger to test for her readiness, her body exploded into seismic shudders that eased into tremors of aftershock as he lifted away. She lay spread and gloriously flushed before him, having reached the first plateau toward fulfillment, and panting for more.

A spear of misgiving shot through him. Her first time shouldn't be on a rough slab of stone, out in the open like some pagan rite of passage. She deserved better. She deserved fresh sheets and champagne and the purr of air conditioning.

"Sheba, maybe we should—"

Her knees clenched tight to hold him between them as she sat up to wrap her arms about his head.

"Shut up, Frank," she told him in a voice so low and gruff it was almost a growl. "Don't talk. Don't think. You do too much of both."

And she pounced upon his mouth like a hungry predator, feeding voraciously, devouring him with provocative nibbles on his lower lip and dueling with his tongue like a master swordsman until the power of speech and thought abandoned him and there was only Sheba. Tasting herself on him.

Without breaking from their kiss, she freed one hand to fumble with the zipper of his cargo pants. When her urgency threatened him with bodily harm, he finished the task for her, wriggling his trousers off his hips so her long legs could circle him, drawing her eager sex up against his aching counterpart.

There was no stopping, no slowing, no time for romantic platitudes or tender considerations. Scooping his palms under her taut bottom, he lifted her slightly and settled her over him. In one smooth move, they were joined as deeply and fully as a man and woman could be.

Sheba gasped into his kisses, her slender body quivering in a moment of shocked invasion and surprise. Then gradually, her breathing deepened and her mouth became demanding once more. And he began to move her in tiny lifts so she could get used to the sensation of him inside her, while he was almost undone by the tight gloving of heat that tempted him toward completion with each increasingly powerful stroke.

Once she caught on to the motion with an unholy zeal, she rode him with a startlingly athletic prowess. She was strong and toned and his equal in every way, able to match his movements and his desires so perfectly, the sense of scalding bliss was more euphoric than any drug. Rising and falling until he was gritting his teeth against the urge to blow like a booster rocket hurtling the Space Shuttle to the moon and beyond. Sheba fisted around him with a savage suddenness.

As he gave one last hard thrust to launch her skyward, her breath sucked in then released along with bone-rattling spasms that shook her all the way to the toes.

Then there was no delaying the earth-shattering send-off, convulsing through him until his knees went to jelly.

They leaned against one another for basic support, breathing in hurried snatches, dazed beyond comprehension.

Then Sheba's lips moved against his, slowly, softly, seeking a response he almost didn't have the energy to give. With her hands still locked behind his head, she leaned back to regard him through slumberous, self-satisfied eyes.

"That was fantastic, and you are phenomenal but I'm getting rock burn on my butt."

His grin split wide. After a long, hard kiss, he yanked up his pants and retrieved her bottoms. Once she was clothed, he wasn't sure what to expect. Shyness, remorse, possibly anger. But it was humor she rallied behind.

"There's something to be said for virgin sacrifice. I regret I have only one cherry to give in the pursuit of happiness."

He continued to grin, wolfishly.

"Who said I was planning to let you settle for just once?"

TWENTY

As they lay side by side on the sleeping bags they'd zipped together inside the privacy of their tent, Cobb made suitably sympathetic noises over the aggrieved state of her scraped backside then looked arrogantly pleased when she vowed it wouldn't sideline her from further activities. Then he pushed her to prove it by stripping her down to the skin and putting her through an exhaustive battery of sensual tests of ingenuity as well as skill.

She excelled in all of them beyond his wildest fantasies, all without him taking off more than his shirt.

When she finally cried uncle, it was more to slow down the moment than to postpone it. Though Cobb promised to let her get some rest, he continued to shape her small breasts within his palms, teasing her nipples into perennial points between thumb and forefinger to let her know it was only a time out, not game over. Then, he paused in his caresses when he came to a two-inch ridge of raised scarring along her ribs just below her left breast.

"What's this from? Knife fight?"

His tone was teasing, but her candid reply scared the hell out of him.

"Pitchfork, actually."

"You're joking."

"I am not. I don't joke about my work. I was collecting some data in a small Slavic village when one of the farmers decided because of my extensive knowledge in matters of the occult that I must be a witch. I must have set a new record in the 800 meter dash that night." When he was silent, she taunted, "What did you think I did for a living? Sat in a hotel room dictating into a tape player about rumors I heard in the lobby bar?"

He got the feeling he was just beginning to understand.

"That's nothing. Check this out." She moved his hand to the back of one trim thigh, where he felt an odd pattern of marks. "Crocodile," she informed him rather proudly, "from the Outback where I was categorizing folklore and decided to take a swim. Lucky for me he was just a little nipper."

"Pretty tough chick, aren't you?" He sounded impressed in spite of himself.

"I am when I have to be. And what about you, tough guy. Show me your scars. From the line of work you're in, you must have a road map of them."

He rolled up on his side to regard her with an indulgent smile. "And what do you know about my line of work?"

Her expression sobered as she reached up to trace the jagged line marring his cheek. He didn't flinch, but she could feel his tension beneath her fingertips. "I know it's dangerous work. I know you put your life on the line over and again for people who don't give a damn about you. But then, you don't give a damn about them either. Why do you do it, Frank? It's got to be more than the money."

"Why does it have to be?"

She could sense him trying to wriggle that impersonal distance back between them. *Oh no you don't, bub.* He wasn't going to escape through either cocky attitude or sly avoidance. Not this time. Not when it was so important for her to understand what made him tick.

"Because I can see past that bad ass act to the decent guy you try to hide."

He put a hand over his heart in a dramatic gesture. "You've found me out. I'm just a pussycat wearing tiger stripes."

She touched his forearm where a thin white line started and ran across his elbow. "Where did you get this? Playing tennis at Club Med? Or Club Fed?"

"I got tossed off the hood of a car cornering at about forty-five miles an hour. The surgeon took out enough gravel to fill a five-gallon aquarium bottom." And he sounded rather smug about that, too.

"And what about this?" She pointed out a small scar below his left shoulder where it was nearly hidden by tufts of chest hair. "Someone try to break your heart? Don't tell me. Knife fight."

"It wasn't much of a fight."

His voice was so soft and empty of emotion, the hairs prickled instinctively at her nape. She flattened her palm over that long-ago wound and felt his heart beat hard and fast beneath it.

"Frank, talk to me."

He had the eerie ability to look right at a person and yet through them, the way he did now as he answered her request, starting at a place she hadn't expected. With family.

"My dad was a private pilot. He had learned to fly in Korea and loved it. He had a corporate job that required him to shuttle industry bigwigs to their meetings along the East Coast. My mom hated it when he was gone. She'd be up all night prowling the house and there at the airport waiting every time he got back. And I'd go with her when I wasn't in school. Only one late night, he was landing in this nasty mix of sleet and snow and something went wrong. He landed short of the runway. They were all killed on impact."

Sheba's eyes teared up instantly. Her voice was choked but gentle. "How old were you?"

"Eight."

"And you were there?"

He didn't have to nod an affirmative. She could picture the explosive impact in the brief glittering shadow that crossed his gaze. But he blinked, and it was gone.

"My mom fell apart. She started with prescription drugs to get through the funeral and then started washing them down with whatever was in the liquor cabinet. She just couldn't seem to get her life on track again. I guess I wasn't enough of a reason for her to hold on." Emotional volumes were spoken in that one flat admission.

"Within the year, we'd lost our house and the cars, and our old friends stopped coming around. Mom's new friends came and went. I stopped going to school to do odd jobs so we'd have money to eat, but there was never enough for rent, even for the crummy dump we lived in. There was rarely any heat and a bathroom shared by the entire floor where you'd have to step over winos and guys shooting up heroin. The filth and noise were everywhere. I couldn't be scared because I had to take care of my mom. She'd stopped caring about anything but her bottle of booze and pills. Then it went from pills to some real bad stuff."

His jaw clenched down on the rest. That's all he could say about the truly dark times when she wouldn't know him or would plead with him to go out in the night to steal enough to pay for her next fix.

"I never blamed her, though. It wasn't her fault that she wasn't stronger. And it wasn't my fault that I wasn't old enough to take her out of that cesspool. Maybe I could have if I'd had enough time, but time ran out when I was fourteen.

"She had a new guy coming around, bad news all the way. I'd gone out to hustle some money shooting pool, and that's when he decided that she'd been siphoning off his drug supply. He was in the process of teaching her a lesson with the butt of his pistol when I walked in. I guess I surprised him. I never even knew he'd shot me until my mom started screaming for help. Then he shot her, too. She died before I could get to the phone at the pawn shop next door. Nobody would help. And of course, nobody heard a thing."

No wonder he'd understood her pain so well. He'd lived it himself.

"What happened to you?"

"I survived. I told the cops everything I knew about the guy, but they just didn't seem all that interested in expending the manpower to track down some drug addict's killer. And were less interested in how I was going to get by. Until the sonuvabitch turned up in an alley with a knife in his throat. Then everybody wanted to talk to me again."

Quietly, she asked, "Was it self-defense?"

He stared her straight in the eye, never blinking. "No. It was justice."

And a dark, savage part of her understood and agreed with

that cold pronouncement.

"Well, to make a long, sordid story short, one of those interested parties was impressed by the rather lengthy rap sheet I'd managed to rack up for my tender years. Just small stuff mostly, petty larceny, truancy, just stuff I had to do to get by. And then he offered me another way to get by, a way that would make the most of my 'talents' and street smarts. He and his associates needed a minor with a cool head to play a role in one of their little games of espionage. I'd had a good upbringing, so I was civilized with just a few rough edges, and that's what they needed. They'd give me a new name, a new past and the means to finish my education. And I'd do things for them."

"They were the good guys?" she asked hopefully.

"Technically, but the things they did for the good of the country the country didn't really want to know about. And I didn't care, either. I had clean sheets, a warm place to sleep and quiet...God, it was so quiet. No sirens, no gunshots, no fighting or sixteen different kinds of music blaring. Clean and quiet. I would have done anything for those things. And I did, Sheba...I did anything they asked me to do, without thought, without question."

He waited for her repugnance, her horror to surface, but instead when she spoke her words were honed to a sharp edge of admiration.

"And I bet you were damned good at it, too."

"Oh, yeah. The best. Men without conscience are always in demand."

Before she could argue that definition, a soft voice intruded.

"Mr. Cobb, your call went through."

Without a word of explanation or excuse, he was up and out of the tent.

And after he'd gone, Sheba wept quietly for the innocence he'd lost at such an early age and out of pride for what he'd risen above.

For although Frank Cobb might paint himself as all black and no white, Sheba knew all about shades of grey. For those were the same shadows she lived in, and it was time the both of them discovered the light again.

***

"Cobb, what's going on?"

Greg Forrester's voice cut across the halves of the hemisphere to slap romantic notions from his head. Like a good soldier, he snapped to to deliver the bad news.

"Lemos was attacked out in the jungle by Alexander. I don't know his status. He was pretty bad off."

Forrester brushed off the young scientist's life with a callous, "Too bad about the project."

Cobb's jaw clenched. He hadn't liked Lemos for a lot of reasons, but the man didn't deserve to be tossed aside like worn-out slippers. "I'll let you know his condition when I have news."

But Forrester couldn't even pretend a polite interest as he demanded, "Tell me about Alexander. Are you sure?"

"Yes. He's here."

He could almost hear Forrester salivating through the air waves. "You've seen him? Talked to him?"

"Let's say I recognize his work. And he's approached me."

"Excellent. Excellent. I want him, Cobb. Alive. Do you have everything under control down there?"

A subjective notion, under control. "Yes, sir."

"Find out all you can about him but make no moves against him. Let him think he's safe for the time being."

"He's threatened Dr. Reynard."

"Who?"

"The ethnologist who met me down here."

"Oh. The problem being?"

"I'd just as soon she not get hurt."

"Then get her the hell out of there. She's served her purpose. We don't need Lemos anymore, so put her on the first plane back to the States. You don't need any distractions."

"But she still has business to take care of."

"I don't give a damn about her business. We don't need another Stacy Kimball mucking things up for us. Take care of her, Cobb. Take her out of the picture."

"Excuse me?"

Just what the hell was Forrester asking him to do?

"Figure of speech. I need you to focus on Alexander. He's your goal. I'm going to have a unit of men briefed and on a plane by tomorrow morning. They'll be at your disposal."

"Sir, you can't send armed soldiers into Peru. Armed American soldiers."

"I can do whatever the hell I please. Do your job, Mr. Cobb. I don't pay you to think, just to act. I want Alexander. Don't you dare let him slip away again."

"Oh, you can count on that. Believe me. I won't let him get away."

"Good. Good man. Take care of the woman. Get her out of the way and find Alexander."

"Isn't that what you pay me the big bucks for, Mr. Forrester?"

And as he said that, he turned to see Sheba framed in the doorway. He had only to glimpse her stony expression to know she'd heard everything.

Oh, hell.

Before he could sever the connection with Forrester, she was gone. And he knew in an instant he'd lost the only valuable thing he'd ever come close to possessing.

***

She was seated in the darkened tent, arms about updrawn knees, her face in deep shadow. Though her breathing was rough with tears, her voice sliced with Ginsu precision.

"You're not packing me off, Cobb, not until I finish what I've come here to do."

"Sheba–"

"No, you listen to me. Sorry if it mucks up your plans, but I'm staying right here. You go do whatever it is you have to do. I won't get in your way."

"Sheba, you're in danger here. I wanted you out of his reach. You don't understand what he is."

"A monster? That's what he is, isn't it? And you're wrong. I do understand, probably better than your boss in Seattle and maybe even better than you. And I'm not the only one in danger. He's after you, Frank. I can help watch your back."

He was so stunned his entire thought process jerked up after slamming into the speed bump of one realization. She wasn't angry with him for doing his job.

She was worried about him.

He went down on his knees in front of her, his palms cupping her damp face so he could pull her up into his fierce kiss. She tasted of salty tears and bittersweet hopes of a happily-ever-after ending to the emotionless void he'd existed in. She didn't respond at first, surprised then rebellious but finally conquered by the persuasive furl of his tongue along her tightly seamed lips. She opened to him with a surrendering sigh.

His hands slid down her arms, lifting them, looping them about his neck. His fingertips burrowed under the bottom edge of her snug tank top and sought out the tiny mounds of her breasts pulled taut by the upraised position of her arms. Her nipples pebbled at his touch, becoming a temptation he couldn't ignore. In a quick move, he had shucked her out of the scrap of white cotton knit. She sucked in her breath as he fastened over one of those rock-hard little nubs, softening it with the attentive moisture of his lips, elongating it with the hard suction of his mouth, shaping it with the curl of his tongue then exciting her into helpless shudders with the nip of his teeth.

Sheba clutched at his short hair, hanging on for dear life, as if by letting go she might lose him. She knew that moment would come eventually, but now, now while he was tormenting her with that sassy mouth, he was hers. And there was no way she was going to surrender even a second of that bliss.

She arched into him, offering everything she had, everything she was, and he took greedily, gratefully. Voraciously. When their clothes were gone and he was firmly implanted within her, she clamped her hands upon his hard flanks to hold him still for one glorious moment, to feel, to revel, in how good he felt inside her, around her. No matter what else might happen, she would always have this moment, this perfect joining. And that made it all worthwhile.

He lifted up on his elbows to look down upon her. In the darkness, she couldn't distinguish his features.

"What? Something wrong?"

"No, Frank. Everything's right for a change."

She could imagine his arrogant grin and pulled him down to meet her urgent mouth, to stop the silly, sentimental words he probably didn't want to hear.

Words crowding about her heart where they ached with longing and, for this moment, happiness.

The words *I love you.*

***

"I'm not leaving, Frank."

He muttered softly, nudging his face against her neck. "I wouldn't let you."

"In the morning. I'm not leaving until all my questions are answered."

He nuzzled her ear. "Isn't that what we've been doing, Doc?"

She started to push him away then ending up hugging him closer. Damn irritating man, anyway. The feel of him was like an addicting drug; she just couldn't say no even when common sense told her to quit. She rubbed her palm over the cap of his shoulder then charted the hard swells of his arm with lingering appreciation. She was a pragmatist. Enjoy while you can.

"I'm going to take the vine to see if it will open up my memories."

He was still, only the soft pulse of his breath stirring against her throat as he considered her words. Finally, he said, "Whatever you want, Doc." Contrarily, his arms tightened about her.

"And then I'm going to help you catch a vampire."

More silence, then a noncommital, "We'll talk about that later."

"We're in this together, Frank. We share the same demons."

They'd just shared a helluva lot more than that.

And in the darkness, with her warm, lithe little body wrapped about him, Frank Cobb's cynical mind touched upon a truly awful logic. Was that what this was all about? Had she given herself to him in order to make her battles his own? He knew first hand how far a woman would go to have her way. Had Sheba gone the distance just to manipulate his allegiance? Was she any different than Forrester, using him to get what she wanted, securing his loyalty with the temptation of exorbitant pay?

He didn't want to believe it.

He didn't want it to matter.

But as she fell into a satisfied slumber beside him, he knew that it did.

***

Dawn seeped in like the ominous cloud of vapor hugging the valley floor beneath them, cloaking all within its impenetrable embrace. Mist smothered their camp, glistening on the hundreds of spider webs strung from plant to plant in a delicate weave. For that slice of time, they were suspended in a world without boundaries, without reference points. An illusion, like Sheba's dreams, with reality just out of reach.

Today, she would grab hold of that truth and learn what was real.

And she was not afraid. Not as long as Frank Cobb crushed her hand in his.

She lay stretched out on the altar, where last night she'd sacrificed her innocence and this morning, she'd try to rend through the veil of her ignorance. Anticipation spiced with just a hint of apprehension tickled through her belly as she waited for something to happen.

"Close your eyes and count back from ten," Ruperto was saying.

"*Chunka, isqon, pusac, k'anchis, soqta, pichq-a, tawa,* three, two..."

Frank didn't like it. Not at all. Her hand went limp in his, and when her eyes opened, they held the blank sheen of catatonia.

"Sheba."

"No," Josef hissed at him. "Do not disturb her dream state. It is dangerous."

So he bit down on his anxiety and watched helplessly as the woman he loved drifted through the surreal planes of her mind in search of the answers hidden there. Answers that might well link his quest to hers. There was a connection.

There had to be.

And this was a damned reckless way to look for it, in his opinion.

Sheba's sudden cry set the hairs on the back of his neck and along his arms up on end in a bristling of alarm. Her gaze was no longer empty but wide and wild and swirling with unknown terrors. The sounds she uttered, those guttural grunts of fear, were the ones he remembered when waking her from her nightmares. Wherever she was within her drug-induced journey, she was no longer alone. Whatever she saw was for her eyes only. And Frank couldn't help her.

So he remained aloof while she wandered through her nightmare. He watched, uninvolved while she struggled with her fears. And he waited, so knotted with dread and tension that he trembled as she ran from the truth within the confused corridors of her mind.

And he prayed. Not something he did often, but this morning, on this sacrificial site, he felt it was the appropriate thing to do. To call upon her parents to help her find her way back to him.

When she bolted upright into a seated position, Frank fought the need to embrace her while her stare still wandered through a world he could not see. Then she blinked, once, twice, and her gaze sought his with recognition.

And confusion.

"It's all right, Doc. You're safe."

The puzzled expression deepened into one of despair.

"What's wrong, Sheba? What did you see?"

She looked to him in a desperate disappointment. "I was right there. I can feel it. I can taste it in my mouth and smell it up my nose. I was there, back where it all happened. And lived through it all again.

"But Frank, Frank, I don't remember any of it. I don't remember what I saw."

TWENTY-ONE

Sheba turned to an impassive Ruperto Lemos. "Why can't I remember?"

"It's there," he reassured her gently. "Closer to the surface now where your mind will be able to reach it. Give it time to accept what it has seen as truth."

"Time? I've given twenty years of my life already. I have no more time to give." She was thinking of Frank Cobb and his superior planning her exit from Peru. "I have no more time. I need to know now. Where is the temple, Ruperto? Everything I must remember is there. I know it."

He shook his head. "No. You must not go there. Not with the key. It is too dangerous. You must leave this place. You must go back home and wait there for the truth to be revealed to you there."

"I am home."

Saying that, she realized the first part of the truth that had eluded her. She was home. This was home. She'd let fear and sorrow keep her away for far too long. Not again. This time, nothing was going to drive her away. Not even the determined mercenary whose goal was not her own and whose motives were still a mystery.

***

At eight o'clock sharp, a strange sound cut through the air. While Sheba and Cobb stood packed and ready, they were astounded to see a state of the art helicopter skimming over the treetops toward them.

Josef chuckled at their amazement. His explanation was simple. “I still work with the military from time to time, and they owed me a favor.” He shook Cobb’s hand with gusto and intimated, “Welcome to the family, bro.”

Before Cobb had a chance to question or deny that statement, the camouflaged chopper landed, kicking up enough debris to have them ducking and shielding their faces. All except Ruperto who stood unflinching in the whirlwind, his features softened with a benign smile. He looked surprised then pleased to be on the receiving end of Sheba’s hug.

“Thank you, Great One. I will finish the journey, and I will honor our people.”

“I have no doubts, child.”

With Sheba and Cobb wedged into jump seats, the military bird swept down off the mountainside like a thermaling eagle.

“Where to?” the crew yelled to them.

Sheba didn’t hesitate. “Txukamayura Lodge.” She met Cobb’s glance with a challenging lift of one brow. “I have to know, Frank. One of them is guilty as hell and will know the significance of this.” She put her hand to her shirt front, over the medallion.

He caught her meaning immediately. She was going to dangle herself as bait and see who snapped. His expression never changed. “You’re taking one helluva risk, Doc.”

“But I’ll have you there to protect me.”

He never so much as blinked. “We’re dealing with more than one problem. It could get tricky.”

“I think our problems are one in the same. I just don’t know how they’re connected. Yet.”

Cobb leaned back, appearing thoughtful. Watching him digest the situation with a professional calm, Sheba realized she would have preferred him to display a little more reluctance over using her to spring a trap. She didn’t expect any grand declaration forbidding her from placing herself in jeopardy, but a bit of concern would have been nice.

But then he’d already told her to remove herself from the jaws of danger, and she’d refused to retreat to a safe distance. He was only respecting her wishes.

Sometimes respect sucked.

***

The moment she saw Peyton Samuels, she knew something was awfully, terribly wrong.

Before she could ask, he came down off the front porch to place hands on either shoulder in a bracing gesture. By then, her heart was beating like crazy.

"He's dead, Sheba. Paulo died before they could get him here. I'm sorry. I know how much he meant to you, to both of us."

It wasn't until Samuels' voice broke on that last phrase that Sheba absorbed the shock of what he was saying.

Paulo was dead.

The enormity of it, atop all else, swarmed up in an unexpected wave of darkness. She felt her knees give as that blackness surrounded all her senses. Even the strength of Cobb's arms around her became a vague and distant reality. Vignettes from the past flashed like stereopticon stills upon the veil of her closed eyes. Paulo as a pudgy boy netting giant morpho butterflies. Paulo as an awkward teen, blushing as he vowed they would be together forever. Paulo as a handsome, self-confident man grinning as he greeted their boat, hugging her up tight and whirling her around until her head spun, like now.

And as the dizziness abated, Sheba realized she was no longer standing on the front lawn of the Lodge. The cloud obscuring her vision became the netting swaddling her bed, and the buzz in her mind the lowered voices of Frank Cobb and Peyton Samuels as they spoke softly on the other side of that gauzy barrier.

"Frank?"

She tried to sit up. A now-warm cloth tumbled from her forehead. Then Cobb was there to support her effort, cupping her elbows to ease her upright as if she were an old lady.

"Easy, Doc. You had quite a shock. Take it slow."

Paulo.

The remembrance brought a sting to her eyes and throat, but she fought that expression of grief because she had to know.

"What happened? Sam, what happened?"

The elder man perched upon the edge of the bed to take up one of her cold hands in his. His painfully tight squeeze conveyed his own disbelief and sorrow.

"The others said they don't know how he did it. One minute, he was too weak to open his eyes, and the next he was vaulting out of the back of the truck to run into the forest. By the time they found him, it was morning and he'd – he'd been gone for some time."

"Where is he, Sam? I need to see him."

He looked away uncomfortably. "We put his body in the freezer. It was the only way to keep him...until the authorities come for him tomorrow. The research center he worked for wants his body preserved."

Ice raced through Sheba's veins.

"Why?"

"They're taking him back to Seattle for study."

The irony of Paulo Lemos becoming part of his own research project was almost too much. Pain wrenched the objecting words from her heart as Sheba cried, "No. No, he'd want to stay here where he belongs. This is his home. He should be buried here with his family."

"I'm sorry, Sheba. It seems he signed some kind of waiver. The matter's out of our hands."

"You're saying Harper owns him?" The fragile tremor in her voice had Frank reaching to put his arm about her shoulders, but she flung it off, anger surfacing to supply the strength she needed. "That's ridiculous. I'm sure Ruperto will have something to say about that as his next of kin."

"You've seen that crazy old man?" Samuels' question held a tinge of bitterness.

"We spent last night in his camp." So much for the element of surprise. But Sheba was no longer thinking about traps and best laid plans. Not when her heart was breaking. "He's not going to let this happen. First they try to steal the country's antiquities and now its citizens. It's not right. I won't let them take him."

"Sheba, now's not the time for hysteria."

"I'm not hysterical. I'm mad. And I'm sick of organizations like Harper pushing us around. Harper doesn't care about Paulo. I don't even want to think of what they have planned for him. But you know, don't you, Frank? You know what kind of people they are and the kind of things they do."

He remained silent and stoic in the face of her question. But he knew. His failure to answer was his answer.

She swung her legs off the bed, blinking into the wooziness that still blanketed her brain. "I want to see him. I can't believe until I see for myself."

***

An armed soldier stood outside the freezer.

Sheba frowned, wondering what interest Peru's intelligence community had in the death of an economic botanist. Nodding to Samuels, the guard stepped out of the way so she could pull open the heavy door.

Seeing was believing in the worst possible way.

Paulo Lemos lay stretched out and frozen on the floor of the Lodge's huge walk-in freezer, like a side of beef waiting to be quartered. Through the clear freezer wrap, his grey features were composed by death's waxy permanence. There was no question about the cause of his demise. Twin puncture wounds scored his throat with ragged savagery. The cross Cobb had fixed about his neck for protection was gone. It hadn't stopped the vampire from making his mark a second, fatal time.

Sheba's single sob expelled in a vapor cloud. Moisture gathering on her lashes crystalized. But she wouldn't weep for Paulo. She would avenge him by helping Cobb attain his goal. Tonight, they would go vampire hunting and perhaps kill two quests with one stone.

"Are you all right?"

Cobb's question struck her as ludicrous. Sheba halted her restless pacing of his room to confront him. Seated on the edge of his bed, he looked cool and unflappable, untouched by the newest tragedy to rock her world. And she resented the hell out of it. "No, I'm not all right. The best friend I had in the world is dead, and the last words I had with him were hurtful. I shouldn't have left him alone. I should have come back with him instead of insisting on going ahead with what turned out to be a useless trip. Now, Paulo is dead and I know no more than I did when I began."

"What can I do?"

"What you should have been doing was your job. You were supposed to be protecting Paulo. Isn't that why they sent you here?"

His expression never changed. He absorbed her attack like an emotionless blotter with no lasting impression to mar the surface. "There goes my resume."

The bland remark brought her up short to quiver with upset and the need to strike out. "That's all this means to you, isn't it? Paulo wasn't a person to you. He was an assignment."

"I can't do my job if I get involved."

"Well guess what? You didn't do the job anyway. Paulo wasn't supposed to die. He was supposed to go on to do great things. He was supposed to..." She took a hitching breath, unable to control the sudden rush of sorrow and regret that clogged her throat.

"Maybe you should go back to the States with him."

His soft suggestion slapped the grief from her. "I'm not leaving."

"You may not have a choice once Harper's people get here tomorrow."

"What? They're going to pack me out against my will?" Her sarcasm died a quick death beneath his steady stare. "Why is the SIN here?"

"Probably to protect Harper's investment."

"Paulo's dead."

"But that doesn't make him any less valuable."

"Talk to me, Frank."

"Tomorrow the troops arrive from Harper. While they ship Lemos back to Seattle to be studied, they're going on a vampire hunt for Alexander. And what you want or I want won't matter a damn to them. They, unlike myself, only follow orders. But now that they have Lemos, Alexander might not matter to them quite so much."

"What do you mean?" She didn't want to hear, didn't want to know, yet still had to ask. Cobb's answer laid it out like cold cuts on whole wheat.

"Why chase after a vampire when you've already got one on ice?"

"But Paulo isn't–"

His meaning took her between the eyes like a sledge.

"Come on, Doc. Think. Do your job. You're supposed to be the expert here. Killed by a vampire, become a vampire. Isn't that how it goes?"

"On the late show, yeah. But in reality, I-I haven't a clue."

"But I know who would. I've got some suspicions I need to follow up on. It shouldn't take too long." He studied her pale features for a long moment, and finally, gratifyingly, his registered reluctance. That conflict of interest she'd been waiting so long to see as he considered his job and his involvement with her.

"Are you going to be okay by yourself?"

"It's daylight and dinner is in an hour. What could happen?" Her crooked smile dared him to name something. He pursed his lips, warning her not to get cocky with him. Then as he started to go, she placed a staying hand on his arm.

"Frank?"

"What?"

"I should have believed you sooner. Then maybe–"

"Then maybe, nothing. Don't second guess yourself, Doc. You did your best, what you thought was right."

There was more she had to say and no better time to say it. "What I said about you doing your job – don't listen to me when I'm being an idiot."

His hazel-colored eyes crinkled at the corners. "And I'm sorry for what I said about you being narrow-minded and self-centered."

"You didn't say that."

"Didn't I? Oh. Sorry." He grinned and planted a quick kiss on the end of her nose. "Stay here."

"I'd look kind of funny coming to dinner in your clothes. I have to go to my room. I need a shower and my own underwear, thank you."

"Be careful. Most accidents happen in the home." With that, he was gone.

Tomorrow. They had until tomorrow when the science Nazis arrived to take control. When that happened, she could no longer count on Cobb's support or Samuels'.

That left tonight to get her questions answered.

***

A small, subdued group gathered for dinner. Because of Paulo's death, Peyton had canceled the incoming group of tourist and university students, and most of the group that had come back with his body decided unanimously to travel to Lima where they would be questioned by authorities, rather than remaining at the Lodge, cut off from civilization. Where Paulo's body lay in state in the freezer. That left Peyton, Rosa Kelly, Frank Cobb, the two botanists who'd remained behind to gather Paulo's notes, and two newcomers. From their dark, unblinking stares, Sheba pegged them as Peruvian government.

Conversation stopped when she entered the room. It wasn't because she was wearing a short wrap skirt that displayed a goodly length of thigh with every step or the silky, sleeveless blouse unbuttoned to the center of her breastbone to reveal the hint of shadowed cleavage. She didn't kid herself. They were all looking at the medallion. Beneath the simple silver cross, it gleamed, old, valuable, unique.

And to someone at the table, worth killing for.

She slipped into the seat next to Cobb. His disapproval vibrated through his briefest touch as he tucked the chair in behind her. She met his flat stare.

Time to bait the trap.

And it almost broke her will to continue when Peyton was the one to snap it.

His stare riveted to the medallion. "Where did you get that?" Voice hoarse and without any polite preamble, he started to reach across the table before remembering himself. He withdrew the hand, but the question hung suspended.

"I've had it since I was a child. Why do you ask?"

"My wife had one just like it. The thieves who took her life stole it off her body. It was never found. I hadn't expected to see it again."

Sheba lifted the heavy oval, letting everyone get a good look at it. "Surely you're mistaken. It was in my mother's things. Perhaps something she inherited. It's very rare. I find it hard to believe there is another like it."

"I don't believe it, either. It looks like the same piece to me. She was always very protective of it. She even wore it while...she never took it off."

"How odd. Ruperto Lemos seemed to think it was the same one he gave to Cipriana, too. He grew quite agitated when I wouldn't let him have it back."

"It should be in a museum," growled one of the Peruvians.

"Perhaps I'll donate it in Paulo's name. He would have liked that."

She waited, but the topic seemed to fall away as the meal was carried in and served around. She found she had no taste for anything but a vengeful truth. Then Rosa blew the conversation wide open again.

"I hear you're leaving tomorrow."

"Where did you hear that?" Sheba asked in feigned surprise. Perhaps she wasn't the only one who learned things listening outside closed doors.

The older woman glanced at Peyton. "It's what the others in Paulo's group were saying. Now that there's no reason for you to stay."

"But Rosa, I have every reason. You see, my memories have started to come back."

Silence. Absolute silence.

"Isn't it amazing?" she continued, buttering her dinner roll while pretending not to feel their stares. Stares of surprise or shock? Or dismay? "After all this time. I guess Paulo was right. All it took was a trip back home. I wonder what secrets my mind has locked away? What a relief if they could put the mystery of my parents' death to rest after all these years. That's what I'm hoping, anyway."

She nibbled on the roll as the silence thickened. Was it because they didn't know what to say or because they were afraid of what she might answer?

Either way, she was certain someone at the table was squirming. Someone or both someones. Slowly, she lifted her gaze to study in turn Peyton Samuels and Rosa Kelly. Her uncle looked stricken, as if a piece of pork had gone down the wrong way. Rosa looked pensive, amused, but at whose expense?

Well, she'd thrown down the gauntlet. Now, let someone pick it up.

Maria Ruis slipped into the room, bending to whisper something in Frank Cobb's ear. He placed his napkin next to his dinner plate and pushed back from the table.

"Please excuse me a moment. There's something I must attend to." As he rose, he glanced at Sheba, the brief look conveying a single command.

Watch your back.

For the first time, she'd put a killer on the defensive, making herself their immediate target. And chances were good they'd strike tonight.

It was up to her to be ready.

***

Peyton Samuels may have built himself a luxury palace of pretended isolation, but he was far from cut off from the outside world. His office boasted a state of the art computer system for marketing and research, linking to a publicist and an expensive advertising firm in New York.

Frank Cobb didn't care about those things as he sat before the keyboard. He was anxious to discover what the reply to his earlier e-mail would yield. Were his suspicions right or off the mark?

He knew of only one source for the research he had in mind, and he'd sent that question a world away, through a guarded system of locked doors and cautious barriers should anyone attempt to follow.

Have a question about a vampire, ask a former vampire.

Besides, Redman owed him. He'd gotten a new start in

life and Stacy Kimball, to boot. And who would have a greater stake in catching Quinton Alexander than the man who'd been tormented by him for a century?

And there on the screen was his question in brackets.

Can they shapeshift into another physical form for an extended period of time?

And the reply.

Yes.

Cobb's smile was small and cold.

"Gotcha, you bastard."

TWENTY-TWO

When Cobb hadn't returned by the end of the meal, Sheba was forced to put her plan into motion on her own. Certain that he would not leave her for long, she began walking back to the bungalow as twilight stretched deepening shadows across the walk ahead of her. Her heart beat fast but not with fear. It was the aggressive rhythm of a hunter on the move. Only this hunter would sit and wait for the prey to come to her. Then she would have her answers and her revenge.

She left the lights off inside her cozy cabin, opting instead to touch off the wick of a single scented candle. The uneven flame sent odd shapes dancing along the walls as she prepared the snare for her victim. When she was finished, she stepped back to observe her handiwork.

Crude but effective.

With light low and the mosquito netting drawn about the bed, the blanket she'd rolled and placed beneath the covers resembled a sleeping shape. Her shape, any intruder would assume. She angled a chair into the corner by the door so she would not be seen by anyone coming in. Not until she had a chance to recognize them and greet them with the gun she'd borrowed from Frank's bedside table. If he had time to join the party, fine. If he didn't show, she'd just have to host it alone.

The waiting was difficult. She struggled to keep her mind clear of second guesses, those dangerous second guesses Frank had warned about. She wouldn't sit and blame herself for Paulo. She hadn't forced him to foolishly run off into the forest alone. She had not killed him.

Closing her eyes briefly to halt the burn of sorrow, she

made a silent promise to her dear friend, the friend preserved by her memories. She would see his death avenged. She would not allow the unfeeling firm he'd worked for to make his death into a mockery. They would not use him in death as they had in life, without care, without an appreciation for the unique individual he was.

She checked her watch.

Soon.

The truth would be apparent soon enough.

The strain made her head ache, or perhaps that was the scent of the candle, burning low now as the hour grew later. It's floral smell, now strong, was almost overpowering. She blinked and rubbed at her temple. That smell. What was there about that fragrance? Her breathing labored. The odor permeated all her senses like a drug until her heart beat loud and fast in her ears. The way it had that night in the jungle when she was running from...

From what?

Not from what. From whom.

A soft click sounded. Alert now in every fiber, Sheba watched the doorknob turn. Careful. She couldn't act too quickly, lest she spring the trap too soon and on the wrong person. It might be Frank coming to check on her.

She held her breath as the door opened slowly inward, momentarily blocking her view. All she could see was the shadow of a man detailed in silhouette upon the floor from the full moon shining in the night sky beyond.

He advanced into the room with a silent step, moving too easily, too silkily for a man of Peyton Samuels' size. She expelled a relieved breath and lowered the pistol.

"Frank, it's about time. I was beginning to think you were going to miss everything."

She stood and started to close the door. Then got her first look at her visitor.

It wasn't Frank Cobb.

It wasn't human.

Red eyes glowed hot in the dimness as lethal fangs snaked toward her throat.

***

Joaquin Cross stood in the Lodge bar making time with the lovely bartendress. As he was the only one in the room, she had no tactful way to avoid his conversation. Her smile was strained and her attention jumped to Frank Cobb with obvious relief.

"What can I do for you, sir?"

"Nothing, thanks."

"Would that she ask me that question. I could certainly think of something," Cross grumbled into his glass.

"I was actually looking for you, Mr. Cross."

"Oh?" His gaze slid from the young woman's cleavage to Cobb. "More questions, Mr. Not a Policeman? I hope you have a fat wallet."

"Fat enough. Actually, it's not a question. If you're not too busy, I'd like you to show me where you found that woman, the one who was killed."

"I told you."

"But I'd like you to show me. It's important. Now."

The Indian sighed, giving the shapely bartender a last lustful ogling. "Pay my bar tab for me?"

"Sure." A small enough price to pay. Cobb reached for his wallet, asking, "How much?"

"That's $87.50."

"You must be a thirsty guy, Mr. Cross." He placed a hundred dollars on the bar and told the young woman to keep the change.

"Thanks, mister," the young lady gushed, grateful on two levels—for the generous tip and for the removal of her creepy customer.

"Okay, *Americano*, let's take your tour. It'll be a short one."

The guide rolled awkwardly off the bar stool onto his good leg, then hobbled toward the exterior door. He moved quickly despite his ungainly stride, and as they stepped out into the night, Cobb ventured, "Mind if I ask you what happened to your leg?"

"Nothing dramatic. I tell the tourists I was bitten by a

caiman." His laugh mocked their gullibility. "Actually, I was born with it. If my family had had money, or if we'd lived in your fancy America, it could have been corrected by operations, but..." He shrugged eloquently. "I make do."

"You seem to do very well."

"Can't complain. The money's good and the pickings are easy. It was right up there, Mr. Cobb, where the walkway branches off."

Cobb preceded him down the planked walk, heading farther from the light of the Lodge and the soft, rhythmic music in the bar. In the silence, Frank listened to another beat: the step-drag of Joaquin Cross's footsteps as he followed behind him. He scanned the dark walk and the dense shrubbery.

"Is this where you found her?"

"Pretty close."

"It's secluded here. I'm surprised she didn't see it coming."

"They never do."

The warning shift wasn't in Joaquin Cross's tone, it was in his walk. From shuffling step drag to a pair of very solid footsteps.

And this time, Frank was ready. He pivoted, swinging with all his might to drive the spike he held deep into the guide's chest.

Caught by off guard, Cross had only enough time to shift his weight so that the sharp point pierced beneath his collarbone rather than through his heart. He let out a roar of pain and surprise as he stumbled back. He grabbed for the silver stake, howling as contact with the precious metal caused his flesh to smoke and sear. As he jerked it from his body, the illusion rippled like water, then faltered and failed.

The crippled Indian, Joaquin Cross became the handsome vampire, Quinton Alexander. A stunned and wounded Alexander. A vulnerable target. As Cobb bent to retrieve the silver stake, he reeled away in an attempt to escape his nemesis.

Cobb raced after the injured creature. He wasn't thinking about capture or his obligations to Harper. The need to put an end to this evil consumed him. The image of Alexander with his hand about Stacy Kimball's throat spurred him on. The sound of her weeping over her slain friend roared over any other considerations. The glitter of that tiny ankle bracelet set obscenely near Sheba's pillow blinded him to all else.

There was no way a monster like Alexander would survive another second if he had anything to do with it. Harper be damned. His career would be shot to hell, but that no longer mattered. Evil spawned evil, and if Harper got their hands on even a portion of what Alexander was, the potential was staggering. Stacy had been right about that; Sheba, too. He would dispose of Alexander then deal with Lemos before he became an equal threat.

Alexander headed for the observation tower. Unhampered by his pretended handicap, he took the steps in great preternatural leaps, slowed only by the crippling effects of the silver coursing through his system. That was Cobb's only chance of catching up to him, that and the hope that he would get another opportunity to drive home his vengeance—right through Alexander's black heart.

If he only had his pistol, he could have ended it without all the effort. But when he'd gone to get it, it was missing from his drawer. He had no opportunity to wonder who had pilfered it or why. He'd just make do with the weapon at hand. It could kill Alexander just as dead, and that was all that mattered.

By the seventh story, Cobb was wheezing. By the ninth, his lungs were on fire.

That's it. No more cigarettes for me.

He rounded the final turn of steps. Alexander stood on the platform, backed up against the rail. His features twisted into a hideous snarl of rage and pain that bared his unnatural fangs. His eyes glowed blood red. Cobb slowed, not underestimating the danger. Wounded didn't mean helpless. Trapped didn't mean caught.

"How did you know, mortal?" the vampire hissed.

"I know you, Alexander. Your vanity is your downfall. I knew you had to be close to admire your handiwork. Your habit for working the graveyard shift gave you away."

Alexander squinted. "Not even you are that good."

"Your forehead."

"What?"

"I noticed it before but thought it was just a birthmark. But it's not, is it? It's a burn. From this." He drew out Stacy Kimball's crucifix. "She put that mark on your forehead when you tried to kill us in her apartment."

The arrogant vampire put fingertips to the fading spot he combed his hair to cover. A spot shaped like a cross. "I'll remember that next time."

"There won't be a next time."

A vicious chuckled rattled from the creature. "And you're going to stop me, Cobb? Aren't you forgetting something? Or should I say someone?"

For the first time, Cobb paused in his headlong rush for revenge.

"Ah," Alexander gloated. "I see you have. Vanity, Cobb. I'm not the only one who suffers from that affliction. While you're here seeking to wipe the stains from your reputation, who's watching over your little lady friend?"

And Alexander watched with an unholy amusement as a sickening realization dawned.

"You thought I was the only danger to her? Once again, mortal fool, you were wrong. In her case, mine was not the prior claim."

"Then I guess I'd better put a quick end to you so I can get back to her."

"You're too late, my friend. Too late."

"Don't count on it, blood sucker. Punctuality is my favorite virtue."

And with that, Cobb attacked, flipping the silver stake from a jabbing to an overhanded stabbing position as he rushed the startled vampire.

Believing his charge to be one of imprudence rather than purpose, Alexander tried to sidestep him, but Cobb anticipated the move, feigning to the left as well. Furious at being outmaneuvered, Alexander's thoughts went to fight instead of flight. A blow to his forearm by one mighty swipe from Alexander numbed Cobb's hand as his attack was flung off.

The silver stake winked in the moonlight as it twirled end over end and disappeared into the night over the tower rail.

Eager to put an end to the game, Alexander grabbed for Cobb's throat, only to scream in fiery injury as he came in contact with Stacy Kimball's gift. Staring at his smoking palm, he cursed the power of the small silver cross and Cobb's ingenuity. Pain and frustration took the fun out of the confrontation. This puny mortal had gotten in his way for the last time.

"I am tired of playing with you, Cobb. You bore me."

And that said, he seized Frank by the upper arms and flung him bodily off the top of the tower.

But he hadn't counted upon Cobb getting a grip on his shirt front first.

They both went over the rail.

For an instant, time seemed suspended. Then the rapid downward plummet began. As vines and branches whipped past his face, Cobb frantically grabbed for a single saving purchase. He found and hung onto Alexander's ankle and, miraculously, his fall jerked up short. Penduluming wildly, he looked up to be stunned by the sight of Alexander hovering in mid-air. But he only had a moment to marvel as Alexander raised his other foot.

"I don't allow hitchhikers, Cobb."

The sole of his boot took Frank full in the face, shocking him into releasing his grip. He plunged several stories before winding his forearm about a clinging vine to halt his fall once more. While he scrambled desperately to find a solid hand or foot hold, the vine ripped away from the tower structure.

Then, there was nothing to stop his six story free fall to the ground.

He hit, the impact shattering through him. As vision haloed and wavered, he got a glimpse of Alexander's mocking features, then all went black. And through that endless void that led to death, a single thought delayed him.

Who would save Sheba?

"Mr. Cobb, stay still."

Samuels?

Frank tried to speak, but his mouth was filled with blood as his crushed ribs refused to allow his punctured lungs to fill. He opened his eyes to see the distraught older man bending over him. He could see his own mortality in the saddened stare.

Dammit, he couldn't die and leave Sheba alone. He'd promised.

Movement woke all sorts of hell through a body broken beyond repair. He managed to manipulate his hand so that it fell atop his open jacket. His fingertips brushed the metal case he carried. Seeing his intent, Samuels drew out the container then stared at the two vials in bewilderment. Frank withdrew one of them, nearly dropping it from rapidly numbing fingers.

"Inject me," he whispered. His words gurgled as he choked on fluid and lack of air.

Acting quickly and without questioning, Samuels filled the enclosed syringe with the dark liquid from the vial. He shoved up Cobb's sleeve and plunged the needle into a vein even as life ebbed from his grasp. And, empty syringe in hand, he waited and watched for some miracle to occur. For it would take at least that to restore a semblance of life to the broken form before him.

It started as a burning at his elbow, a pain keener and more centered than the agony of having his skeletal structure smashed into hundreds of puncturing pieces. It spread slowly because his heart had begun to labor and falter, moving Stacy Kimball's serum through his system at a maddeningly slow pace. But it was moving, streaking up his arm like fire, spreading into his chest upon tingling threads that reached out to battered and ruptured organs, supporting and rebuilding caved in ribs until his first decent breath pulled in life and hope in a ragged gasp.

His first faint words puzzled Samuels.

"Thanks, Doc. Now we're even."

The serum created by Stacy Kimball from the same vampiric elements that had made her lover an immortal, had cured her cancer and now repaired in him what went well beyond simple healing. With every beat of his heart, his strength increased and his senses sharpened. He knew...he just knew that Alexander was gone. And that left his thoughts clear to turn to another.

"Sheba." He sat up without even the slightest residue of pain. Samuels was gawking at him, dumfounded. "Sheba. Where is she?"

"I thought you'd know. I came looking for her when I heard the commotion overhead and saw you...fall. What the hell was that up there with you? Was it a man? It looked as though he was...flying."

Poor Peyton. He really hadn't a clue.

"I have to find her. She's in danger."

But if not from Alexander, then from whom?

He headed for the Lodge at a run. Amazingly, there was no restrictive tightness in his chest from years of abusing nicotine. His breaths came full and easy even when his pulse began to race. The wonder of it paled next to his worry over Sheba. What if something really had happened to her while he was absorbed with the need for his own revenge?

The kitchen was dark and smelled of pungent spices...and of something darker. A scent he recognized even before he saw the guard sprawled out upon the newly patterned tiles.

He didn't need to look inside the freezer to know that it would be empty.

Paulo Lemos had woken up hungry.

And now he was after Sheba.

TWENTY-THREE

Paulo Lemos stood before her, looking much like she'd last seen him. His skin was grey. His lips and lashes wore a thin crusting of ice. The ragged wound at his neck seemed shriveled and old. And his eyes, his eyes burned with unnatural fire from out of that frozen shell. His eyes were alive, but they didn't belong to the Paulo she'd loved since childhood. That Paulo was gone, killed by a fiend and now become one himself.

Monsters were real, and if she was going to escape this one, she had to act fast.

The gun with its silver bullets. All she had to do was point and shoot.

She lifted it with determination. It was not Paulo, she reminded herself. Paulo was dead. This was some unholy form using his body, staining his memory. Still, looking upon those beloved and well-remembered features gave her just an instant of hesitation. And that was all the time the ghoul needed.

He sprang.

Sheba pulled the trigger, but a swat of his hand to her forearm sent the bullet flying wide and the gun sailing in an impotent arc. He was fast, so fast. Sheba dropped and rolled, coming up to her feet next to the bed. Diving beneath the mosquito netting, she scrambled across the mattress, watching the flicker of his shadow through the filmy curtain. An involuntary cry escaped her as a powerful hand gripped her ankle and began dragging her, belly down, toward the bottom of the bed. His hand was cold, as cold as death. Wriggling wildly to free herself, she clawed up the covers and kicked at her unseen attacker.

And then, the loud crack of a pistol shot rent the night air.

Sheba screamed and broke loose as the thing that had once been Paulo fell forward into the netting. It shrouded his form in a gauzy wrap as he toppled onto the bed, tearing the curtains down around him.

Panting hard, Sheba looked up to see her unlikely savior. Rosa Kelly's bulk filled the door frame. She held Cobb's pistol in her hand. Her features were grim.

"We must go. Hurry."

Sheba skirted the motionless figure. "Go where?"

"To a place of safety. It's Sam, Sheba. It's been Sam all along. We've got to get out of here before he discovers that we've killed his creature and are on to his tricks."

"Uncle Peyton? I don't believe it!"

"Don't believe it. Stay here and be as dead as your boyfriend there. Or come with me and help me defeat him. Decide now, or I'm leaving without you."

"But Frank—"

"Is dead."

That stopped her like one of the silver bullets. Everything that was living and breathing inside her shuddered to a stop. "No."

"Samuels killed him. He figured it out, smart boy. But he wasn't smart enough to save himself. Would he want you to stay here and die or to live to fight another day? Sheba, he must have heard the shots. There's no time for tears now. We have to go. Now!"

She couldn't help Paulo. She couldn't help Frank. She could only survive.

So she ran into the jungle with Rosa Kelly.

***

A sick sensation spread through Frank's gut as he stood at the threshold of Sheba's room. Paulo was destroyed and Sheba was gone. No blood trail, no signs that she'd been injured. But where the hell was she?

He voiced that question to the man behind him.

"She's with Rosa," he answered glumly.

"And where would they go?" He grabbed the dazed entrepreneur's shoulders and shook him out of his stupor.

"Where would they go?"

"To where this whole nightmare started. To the temple. Sheba has the key, and Rosa's been waiting twenty years to get to the treasure inside."

"Rosa? I thought she was an environmental activist."

"She's a thief. We both were. We were using the Reynards and their contacts in the States to smuggle artifacts out of Peru. It was a great game while it lasted."

"What happened to Sheba's parents?"

"I don't know. Honest to God, I don't know. When my Cipriana died, I put my illegal ways behind me. It's what she had wanted while she was alive and the least I could do for her memory. Memory..What does Sheba remember?"

"Nothing. Not yet. It was a trap, and now she's caught in it."

Because he wasn't there to protect her.

Samuels wasn't through with his mournful confession. "I should have told her...about me and Rosa. I kept silent because I'm a coward. I didn't want her to be disappointed in me. She and Paulo were my only family. Are you going to tell her?"

"I'm not the morality police. What you did in the past isn't my business. Finding Sheba safe and sound is."

"You're in love with her." The statement voiced both surprise and, surprisingly enough, approval.

"Yeah."

Not exactly an overwhelming admission, but he felt it warm all the way through him with a power not unlike Stacy Kimball's serum. It left him feeling stronger. He had to tell her. With all the secrets he'd kept during his lifetime, this was one he needed to share. If he had the chance.

With a last look about the room and at the creature left behind, Cobb let his chill professionalism control his head and block the panic seeping in to fill his heart.

"Take me to that temple. I have a feeling we'll get all our answers there."

***

It was all so familiar.

The jungle. The darkness. The scent of decay and

dampness and that other scent, the sweet, cloying smell she couldn't quite place.

For a large woman, Rosa moved with amazing agility. Sheba was pressed to keep up, dodging fallen limbs and evading ankle-twisting vines. The big lantern Rosa carried flooded the path before them, while shadows crowded close on all other sides.

Tears blurred her vision, making Rosa's figure and the light on the forest floor waver in uncertainty. Sheba tried to hold in the anguish, the all-encompassing sense of loss. Frank...Paulo. Peyton Samuels. But mostly Frank. What difference did knowing the truth make if there was no one left with whom to share the rest of her life?

Knowing the truth wouldn't alter what had happened, and it shouldn't have made such an impact on the way she'd chosen to live. She knew that now with a twenty-twenty hindsight. She'd thrown away her past, her future, dwelling on what she couldn't change instead of changing what she could while it mattered. Frank Cobb had mattered. So had Paulo, and her relationship with her uncle. But only her feelings for Frank had been real. Paulo and Peyton had been immortalized slices of memories she could no longer rely upon.

She had no past and no more future. The truth was all that was left her.

She stumbled, falling hard to hands and knees upon the springy ground. A sound echoed in her ears. Breathing, harsh and labored and right behind her. She looked over her shoulder, but there was nothing there but unrelieved darkness. No one was following except the phantoms of her past. Something had been chasing her on that night twenty years ago. Someone. Those same sensations pushed in all around her—the sounds, the scents, the crawly panic and choking terror even now clawing at her throat. The same as in her dream.

The same as in her dreamquest.

And then she saw it, rising up out of the forest green, a pyramid of ancient stone thickly cloaked in decades of smothering growth.

The temple of the Fanged Deity.

"I've been here before."

Rosa turned at her hoarse claim. The glare of the powerful flashlight beam made ghastly jack-o'lantern-like patterns upon her face.

"So, you do remember."

"Not all, not yet. But everything here is so familiar. It's like it happened yesterday. Ruperto said it would come back to me in a rush if just the right spark was struck. When we were in the jungle, it was my dream come to life. The sounds, the...smells."

The scent overwhelmed her. The strong, sweet odor of gardenias. The smell that permeated her every nightmare.

The fragrance that had clung to Rosa Kelly for as long as she'd known her.

Understanding must have dawned like a sunrise in her expression, for suddenly she was facing Frank's pistol.

"It was you."

Rosa smiled thinly. "It's always been me. Me and Sam at first, then just me. You see, Sam forgot the golden rule of thievery. You never get involved with the mark."

Frank Cobb's exact sentiments.

Sheba fought off her choking anguish to put the pieces together.

"Cipriana Lemos."

"We had it planned out so perfectly. We'd heard the legends about this place and the treasure concealed inside. Sam was just supposed to romance her long enough to find the location and to steal the medallion. But he ended up being seduced by that insipid little twit. He couldn't even see that she stayed a virgin long enough to—"

"You were going to sacrifice her because of some silly legend?"

Rosa shrugged philosophically. "Not because we believed but because others did. If they thought we controlled their ancient god, we could control them."

Sheba shuddered at the horrible simplicity of it.

"So what happened to your perfect plan?"

"Sam nearly ruined it by marrying her. Then he refused to

have anything more to do with me. I couldn't let him just walk away. It was just a phase, just a passing lust for her pretty face. I knew he'd get over it when he focused on the treasure again."

"You arranged for Cipriana's death, didn't you?"

"I paid well to have it look like an accident. She was out of the way, and I had the medallion. But I still didn't know where the temple was."

Sickness stabbed through Sheba's belly. "But my mother did."

"Yes, she did. And she was very obliging about leading me right to it." Rosa gestured with the barrel of the gun. "Let's go inside, shall we?"

Sheba took an involuntary step back and found her arms caught in a crushingly powerful grip. She flung her head back to look into the face of Frank Cobb's demon.

"I thought it was time we were properly introduced. Or perhaps you don't recognize me without the limp."

"Cross. But how—"

"Magic. I'm at your service."

"Really? Then let me go."

"'Fraid not, doll. Let's go inside and take a look-see, shall we?" He propelled her forward, almost driving her to her knees. It was then Sheba realized the hopelessness of her situation. She was going to die here in the same place her parents' lost their lives and for the same purpose: Greed.

Rosa pulled down a tangle of overgrown vines, revealing a black hole leading into the heart of the tomb. With the lantern to light the way, she guided them inside where the air tasted of timelessness and an eternal wait.

Waiting for Sheba's return.

"So it was the two of you working together to scare the natives out of the forest." Get them talking long enough and maybe she could figure a way out of her dilemma.

"A stroke of good fortune, actually," Rosa boasted. "I was in Seattle, visiting Paulo. I'd grown tired of waiting for your return and decided I'd go track you down. Sam, damn him, would never tell me where you were. He must have suspected my motives went beyond mere fondness. So I figured I'd worm the information out of Paulo, the stupid boy. But I got distracted from that goal by a certain scandal whispering through the lab where Paulo worked. Whispers of a creature they'd captured in order to research immortality. Mr. Alexander, here."

The monster behind her gave a quiet chuckle. "Imagine my surprise when the ingenious and oh, so avaricious Ms. Kelly hunted me down and made me an offer I couldn't refuse: escape from my current and rather dangerous situation to a place where I would become a god."

"By pretending to be our people's resurrected deity. Very clever."

The sarcasm in her tone had him jerking her arms up higher behind her back, but she refused to cry out.

"You see, my naive little friend," Rosa continued, "this jungle has always been ripe for the picking, and I planned to pluck a king's ransom. Sam and I used your parents for our own gain, did you know that? No? We hid artifacts in the useless junk they sent back to the States. Who'd think to search gifts sent by godly missionaries. Don't look so shocked. You're as ignorant as they were."

Sheba's glare grew as hard as the surrounding stone. "Not any longer."

"There. I've completed your education at last. You were always so eager to learn all there was to know about worldly matters, much to your godfearing parents' dismay. After Sam and the Reynards were out of the picture, I kept my little industry going by threatening the silly natives with their own folklore. If they didn't appease their god with gifts of gold and treasure, he would return and slay them...the way he did that missionary couple."

"What?"

"In due time, my dear. Be patient. Your mind has conveniently locked out the truth for twenty years. Don't rush my story now. Anyway, they brought riches beyond belief, except the fools would only leave them in the place for traditional offerings, a very annoying little slide that shoots their gifts right into the heart of the temple."

"Where you couldn't get to it." Now Sheba laughed. "My ancestors prepared for vultures like you."

Rosa smiled bitterly. "Yes, they did. For years, my treasure has been safely growing, until those *huaqueros* exposed my new partner here where we had him safely hidden away. We had to move fast then, lest the curious start swarming. I enlisted Paulo's help, all very innocently on his part, of course. I had him bring you here by building up his hopes of romance."

Pain twisted through Sheba's heart. Hopes she'd cruelly crushed. She tried to distract herself by concentrating on the other pieces of the puzzle.

"So you paid off the two tomb robbers?"

"No. That must have been Sam. He didn't want the secret exposed any more than I did. And he tried his best to keep you away. But you couldn't stay away forever, could you?"

Sheba turned away from the smug look on Rosa's face.

"I knew you had the key, but the trouble was, you didn't remember. The tricky part was getting you to recall the past without exposing my part in it first. Quinn here was doing a wonderful job at keeping the unwanted out of the area to give us more time."

"And then my old pal Cobb tries to throw in the monkey wrench by seeing through my disguise." Alexander's tone held a grudging admiration.

"You killed him." Her voice shook with eddies of suppressed agony.

"I'd always planned to, but the time wasn't right the last time we met. I rather enjoyed the challenge he presented. But it was time to remove him from the equation."

Sheba winced at his callous dismissal of the man she'd loved. Her tone strengthened. "Because you knew he would have beaten you eventually."

"He would have tried."

"But why Paulo? Why did you have to kill him?"

"That was Rosa's idea completely. And they call me bloodthirsty. Not that I wasn't happy to oblige her."

The other woman paused to convey her vile logic. "That was to get back at Sam for deserting me. He and I were supposed to share this adventure together, but he chose family and sentimentality over wealth."

"And that was impossible for someone like you to understand."

She laughed at Sheba's scorn. "Fortunately, I suffer from no pangs of conscience or regret." Her smile grew malicious. "You've only yourself to blame for this turn of events. You had to display that medallion over dinner. I couldn't risk Sam's guilt getting the better of him. I couldn't let him spoil everything by spilling his guts, so we had to move fast."

They stepped into the huge central chamber. Rosa took out her lighter and touched off the torches bracketed upon the walls to illuminate the cavernous room and the monstrosity it contained.

Sheba cried out, sagging against the demon at her back. Horrible images assailed her, not dreams, not nightmares but memories more terrible than any imagined scene. This place lit by torches, a much younger Rosa using the medallion to open the lock at the base of the statue. Her poor unwitting parents leaning in close out of fatal curiosity as the pedestal opened and hell was released once more.

Sheba squeezed her eyes shut, but she couldn't block the graphic visuals that came pouring back across the barriers of time. Her mother's screams. Rosa falling to her knees in abject horror. As the monster worshiped by her people for centuries sprang from his imprisoning tomb to hungrily leap upon Reynard to feast upon his blood.

Sheba had seen it all from where she crouched in the shadowed corridor.

As the demon drained away her father's life, Rosa peered into the crypt, her features aglow with lust for the gold glittering just beyond her reach. And then...and then as she watched in silent horror, Sheba saw her mother's sacrifice. Not at Rosa's hands, but at her own.

"That bitch," Rosa spat out. "That sanctimonious bitch. She cut her own throat and threw herself into the creature's lair just to spite me and deny me what was mine."

Standing taller, prouder now that she understood it all,

Sheba said, "No, not for you. For our people. It was her duty as our guardian to keep the beast contained. She knew the only way to return him to his rest was with the sacrificing of her own blood. And after witnessing my father's death, her grief overcame her reluctance to do that duty, no matter how awful. It was a time to be brave."

No matter who it left behind. A young girl hiding in the shadows who saw her whole world collapse in an instant as the monster dove back into the tomb, her father's emptied body still impaled upon its claws, to claim it's royal blood offering.

Sheba saw that girl in her mind's eye racing across the chamber, screaming her mother's name. In her anguish and terror as she saw the opening begin to close, she gripped the medallion key, trying to turn it, so she could join her family. But the key wouldn't turn. It came loose in her hand. And that's when Rosa saw her.

"It was you chasing me that night."

"And I would have caught you, too, you brat, if I hadn't twisted my hip when I fell." Then the flash of fierceness was gone from her expression and she smiled, all benign and totally false charity once more. "But I caught you this time, now didn't I?"

At last, Sheba understood everything. It all made a horrible kind of sense. Peyton's guilt, Paulo's unexpected passion spurred on by Rosa's goading, even the memories that had escaped her. The shock of what she'd witnessed combined with the illogical idea that her mother chose to join her father in death rather than life with her, topped by Rosa's betrayal, had driven all knowledge of the event from her adolescent mind. And while she had spent her life lonely, separated from family and the comfort of the truth, Rosa Kelly waited like a giant spider spinning her web of lies and murder to reap her reward.

Well, she wouldn't profit from the death of those Sheba loved.

"Give me the medallion."

Rosa extended her hand, impatient now after her twenty-year wait.

"Why? So you can wallow in your riches?" She twisted to look at the vampire behind her. "Is that what she told you? That this key opens the door to wealth untold?"

Quinton Alexander frowned suspiciously at her sudden, hearty laughter.

"Did you think she'd be honest with you after she's lied to everyone else she's ever known? Then you are a fool."

His grip tightened on her arms as he leaned closer. His breath brushed cold as impending death upon her cheek. "Fool, am I? And why is that? Tell me so I might share the joke."

"Don't listen to her, Quinn. She's just trying to make trouble."

"Then what harm can her words do?" he snapped, and Sheba saw a possible way out of her dire situation.

Divide and conquer.

"Why do you think she brought you all the way down here? Just to scare a few natives? For pure humanitarian reasons? So she could split her treasure with you? Think about it."

Alexander had no quick and cocky answer. That was good. He was thinking. Sheba pushed harder.

"She brought you here to do her dirty work, to take all the risks, to be her fall guy. Did you really think she was going to make you into a god? And share the power she's hungered for all her life? I don't think so. What do you think?"

Alexander looked from her to the increasingly agitated Rosa. "Why did you bring me here? Just so you'll have a trophy body to show while you hoard all the gold to yourself?"

"Don't be ridiculous. She's playing with your weak little mind."

"No more than you, I suspect." He hugged Sheba up close. "So what's your theory, smart girl?" His icy cheek rubbed against hers. "Cobb, for all his annoyances, did have excellent taste in women, did I tell you that?"

Sheba shut her eyes. Now wasn't the time to give in to her mourning for Frank. She had a lifetime to grieve for him, and that time would be painfully short if she lost her focus now.

She had her people to protect. She opened her eyes to glare at Rosa, concentrating on the treacherous female who had abused her trust, stole her family and her future but who would not feed off the superstitions of her mother's heritage.

But they weren't just superstitions, were they?

And now she knew why Alexander was here.

Her laugh was short with the irony of it.

"What?" Alexander demanded. "I grow tired of your games."

"Rosa brought you down here to distract a demon while she made off with the gold. You've been her expendable pawn since the start. You're the monster they'll hunt down when she's finished here. You'll be the scapegoat if you manage to defeat what waits inside that tomb of stone."

He took an anxious breath. "What's in there?"

"If it was just gold, why do you think she's waited so long to go after it?"

"She needed the key," he explained weakly.

"She needed me and she needed a way to stay alive long enough to use me. There's a monster inside there, and when the door is opened, it's coming out for you. Then, while it's tearing you to pieces, Rosa will use me as an offering to gain control of it. Her virgin sacrifice."

"She's lying to you, fool," Rosa insisted angrily. "Why are you laughing, stupid girl?"

Sheba smiled tightly. "Because I gave Frank Cobb more than my trust...and my love."

"Bitch!"

Rosa's fisted blow rocked Sheba's senses. While she tried to shake off the pindots of pain and disorientation, the medallion was snatched from around her neck.

"Nothing but trouble, your whole damn family. Cipriana with her naivete and harlot's body tempting Sam away from our plans, your mother with her grand gesture of martyrdom. And now you think to steal away my future for a few minutes of blind rutting with a stranger. What a waste."

"You're the fool if you believe that," was Sheba's soft reply. "Obviously you know nothing about love, or you'd understand why the women of my family acted the way they did, the way I plan to."

"What, by dying well in the name of nobility? In the name of love? Fine. I won't stop you. But die, you will. And now."

With that, Rosa strode across the chamber to insert the medallion at the base of the statue.

And turned.

TWENTY-FOUR

"Wait!" Alexander squealed as the stone began to rumble and shift upon the dirt floor.

Rosa stepped back, her features flushed with greed and eagerness. She pointed the gun with its silver bullets at her former partner. "Let her go, Quinn and get ready to meet your match. Thanks for all your help, but you're one loose end I don't want to have to deal with later."

Sheba stumbled free as Alexander watched the black hole yawning wider and wider as the stone rolled back. Fear panted from him in short, harsh bursts. Rosa gestured to her with the pistol.

"Come over here, Sheba. While Quinn keeps the creature busy, you'll help me remove the treasure."

"And as a reward for my help, you'll cut my throat and throw me in that hole so the monster will return and leave you with its riches?"

"That's the plan."

"Your plan stinks."

"I agree."

The sound of the intruding voice nearly brought Sheba to her knees.

"Frank."

Before Quinton Alexander had a chance to turn in amazement to greet a nemesis surely resurrected from the dead, he winced at a sudden sting in the side of his neck. Stumbling back in surprise and dismay, he put his hand to his throat and glared at his enemy.

"What was that?" He staggered, expression contorting as he felt the first stirrings of change burning through his body.

He went down to the dirt floor on hands and knees, snarling in rage and pain.

"A little gift from Stacy Kimball. Enjoy." To Sheba, he said, "Always ready, but unfortunately not quite as punctual as I'd like to be."

A silly smile spread across her face as his marred but oh, so beloved features blurred through the veil of her tears. "You're forgiven, this time."

"No!" Rosa stood by the still-opening stone, looking from the portal leading to riches to the interlopers bent on snatching it from her. She pointed the pistol at Sheba's breast. "You will not keep me from what is mine!"

The shot echoed in the cavernous chamber, but it was Rosa who clutched at a mortal wound, not the equally startled ethnologist. Through rapidly glazing eyes, Rosa stared at Peyton Samuels.

"Nothing's keeping you now," he said softly. "You've gotten what you deserved."

As Rosa collapsed back against the foot of the altar, Sheba ran into Frank Cobb's open arms, hugging to him with a desperate possessiveness. For a long moment neither said anything, then she leaned back to strike his chest with her fist and complain in a wobbly voice, "You scared the hell out of me."

He stroked her hair back with a tender gesture, his grin full of cocky certainty. "Oh, I think you have plenty of hell left over."

Her brows knit together in concern as she noticed the crusted blood stains on his chin and shirtfront. "Are you all right? Alexander said he'd killed you."

"I'm sure he did his best, but thanks to your uncle, he didn't quite succeed."

She glanced over his shoulder to where Peyton Samuels stood uneasily awaiting her judgment. A riot of emotions swirled through her, not the least of them hurt and fury at his betrayal of her parents, then sadness at his many losses. "I think we have some talking to do, Uncle Sam."

"You're willing to listen?"

"And to learn how to accept what's done and over and move on."

As they spoke, Rosa Kelly was breathing her last. Bright splashes of her blood fell upon the stones and down into the maw of the tomb. Her thoughts were of the treasure, of seeing it close up, of touching it, claiming it. She tried to drag herself toward the opening. And as she tried to focus her failing eyesight, she was mesmerized by twin points of light, fiery dots that grew larger and more compelling. Her hand dropped away from her mortal wound as she stared, hypnotized by the steady glow of red.

And when she finally realized what came with those fascinating beacons, it was too late to even scream.

With a ravenous roar, the ancient deity sprang from its imprisoning bastion, lured by the scent of blood and its eternal hunger. While Sheba, Frank, Samuels and a writhing Alexander watched in helpless horror, the beast fell upon Rosa Kelly to suck up the last of her life force.

It was the nightmare of Sheba's restless dreams, the horror that had destroyed her family and now threatened the others that she loved. As it straightened from Rosa's drained corpse, her blood dampening its hideous teeth, Sheba beheld the stuff of legends—all the terrors, all the evils, all the destructive powers embodied in the creature before her. She recognized it from the descriptions told to her in frightened whispers. Half-beast, half-man with red eyes and fangs.

And she'd scoffed. She hadn't believed, not until this moment, not even when her memory returned. After all, how accurate could the recall of a traumatized child be? Some of the details must have been exaggerated. Nothing could be as horrible as the tales told around her ancestors' fires.

Until she saw it with her own eyes.

Logic couldn't deny it. Reason couldn't explain it away. It was what it had been for centuries— the bane of her ancestors' existence, the force behind their fears and the focus of their worship.

And it would not be satisfied with only one sacrifice now that its rest was disturbed.

"Run!" Samuels cried in panic. But then he stood paralyzed as the creature growled and pinned him with its red glare.

"No," Sheba cautioned. "We've got to get it back in the tomb. We can't let it leave here. It mustn't escape. It will destroy my people. It's power will be unstoppable once it's had its fill of victims."

"I, for one, never cared to play the victim." Frank set her behind him as he measured the distance between them and Rosa's body. "I think I can make it."

"What do you mean?" She gripped his arm.

"To the gun. It's still got nearly a full clip."

"Silver bullets aren't going to stop this monster!"

"I'm open for other suggestions." He pried her hand off and began to slowly circle to the right. The beast immediately tracked his progress, the spines bristling up along its backbone. "Sam, distract it for a second. Don't be a hero. I just need a second."

"Any longer, and I'll be a late snack," the old man muttered. But he obligingly waved his arms and called, "Over here, you spawn of hell. That's right. I may be old, but I've still got juice. Come and get it."

It moved like heat lightning, streaking across the room in a flurry of teeth and claws and bloodied froth. As Samuels did his best to evade the charge, Frank dove, coming up with the pistol. As the creature snapped for Peyton's throat, Cobb fired, again and again, the bullets penetrating the unnatural form without effect until his clip was empty.

They were going die.

Sheba couldn't let it happen. She couldn't surrender up these two men who meant everything to her, not for the sins of ignorance and greed of her people's past. Only she had the power to stop it now. She, with her royal blood and trembling nobility, could save them.

"Here!"

At her shout, the beast turned, lips peeling back from the enormous fangs in the face that was almost human.

Sheba stood at the gateway to the tomb holding the blade Rosa had planned to use for her sacrifice. As she brought the blade to her throat, she met Cobb's agonized gaze. She smiled as she told him, "I love you, Frank. Don't ever doubt that."

Realizing in a splinter of a second what she meant to do, Frank Cobb ran. He poured all his energy, all his strength—both natural and enhanced by Stacy's serum—into that frantic dash across the chamber. His churning feet kicked up ancient soil. His desperate gasps for extra deep breaths drew in the air of another civilization just beginning to mingle with their own. From out of the corner of his eye, he glimpsed the creature as it streaked toward Sheba, but Frank was centered on one thing only, on the slender hand that began a martyred stroke.

He hit her like a linebacker. He heard the breath punched from her lungs in a grunt of surprise and impact. He caught the blade with one hand, his other arm encircling her waist to pull her away from the entrance in a violent roll just as the demon pitched at her in a frenzied rush that led it right through the opened hole and into the tomb. Cobb reached with a savagely sliced hand, grasping the medallion, turning it and wrenching it free. As he fell back on top of a winded and wide-eyed Sheba, the stone rumbled closed, sealing the beast in.

When he had his breath back, Frank levered up to adore her with his gaze.

"That was a stupid, stupid, stupid, brave and incredibly stupid thing to do," he admonished gently. "And I love you for it."

"You—?"

He halted the rest of her astonished question with an exquisitely eloquent kiss that answered all doubt in the matter of a few delicious seconds.

Heaven. It was heaven, the taste of his mouth, the taste of victory and accomplishment. And peace, at last. She could lay the past to rest and go on.

Suddenly, she pushed Frank away.

"Your hand!" She gripped his hand, dismayed by the pool of blood forming in his palm from the cuts across his fingers.

"I'll survive," he chided on the receiving end of her worries. "More scars, more stories to tell, Doc Sheba. Don't cry. I'm fine."

"I know. That's not why I'm crying. It's just..." Her words trailed off as she tore a strip from her shirt to wrap crudely about his hand.

He didn't question as he enjoyed her care. He knew. It was everything. Every overwhelming piece of a fantastic puzzle finally forming a picture for her to see. And now that she'd seen it for what it was, she could put it aside without looking at it again with the same horror and painful revelation.

"Where's your friend?" Samuels' question pulled them from their tender study of one another.

Cobb glanced about, but Alexander was gone. "He's no friend, believe me, and I won't mind leaving him behind. Let's get the hell out of here."

They exited the temple to find the jungle and the ancient stones bathed in the pure silvering of dawn. A silent gathering stood at a distance, watching, waiting to see who or what would emerge. In that group was Ruperto Lemos and his nephew, Josef. Josef smiled and nodded as Cobb displayed the medallion in his bandaged hand.

"Seal it," Josef instructed his people. "Hide it so it might be another century before the greed of man leads him this way again to look for what he should never find."

Sheba took the medallion from Frank and carried it to the two Indians who were family by blood and tradition. She handed the sacred key to Josef and pressed her palm over it.

"This should be yours. Guard it with care and lead the people wisely."

"You won't stay?"

She shook her head and glanced over at Frank with all the meaning in the world. "No. I've put all my demons to rest. There's nothing left for me to do here, and my whole life is waiting. But I'll be back. This is my home."

"There's more to do, cousin. There's always more to do. Remember that another time and come back to see us." He raised a hand to Frank. "Take care, bro. And take care of her."

"I plan to."

Just then the jungle stirred with the downdraft from a sleek, unmarked helicopter flying low over the trees.

Harper's cavalry.

"That your ride, brother?"

Sheba waited for his answer, relieved when he shook his head.

"Not mine. I'm flying commercial from now on."

***

The security team sent by Harper wasn't pleased with Cobb's report that the botanist, Paulo Lemos and the vampire, Quinton Alexander had both been destroyed and burned by the superstitious Indians. With nothing to take back with them except excuses and the unacceptable sting of failure, they had no reason not to honor Cobb's decision to stay behind. He wouldn't be welcome where they were going, where Forrester waited anxiously with his future in the balance for career-saving news that was not forthcoming.

Frank watched the helo lift off, with his arm firmly wrapped about his future. He didn't envy the crew the job of telling Forrester to start sending out resumes. He didn't envy anyone at all because he finally had everything a man could want. He turned to take Sheba fully into his embrace.

"Where to, Doc? I'm at your service."

Her smile was naughty. "I sincerely hope so." Then she looked pensive. "I heard of a tribe in New Guinea that was plagued by a supposed ghost walker..."

Frank touched his fingertips to those lush, unbearably kissable lips. "Haven't you had enough excitement for one lifetime?"

"What did you expect? A house, a yard, a mortgage and two point six kids?"

"The kids might be nice, but the rest is negotiable." His hands were busy roaming the sweet curve of her back and backside until she slapped at his bandage to make him wince.

"About New Guinea?"

"No vacation first?"

"We can honeymoon in the bush."

He grinned hellishly. "I plan to. But a little R & R would be nice."

"Come on, tough guy. I thought you liked it hot."

He squeezed her up tight against his chest. "The hotter, the better. Now, you'd better go talk to your uncle. He's got a load of guilt to dump. And be nice." He slapped her delightfully taut little fanny. "He's family."

Her gaze grew somber and serious as she studied him. "I love you, Frank."

"Scars and all?"

"Especially the scars."

He leaned forward to buss a kiss upon her brow. "Good. Now, go take care of family business. I'll be waiting."

She kissed him back, hard and quick. "You'd better be."

***

The underground corridors were endless black ribbons leading him nowhere except back to the central chamber of the inner tomb. There, Quinton Alexander sat down to rest. He was no longer distracted by the heaps of gold and ancient treasures that had delighted him at first when he'd dodged into the cavern to evade Cobb and possible consequences. How ironic that he would end up with the fortune Rosa Kelly coveted. He chuckled to himself.

He hadn't been alarmed when he discovered the stone had rolled across the opening, sealing him inside. He'd hoped there would be another way out other than the narrow slot through which the ignorant natives had fed their tribute. There wasn't. But that didn't really matter. He could become smoke and mist and easily escape through even the tiniest chink in the wall. He would get help from other greedy and unscrupulous men such as himself and retrieve the treasure later. He didn't know what had happened above in the battle between the demon and his enemies. Part of him hoped the beast had slain them all, but another part would miss the chance to exact a more personal revenge. Whichever it was, he couldn't linger. He didn't know where the creature had gone, and he wasn't interested in a confrontation in his strange state.

His mind felt foggy, his body strangely weak. What the hell had Cobb done to him? Once he got out, if Cobb was still alive, he would demand to know, just before he tore the bastard's throat out once and for all. He would toy with Cobb's woman for a while until she began to bore him and finish her for dessert. Then he would claim the treasure and, as a wealthy man, maybe he'd go back to the States. He had no enemies there now. Yes, the States. He'd had enough of the heat and the bugs and the inconvenience of jungle living.

That decided, he stood, summoning a change of form. And waited. Nothing. Again, with more concentration, he willed himself to thin and disperse in a fog so he could seep through the chinks in these cold, ancient walls to freedom.

Perplexed to find he was still whole, Alexander put a hand to his chest to discover an alarming alteration. He felt his own heartbeat beneath his palm.

"No. It can't be."

He drew a fearful breath that shook with the numbing truth just beginning to reveal itself to him.

Something bright flashed across his eyes. He lifted his face heavenward and received his stunning answer.

The sun shown down through the small opening above.

It was daylight.

And he was human.

And he was trapped inside the tomb.

"Cobb!"

His scream reverberated through the cavern. As it died down, he heard, to his horror, a soft snuffling growl from behind him in the darkness. His breath shivered to a stop. He was alone and helpless and now mortal.

And he was trapped inside a tomb with the embodiment of all his sins.

"Cobb!"

***

His wail went unheard by the couple lifting off out of Lima.

"You can open your eyes now, Mr. Cobb. We're off the ground."

One cautious eye opened, then the other. "You needn't sound so smug, Mrs. Cobb. You've managed to keep me up in the air since I met you."

Happily, Sheba snuggled against her new husband's shoulder. Her uncle had pulled a handful of strings to arrange their marriage at the Lodge where he could give her away. He'd spared no expense with flowers and a white, silky sarong for her and a promise that he'd be expecting them to visit when they got back from ...Where was it? New Guinea?

Sheba watched the jungle disappear below her, swallowed up by the clouds the way the torments of her past were devoured by the truth. Securely wrapped up in Frank's possessive arms, she leaned her head against his strong shoulder and finally let herself sleep.

And her dreams were wonderful.

ABOUT THE AUTHOR

With 43 sales to her credit since her first publication in 1987, Nancy Gideon's writing career is as versatile as the romance genre, itself.

Under Nancy Gideon, her own name, this Southwestern Michigan author is a Top Ten Waldenbooks' best seller for Silhouette, has written an award-winning vampire romance series for Pinnacle earning a "Best Historical Fantasy" nomination from Romantic Times, and will have her first two original horror screen plays made into motion pictures in a collaboration with local independent film company, Katharsys Pictures.

Writing western historical romance for Zebra as Dana Ransom, she received a "Career Achievement award for Historical Adventure" and is a K.I.S.S. Hero Award winner. Best known for her family saga series; the Prescott family set in the Dakotas and the Bass family in Texas, her books published overseas in Romanian, Italian, Russian, Portuguese, Danish, Dutch, German, Icelandic and Chinese.

As Rosalyn West for Avon Books, her novels have been nominated for "Best North American Historical Romance" and "Best Historical Book in a Series. Her "Men of Pride County" series earned an Ingram Paperback Buyer's Choice Selection, a Barnes & Noble Top Romance Pick and won a HOLT Medallion.

Gideon attributes her love of history, a gift for storytelling, a background in journalism for keeping her focused and the discipline of writing since her youngest was in diapers. She begins her day at 5 a.m. while the rest of the family is still sleeping. While the pace is often hectic, Gideon enjoys working on diverse projects—probably because she's a Gemini. One month, it's researching the gritty existence of 1880s Texas Rangers only to jump to 1990s themes of intrigue and child abuse. Then it's back to the shadowy netherworlds of vampires and movie serial killers. In between, she's the award-winning newsletter editor and former vice president of the Mid-Michigan chapter of Romance Writers of America and is widely published in industry trade magazines.

A mother of two teenage sons, she recently discovered the Internet and has her own web pages at: http://www.tlt.com/authors/ngideon.htm and http://www.theromanceclub.com/nancygideon.htm.

She spends her 'spare time' taking care of a menagerie consisting of an ugly dog, a lazy cat, a tankful of pampered fish and three African clawed frogs (adopted after a Scouting badge!), plotting under the stars in her hot tub, cheering on her guys' hobbies of radio control airplanes and trucks, bowling and Explorer Scouting or indulging in her favorite vice—afternoon movies.

Don't Miss
Nancy Gideon's

Novelization of the Horror Movie

In The Woods

ISBN 1-893896-52-8 Price: $12.95

"Horror at its finest and most eerie!"—Midwest Book Review

In the woods a creature was buried centuries ago...a creature of unlimited power and capable of unspeakable terror. Unleashed upon the world during the Medieval ages, its rest has been undisturbed...until now.

Two firefighters entered the forest and found a grave. Not knowing whether they would find the remains from another victim of the serial killer stalking their town or simply someone's pet, they dug. The two men ran out of the forest that day, only to bring hell with them ...

"Horror and mystery combine to delight readers with a work reminiscent of early King." —The Mystery Zone

"Horror fans be on the look-out for this terrifyingly delicious novel!" —Vampyres